ORDINARY DEVOTION

KRISTEN
HOLT-BROWNING

ORDINARY
DEVOTION

a novel

Monkfish Book Publishing Company
Rhinebeck, New York

Paperback ISBN 978-1-958972-47-2
eBook ISBN 978-1-958972-48-9

Library of Congress Cataloging-in-Publication Data

Names: Holt-Browning, Kristen, author.
Title: Ordinary devotion : a novel / Kristen Holt-Browning.
Description: Rhinebeck, New York : Monkfish Book Publishing Company, 2024.
Identifiers: LCCN 2024023382 (print) | LCCN 2024023383 (ebook) | ISBN
   9781958972472 (paperback) | ISBN 9781958972489 (ebook)
Subjects: LCGFT: Novels.
Classification: LCC PS3608.O49435983 O73 2024 (print) | LCC
   PS3608.O49435983 (ebook) | DDC 813/.6--dc23/eng/20240529
LC record available at https://lccn.loc.gov/2024023382
LC ebook record available at https://lccn.loc.gov/2024023383

Book and cover design by Colin Rolfe

Monkfish Book Publishing Company
22 East Market Street, Suite 304
Rhinebeck, New York 12572
(845) 876-4861
monkfishpublishing.com

For Jack Holt (1942–2010)

" The paths were so full of thorns and briars and other obstacles that I could hardly make any headway. ... I at last reached the summit of the mountain ... and made my way towards a gully where I had to descend. But there I stopped and looked. Vipers, scorpions, lizards and various other species of reptile were hissing their tongues at me and blocking the way down! . . . It was then that I heard my mother's voice speaking to me, "Run, my daughter, run, for you have been granted wings to fly with by the great Giver whom none can resist. Quickly, therefore, fly over all these creatures opposing you." And then, with a great feeling of comfort and release, I took up my wings and flew . . ."

HILDEGARD OF BINGEN, *Scivias*

" And she asked herself, How is it possible to be at once enclosed and illuminated."

ANN LAUTERBACH, "Nocturne"

" The pleasure of abiding. The pleasure of insistence, of persistence. The pleasure of obligation, the pleasure of dependency. The pleasures of ordinary devotion."

MAGGIE NELSON, *The Argonauts*

1
—

STONE AND DIRT. Disappearing light. The door to the cell, behind me, closing. Heavy, carved from oak. The men are pushing it closed. I could still turn and flee. I could run back out of this cell, past all those men out there in their brown robes, up the nave and out of the church, down the hillside path, past the placid, grazing sheep, the whole world before me, my feet galloping over the grass, all the way back home.

But nobody lives there anymore.

The door is closing. The wall of the cell across from me, already dim, grows darker.

The light behind me—edged with red, filtered by the stained-glass windows of the church connected to this cell—pales, withers, and dies, as the door keeps groaning across the ground. The final slip of light at my feet fades to pink, then shrinks to nothing at all.

The door is closed. Black everywhere. The dark is all. More dark than I thought there would be. How can such a small space hold so much darkness? But also, there is less: less air, less light. Less me. As if, already, I am shrinking to fit this enclosed place.

Scraping and shuffling on the other side of the door, its outline hardly visible within the stony wall. It is being bricked up again, enclosing me—no, *us*.

Joseph and all the other monks out there, all of them adding bricks to the rising stack, under the watching eyes of the abbot and the priest.

When my father first told me of his decision to send me here, as baffled and mad as I was, I also felt a seed of pride take root. *I had been chosen for this weird fate*, not my sisters, not any of the other girls in our village. Father said Mother had seen something in me, wanted more for me than farm life. I was afraid, but even so, that deadly sin, that haughty self-regard, sprouted in me.

But no longer. That foolish feeling has already wilted in this darkness. It is too late for me. As if I could tell my father, and the abbot, and the priest, even Joseph and the other monks: *I confess my sin of pride, now please let me out*. As if they would calmly accept the demands of a silly girl with her changeable mind. As if I have any say in the matter of my own fate.

Too late. No way out now. It is done. It is silent. The door has been closed, the other side of it bricked up again, and the monks have left, back to their endless little hours of prayer.

No, it is not full quiet: I hear the thud and rush of my blood beneath my skin, thrumming in my ears.

It is morning and the sun must be risen high, but it is like night in here. The window is set in the north-facing wall, and covered by a heavy hide curtain. A small, narrow slot cut in the opposite wall faces into the dim church, offers nothing bright.

I should feel holy, shouldn't I? Favored by God, smiled upon. Holiness would be a warmth, I think, a soothing heat under and over my skin. But I am a cold beast, cut off, closed in. Untouched.

There is no handle on this side. Nothing to grab and hold. I am trapped. My blood so loud in my ears I fear it will pour out onto the hard dirt floor.

I hear her breath, but I can hardly see her. She is mere shape curled into a black fog. I am alone, truly. I know God is everywhere, but I cannot believe He is here. Which shows what a sinner I am. Which shows that this is where I belong. I can learn so much.

I wait for some sign, any message at all from God.

Nothing.

Last spring, a sailor came through Fossbury on his way to the coast, that place where the land ends and next comes only water, until there is more land again, he said, where people speak in strange tongues. Father offered him a place in the barn for the night. I stayed behind, after Margaret, Anne, and Mother climbed up to the sleeping loft—Mother swaying on the ladder, the baby still in her belly then. A single candle on the table between Father and the sailor, who spoke in the half-light. I sat in a dim corner; men deep in talk do not notice a scrawny, lurking girl. I could not stop thinking about all that water—what the sailor called the "sea." I asked in a voice little more than a whisper, "how can water be so big that you can see nothing else?"

I was a child then. That was only a few months ago. How can that be? I am still twelve, and yet that was a different life, in another world, a warm and candlelit place, nothing like this cell.

"Imagine nothing but water and sky, no land, no village, no cottages or churches, just water everywhere you look," the sailor replied. "The water goes on and on until it meets the low edge of the sky in the farthest distance. It seems a world unto itself. You must remind yourself, there is a new shore ahead somewhere— you must remember this when you are so far from home, and your destination can't yet be seen. Otherwise, you begin to think the ocean has no beginning and no end, and that way madness lies."

God has no beginning and no end. That is what Father Everard says. I do not understand that either. I fear God ended when the door shut behind me, and I entered this stone room.

Dear Jesus, I do not need endless water and sky. Mother is dead, and the baby too.

Father and Margaret and Anne are far away in the city, and I am locked in darkness. But I believe I could accept it all, if I could have a little more light, please.

Something in me flutters, rattles in my chest. There is no way into this dark place, and no way out, not anymore. They shut the door and covered it with bricks. I touch my face. The doorframe faint in the stone. My cheek quivers under my hand. The dark is in me. The devil is dark. I am buried alive. How can I serve God in here? Satan lives in the dark places, says Father Everard.

Rustling in the corner. A gray shape. A gown. A woman. My eyes are learning to see here. She is on the other side of the cell, in the corner, but I could reach her, I think, in just a few steps.

I should speak.

No, I should wait for her to address me; she is noble, and thus must speak first.

I should not be here.

I would very much like an open door.

I should pray. *Holy Mary, guide me in all this dark.*

Please.

Mother?

See me.

2
—

I MEANT TO FIND POETRY, but my feet brought me to Religion. I was done teaching for the day, but before heading home, I stopped at the college bookstore. Did I need more books atop my to-read piles, towering on my nightstand and desk? Of course not—the semester had only started a few weeks ago, but already I was drowning in stacks of stuff to read: books I had meant to get to over the summer, new additions to my course syllabi. I had just visited the bookstore a few days ago, scanning the shelves for potentially relevant new scholarship that might overlap with my own research, or, even worse, might say what I want to say before I've even published my own (unwritten) book. I'm a creature of habit, and books, so there I was again, even though my budget definitely did not support any more book purchases.

I walked around the front-and-center display of blue and gray sweatshirts, tumblers, and baseball caps emblazoned with the University of Northern New York logo; once I made it past those pushed-together tables full of school-pride paraphernalia, the sterile rows of fluorescent-lit bookshelves stretched before me. No attempt to evoke dusty, cozy academia here. A public-university budget only supported soulless and straightforward six-foot shelving under glaring bulbs—although the lighting in the front of the bookstore was softer, bathing the school logo, repeated across all those t-shirts, phone cases, and bumper stickers, in a reverential glow. There were only a couple other people in the aisles, since most students bought their books online. Voices floated over from the campus coffee shop next door, which shared the building with the bookstore and was connected to it by a wide doorway. The smell of the coffee itself wafted over too, pungent and sharp.

The familiar titles perched on their shelves, probably untouched since my last visit, even though many of them appeared on my colleagues' syllabi, as well as my own. *Contemporary Trends in American Religion. No God but God: The Origins and Evolution of Islam. Visioning the Divine Feminine in the Hindu Tradition.* And, more along the lines of my own work, *An Empire of God: Christendom and the Medieval West.* But I wasn't there to pick up anything for my own research, or for any upcoming classes I would be teaching. I was there to keep up to date on the latest research on long-dead people and their ancient, often mystifying, cultures. And to remind myself that I was part of the conversation, even if it was only occurring in a minor corner of the academic world, even if we couldn't talk directly to the people to whom we had devoted our lives.

I was also looking for the newest translation of *The Divine Comedy.* I owned several earlier translations, but for a medieval Christianity scholar like me, it's a foundational text, in all of its interpretations and editions. I scanned the shelves for several seconds before it hit me: I was in the wrong place. I turned and left Religion, walked three aisles over to the slightly larger Poetry section. More space devoted to poetry than religion: academia is the opposite of the rest of the US.

I skimmed the shelves until I spotted it: a stark abstract cover, splashes of orange and a dribble of red against a white background, intended to appeal to contemporary readers and downplay any old-fashioned, Western-canon mustiness. I thumbed through the familiar pages of the second volume, *Purgatorio,* to see how the medieval Italian had been rendered and refracted into twenty-first-century English. How did this translator cross the chasm of centuries? Did her words, shadow-sisters of Dante's own, bridge the expanse of time? The electric hum of the modern world receded as I read: *What I sing will be that/ second kingdom, / in which the human soul is /cleansed of sin,/ becoming worthy of ascent to Heaven. Purgatorio,* sandwiched between the more famous and gory *Inferno,* and the culminating relief of *Paradiso.* Everybody knows about heaven and hell, but purgatory remains familiar to only a few elderly Catholics. And the Pope. And me. It's where I spend my days, it's where I work. Purgatory *is* my work.

I imagined a fourteenth-century peasant, or a medieval monk, there in the bookstore with me. I tried to explain it all in my mind: *these bound manuscripts are books. We mass-produce them now, with machines. You don't have to write and illustrate them by hand anymore. That buzzing glare? Fluorescent lighting: we don't need to use lamps or candles anymore. You just flip a switch*—wait, how would I describe a light switch? *The lights are electric*—but what would electricity be to a medieval mind? A word with no meaning, sounds linked to nothing concrete in the fourteenth-century world. I tried again: *That smell is coffee. It comes to us on ships, across oceans. We drink it because it gives us energy. It comes from a bean*—but I was yanked out of my game as the bitter, cloying smell swam up into my nose, and waves of nausea roiled my stomach. I took slow, deep breaths, and the queasiness eased. I let myself play some more. *You can take one of these books, or many as you like, and sit at a table and read them while you drink a mug of coffee and perhaps eat a light meal. Yes, anyone can: even a woman or a child. All of these people, with all these shades of skin, are literate. Now, most of us read, at leas, in this country that didn't exist when you did, that was built long after your death on lands already home to others who were removed in cruel and monstrous ways that would be familiar to you. That violence—an aspect of this world you would recognize and understand.*

I had done this before, this pretending to describe the twenty-first century to a medieval person. It was unscholarly. It wasn't academically rigorous. But it let my brain flit and jump, and create imaginary connections. I could almost see the confused horror on the face of a scribe who regularly devoted days or weeks to the writing and illuminating of a few letters or phrases, as he took in the sight of the untrained and unpious masses picking up these cheap books, perhaps cracking their spines, flipping through a few pages, brushing away crumbs. If I were to try to explain this place to a poor peasant or confused monk, the words would be a jumble of sounds, signifying nothing.

No bridge to cross, no way back. But why not reach across this distance of language, of time? How would it feel to find someone, understand them, despite the years and years stacked between us?

I looked at the page again and read: *the only road I could have taken / was the road I took.* I probably would have translated "road" as "path."

My hand went to my belly, still flat at ten weeks. Too early to feel movement, but even so, I imagined a fluttering in the dark. I knew it was a cliché, but my hand spread protectively across my middle, a gesture anybody, anywhere across time, would understand.

I put *Purgatorio* back on the shelf, in its place between heaven and hell. I thought about buying yet another what-to-expect-when-you're-pregnant book, but I wasn't sure if the college bookstore carried those, and I had a sizeable stack on the coffee table back home anyway. And I certainly didn't need to spend the money. So instead I returned to Religion, and, just like during my last couple visits, I picked up *Holy Enclosed in the Dark: Anchoresses in France and Italy, 1100–1400.* The author, Dr. Sloane Lanham, smiled wide in her author photo: bright white teeth, chunky black-framed glasses, simple black turtleneck. I imagined my own name on the cover, the words mine (and yes, my smiling face, me sleek in that top too, never mind the baggy cardigan I was actually wearing). But I was too far along a different path by now. I had let my advisor, Dr. Gower, talk me out of medieval gender studies back in grad school. I've devoted so much time to purgatory, and it's gotten me this far, at least. But the questions shimmered hot in my mind: why did some devout people agree to spend their lives in a cell, cut off from the world? Why did women, especially, choose the strange and difficult path of becoming an anchoress in the twelfth, thirteenth, and fourteenth centuries? And why couldn't I just let myself buy this damn book, my meager income notwithstanding?

It wasn't too late. There was still room for me, for my work, for the work I wanted to do. I could finish expanding my dissertation on purgatory into a book, use that to find a tenure-track position (maybe?), and then pivot to medieval women and enclosure. Maybe I could even find some way to link purgatory and anchoresses. *Holy Enclosed in the Dark* was just one book. If I read it, maybe I would see something the author had overlooked or didn't examine thoroughly enough. Maybe she gestured toward some other potential research possibilities. But I'd still be scooping up her leftover research breadcrumbs. She had beaten me to it, there was no way around it. But academic success isn't always about being the first; I just needed to come at the same ideas again, from a new angle, or apply a shiny new layer of theory to them. Just like the other times I had been here, I studied the author photo in an attempt to figure out how old Sloane was. (Yes, in my head, I called her Sloane.) According to the bio beneath her photo, she was an assistant professor of religious studies at a respectable, small liberal arts college. She looked to be around thirty-five, same as me. Maybe a little older? Yes, she could definitely be in her late thirties, maybe even forty. So I still had time. I could finish my purgatory book, finish what I had started—yes, I could continue on a clear path.

Fluorescent lights hummed, books stood in rows and rows on all the shelves covering the walls.

I slipped the book into my tote bag and glanced around, but I was alone.

I wouldn't be cast into hell for this. Or even purgatory. There's no such place. I've devoted my life to an imaginary realm.

I strode out of the bookstore calm, my hand on my belly, my steps as sure as those of a saint.

No—that was who I wanted to be. Someone steady, trusting in my own instincts, knowing my steps were the right ones to take. But in fact, I walked quickly, sweat spreading in my armpits, shoulders tensed, waiting for the shout of "Stop, thief!" I scurried to the bus stop in front of the main entrance to campus, and only when my bus arrived and I took a seat did I begin to breathe normally again, even as I looked behind me, craning my neck to look for the flashing lights of a police car.

My hand, still and truly, settled, protective, on my belly.

3
—

THESE THICK STONE WALLS, stern, ungiving, are so unlike those of the house I left behind, the home I shared with Father and Margaret and Anne, and Mother before she died. Our house was framed with wood walls, the gaps and holes patched with mud and straw. The dirt-and-barnyard smell of it. Comforting, warm, embracing us. Here, in this cell, I smell only the stale damp that clings to the stone. No—there is also the sour tang of a body not far off. But this hint of something living brings me no comfort.

How did the anchoress feel as the door disappeared, and the light along with it, when they buried her alive in this cell four years ago? Why can she only find God, why can she only serve him, in a dark stone tomb? So many questions I want to ask her. *Why did Mother die, even though she prayed to you for a safe birth and a healthy baby?* Last year, the five of us—there were five of us then—came here to the abbey when the baby was still in Mother's belly. Now we are broken apart: some gone to the city, some buried in the ground, and me, here.

But I cannot make words. She has not yet addressed me. I cannot move my feet. There is no place to walk, regardless. A few steps, and I could cross this entire little kingdom of black.

—

My feet throbbed as Father Everard and I walked all morning, into the middle of the day, on our way here to Wenfair Abbey yesterday. The sun was high and hot, but I did not mind the heat, nor the thick dry feel of my tongue in my mouth. I welcomed the warmth sinking into my shoulders from the sun above, as if it might burrow beneath my skin, and stay within me, warm me in the days to come.

I would find a way. Mother called me special. She thought I was made for this. I lifted my head, kept my eyes on the path between the trees before me, and silently formed the words with my lips—*made for this, made for this*—to the pace of my steps. *Made* as my left foot met the ground, *for* as my right foot lifted, *this* as my right foot touched the earth. But after several steps the words became mere sounds. I felt them in my mouth, I enjoyed the shifting shapes of them there, but they had lost their meaning.

I did not speak to Father Everard. At Mass, the priest stood with his back to us, facing the altar and the crucifix, praying for our souls in a language we neither spoke nor understood. And now I was alone with this holy man, on the path to Wenfair Abbey. The priest was tall, and had a way of looking down his nose that left me feeling like a small and sinful creature. But after we had been walking for an hour, without saying a word, he reached over and removed my sack off my shoulder, and slung it over his own. It was not heavy; I had only my extra smock, my other gown and tunic, hose, my winter coat and gloves, and a veil. I did not wear a veil, of course, as I was not married, but I took one of Mother's with me. My distaff, wound with a length of wool. Still, I understood his act as a kindness, and I smiled, but said nothing. My tongue felt too large and stupid in my mouth. He did not smile back; he did not look at me, as he carried my sack.

Sweat gathered on my neck and trickled down my back, despite the shade offered by the trees along the way. Mostly beech, some rowan, and then a cluster of hazel as the path widened. I realized we were nearing the town of Wenfair. Everyone knows hazel trees protect against witches; they must have been planted here to keep evil away from the town. The Church frowns on such old ways, but they linger. Father Everard looked up at the hazel branches as we walked under them, and crossed himself.

Soon I heard hammers striking against wood, and goats bleating. The path brought us through Wenfair; we passed in the shadows of wood and stone houses so close they seemed to lean toward one another for support, as well as a blacksmith, granary, cobbler, farrier, and tavern. Children near to Anne in age galloped around us in shrieking bunches. Chickens scratched in alleys between houses. Women chatting, washing garments in tubs outside their doors; dogs slunk about, seeking scraps. My chest ached; I longed to be doing such washing myself, my arms plunged in water up to my elbows, then drying quickly in the sun, talking with Margaret at my side, splashing her to make her shriek while I giggled. Two years older than me, she tried to pretend she was above such childish games, but she always splashed me back and smiled, then laughed, too. In the sunlight, near my sisters, to be in the place I had always known, where I had rooted and grown—I pushed my silly wishes away, focused on the path before me.

The space between the houses widened as we began to walk uphill, toward the abbey, which towered over the busy alleys. There were no other people on the path up here, which ended at the gates of Wenfair Abbey. I remembered this from my other trip here, months ago, with my family in winter: a mass of gray looming over me and the valley and village below.

I looked to the left of the gate and saw, some way down the abbey wall, the cell, bulging, as if the wall of the church had been pulled outward and rounded by God's hand. A part of the building, like a goiter is part of the neck.

Father Everard lifted the stern black knocker, let it drop against the solid stone door. It creaked open, and a man in a brown robe stepped toward us, his hands clasped before him, as he bowed and said, "Welcome, brother." Although I kept my head bowed, I sensed the priest stiffen next to me, and I glanced up to see the quick frown on his face—he was accustomed to being addressed as "Father"—but another moment and the priest managed to hide his displeasure, replying, "Thank you, brother. This is the child, Elinor, chosen to serve the anchoress. Her father entreats the Lady Adela, and the good brothers of Wenfair Abbey, to pray for her as she enters into enclosure and holy service with the blessed lady, for the glory of God and the salvation of her own soul."

I kept my gaze on the ground, as I knew I should—"look down, look down," Mother always whispered in church, while the priest murmured and chanted. But still I could feel the monk's eyes on me.

"Welcome. Please, follow me. The abbot awaits you both."

We followed the monk through the door, which opened onto a long corridor walled only along one side. Along the open side of the corridor, beneath the clear sky, herb gardens blossomed. I glanced at the plants and named them in my head: sage (with which Mother flavored stew); hyssop (she rubbed it on Anne's bruises and scratches); chamomile (brew in hot water to soothe stomach and throat—Margaret showed me how once, when Mother was with child); and others I did not know. I did not see any of this last winter—the gardens and grounds were brown and bare then. Now this lush landscape seemed a mockery—so much life, so much green, so many useful growing plants, thriving in the sunshine.

The long walkway continued alongside a sunny, roofless courtyard. A fountain stood in the middle, and two monks walked the pebble paths around it, their heads bare and shiny. Bees hummed among the flowers filling the beds around the fountain—calendula, nasturtium, lilies, daisies. The hallway continued into the church itself, and we left the garden behind. I saw the altar up ahead of us, the familiar, sad figure draped on the Cross above.

Even at midday, the church allowed little light. The small flames of many candles flickered across the walls. A gray-haired man stood waiting for us just over the threshold.

"Father Everard, Elinor, welcome. I am the abbot of Wenfair

Abbey, Father Hugh. Brother Paul, thank you for your service, you may leave us." The monk who had opened the gate for us nodded and departed.

"We have prepared dinner for you. I imagine you are hungry after your travels from Fossbury. Please, this way." We followed Abbot Hugh out of a door at the back of the church, across a cloister, into the refectory. Empty, save for two meals of bread, cheese, and ale waiting for us at one of the tables. It was odd to eat in the presence of these two men, especially because the abbot merely sat there watching us, but I was hungry, and the bread was soft.

After we ate, Father Everard asked to see the cell. The abbot led us back through the cloister, across the threshold, and into the church. I heard the singsong drone of chant from the shadows. I knew the monks prayed at certain hours, several times a day; I supposed I would become familiar with their daily devotionals. Maybe I would learn the words and whisper them along with the monks from my cell. I would only understand a tiny portion of the Latin, but with time my mouth might remember more and more of the shapes and sounds. Will that count as prayer, if I say the words, but do not understand them, even if I know I would mean and believe them, if I could?

To the left of the altar a small door was set into a wall, only the top half of it visible, as the bottom portion was covered by bricks; some were stacked and scattered around the base of the door as well. It was a dark, dusty wood, and looked heavy and firm. The lady within the cell must have known that the door had been partly unbricked for my arrival; she would have heard the scratching and scraping. Did she imagine trying to push it open, stepping into the church, running out the door? It was probably easier with the door sealed and shut up tight; better not to have the choice to open it and leave.

Could she hear us? Or was she too deep in prayer, in communion with God, to notice us?

Father Everard made approving sounds as he looked at the partly uncovered cell door, and then the abbot said, "Tonight, the child may sleep in one of our guest chambers. She will take her supper there, as we cannot have a woman present at mealtime with the brothers. Tomorrow morning, after Prime, we will offer the child to the lady." Abbot Hugh removed a small bell from the folds of his tunic, and when he rang it, a young monk entered the church and hurried up the nave toward us.

Father Hugh continued, "Brother Joseph will show the child to her chamber." He turned toward the younger monk, who stepped forward, lowered his head, and said, "If you please, Miss, follow me." I looked to Father Everard, who was now my familiar constant, the only one I had left, but he nodded as well, encouraging me to follow the young monk. "Elinor, get some rest. Use these hours to pray and prepare yourself for tomorrow. I will see you in the morning when you are brought to the lady." He must have seen the fear in me, because he stepped forward and placed his hand on my shoulder as he said, "It is all going to be well, child. God is surely smiling on you. Go now with Brother Joseph." I followed him down another long hall, smooth stone under my feet, another garden to my right: a green square, surrounded by the long hallways of the monastery on every side. Although the hallways were under a firm roof, the garden was open to the sky. I looked at the herbs and flowers there, and envied them.

This is a gift from God, I reminded myself. *I will learn from the example of this wise and holy woman, and I will serve and assist her, I will be of use, and someday, when I die, I will go to Heaven, and there will be Mother, and the baby, and it will be full of light always, all the time.*

I swallowed, and I felt something thick and tight in my throat, as if these thoughts had caught and withered there in the dark.

4
—

I TRIED NOT TO THINK ABOUT WHAT I HAD DONE AS THE CAMPUS DIS-
appeared behind me, those boxy brick buildings giving way to
Victorian houses in various states of repair, and then modest
ranch houses. But as I got off the bus, I couldn't stop chastising
myself, wave after wave of shame breaking over me, as I walked
the two blocks to our townhouse. *How could I have stolen a book?
What if I had been caught? I could lose my job, the university could decide
not to renew my contract for next year. What was I thinking? I wasn't
thinking. I'll go back tomorrow and buy two books to make up for it.*

What would Dad think? Ever since he died in the spring, I
found myself doing this: imagining his reaction, or, more ridiculously, imagining him looking down on me from heaven, like
an omniscient angel. He'd find an excuse for me; he'd give me a
chance to explain. Even if I had no excuse, no compelling reason,
beyond a moment of pure and simple want.

Still, I tried to understand why I had done it. I had never stolen
a thing in my life—sure, I'd watched middle-school friends swipe
packs of gum and candy from the corner store, and after college
some friends ran an elaborate scheme of buying and returning
clothes from The Gap that somehow made money by gaming their
refund policy. I couldn't come up with any logical explanations: I
just wanted the book, so I took it. I was tired of drifting over to
that shelf in the campus bookstore again and again, staring at that

photo, trying to figure out how old Sloane Lanham was, comparing myself to her. But now that I had the book in my bag, I didn't feel competitive or anxious or jealous. Instead, I felt protective of the book nestled in the bottom of my bag, beneath my wallet, my phone, a notepad, several pens, and a sleeve of crackers.

Could I blame this on being pregnant? Some kind of hormone rush or imbalance leading to confused thinking, poor choices? That felt too easy, like I was leaning on a convenient biological imperative—*I've got a bad case of mommy brain!* No, I didn't want to do that—I was pregnant, but I was still myself. Although, I didn't want to admit it, but I was relieved to be pregnant; it felt like I was on the "normal" path for once. Maybe I was a stalled-out medievalist, but at least I could take this societally approved step. Never mind that I didn't even have my own health insurance—I was on Nick's plan, because he's tenure track.

The first fallen leaves crumbled under my clogs as I navigated the uneven sidewalk and let myself turn away from thoughts of my body, the life it was creating, the book it had stolen. I pushed that away, tried to focus on work, to let myself settle into that abstract place we call "the mind." Maybe I could do a translation myself—a modern updating of something medieval? My Middle English was strong. I could probably pitch something to a decent university press. The best translations of Julian of Norwich's *Revelations of Divine Love* were a couple decades old. I could translate the writings of an anchoress, I could dust and shine her words, place them in the bright, modern light.

But those were recycled thoughts, words with no heat behind them. If I was going to see my name on the cover of a book, I wanted all of the words within those pages to be entirely my own. That's the kind of pride-driven thought I would never want to verbalize, but it would surely help me on my quest toward a full-time, tenure-track position. The articles I'd published in journals (*Medieval Christian Studies, Historical Christianity, Journal of the Medieval West*) had helped me earn my place here, at the University of Northern New York, and they were a good addition to my CV.

But if I wanted to advance, I needed to put more words out into the world—well, out into the tiny world of academia, at least.

I reminded myself, for the hundredth time, that my best bet was to stay focused on revising my dissertation and turning it into a book. I had distilled the essence of my dissertation into a paper titled *The Third Place: Developing a Theology of Purgatory, 1100–1300* (with thanks to Martin Luther for describing purgatory as the "third place") and submitted it to the next Kingmore Conference on Medieval Studies, in Pennsylvania next March. If I was lucky, a conference presentation might lead to a book contract: slow and steady steps out of my own little academic purgatory, onward toward—hallelujah!—a full-time, tenure-track position. The annual conference was the hallowed site where I might find my holy grail: interest from an editor at one of the prestigious academic publishers. Kingmore was one of the few places where medievalists didn't feel like marginalized, dusty relics.

Which was definitely what I felt like at the U of NNY. Gray winters that lingered into April, and humidity-drenched summers in a small city, not far from the state capital, that was still struggling with the loss of its cement industry decades ago, despite the handful of New York City expats who spruced up the dilapidated Victorians and opened a couple decent coffeehouses. Thousands of students and many brick buildings. It was a vast place, and my own place in it was in-between, and easily overlooked. Technically, I was based in the religious studies department, but most of the courses I taught fell under the umbrella of the program in Medieval and Early Modern Studies (MEMS). Hundreds of years collapsed into a "program," not even a department proper, for a handful of majors: a few pale girls in long velvet skirts, the occasional serious boy in wire-rimmed glasses and a cable-knit sweater.

I taught "Early and Medieval Christianity" in the fall and "Medieval Theology: Essential Texts" in the spring, along with a more advanced seminar each semester. That fall I was teaching "Holy Madness: Religious Women in the Middle Ages," and next semester would be "Monks, Monarchs, and Medieval Art." I had gnawed at my thumbnail when Dr. Manheim, religious studies professor and MEMS program director, had asked me to teach the latter. I replied, "I'm so grateful for the opportunity, Dr. Manheim, but I'm not an art historian, as you know, of course, and I just want to make sure I'm serving the students the best I can, I'm sure you understand." But Dr. Manheim (I still couldn't bring myself to call her Helen—which she had only asked me to do once—not even in my mind) barely looked up from her iPhone as she replied, "Elizabeth, I absolutely hear your concerns and thank you for expressing them, but it's not an especially advanced course, and you can draw on medieval Christian topics. All of our MEMS courses are supposed to be at least somewhat inter-disciplinary. You can contextualize your approach from a reli-gious-studies perspective, given how central Christian themes are to the art of the period. It's not ideal, but the existence of this pro-gram is so tenuous, we must make do. And I'm sure Nick can give you some pointers. We appreciate you adapting your expertise to our needs so, so much." She had slid her hand over her hair, a sleek white bob, while I had tried not to think about my tired, careless ponytail, limp and drooping on my neck.

—

"Nick?" I called as I opened the creaky door to our townhouse. Safe—I half-expected police cars, sirens blaring, bearing down on me for my crime. One of our cats, gray-and-white Gawain, brushed past my ankles. As I dropped my tote bag (*Oxford University Press: Books of Distinction*) onto the rickety hard-backed chair next to the door, which we had plucked off the sidewalk a couple years ear-lier, I heard Nick call, "Hey, I'm in here," from his office, a modest alcove off the living room. I walked over, rested my hands on his shoulders, and leaned down to place my lips in his curls. I couldn't tell him what I'd done.

Instead, I let myself wonder, as I often did: what if I hadn't gone to that party back in grad school in Connecticut? What would the world look like if I had just stayed home, as usual? Two people reaching for the same bottle of cheap red simultaneously, awkward protestations leading to awkward small talk. Almost seven years ago now, already. I'd been twenty-eight, classes finished, focused on completing my dissertation. But I had noticed his dark brown curls right away.

—

"Let me get that for you." He had beckoned for me to hold out my glass, and poured a generous amount of the astringent stuff. We introduced ourselves and he said, "I don't think we have any seminars together, do we?"

"No, I'm not in art history. I'm here with my housemate, Eugene Chan. What are you working on?"

"The Renaissance. I'm doing a deep dive on Andrea Mantegna and his innovations in perspective. But I'm interested in material culture, too. What's your research focus?"

"Medieval Studies. Christianity. Purgatory, actually."

"Where unbaptized babies go?"

"Technically, no, that's Limbo, which was initially considered distinct from purgatory, or at least a separate realm of it. Purgatory is the stage people have to pass through before they can ascend to Heaven. They undergo punishments for their sins before they're pure enough for Heaven—well, unless they're saints, then they can go straight to heaven. Dante devoted the second volume of *The Divine Comedy* to it. It wasn't really codified as official church doctrine until the medieval era, which is what I'm going to be primarily working on—" I blushed as I paused. "Sorry, not the most fascinating party chitchat."

"I could tell you all about the interplay between patronage and materiality during the Renaissance, and the relative value of tapestries versus paintings as signifiers of political influence. You know, just to *really* impress you. But how about, instead, you tell me how you ended up focusing on purgatory?"

21

I laughed and told him how Dr. Gower had convinced me to put my first passion—intersections between gender and medieval religion—aside for the sake of my career, after I submitted a paper on purgatory to his Dante seminar. As he had pointed out, there wasn't much new scholarship being done on purgatory, so it offered me a little room of my own.

"So," I said to Nick, "I'm sticking with purgatory for the foreseeable future. Does that make me a craven careerist?"

"A dissertation on purgatory and an advanced degree in religious medieval studies? You're a total sellout."

"Thank you for confirming my worst fears about myself. Now what were you saying about patronage and materiality?"

It felt good to be with someone who understood much of the world I had decided to situate myself in—but not all of it. Like we both spoke a dying language, something diminished and diminishing that nevertheless lived comfortably on both of our tongues. But even so, some vocabulary was mine alone. Like a dialect: distinct, yet related, overlapping.

I saw it in Nick, too: the focus on what we would never actually refer to as "the life of the mind." We talked about travel only as a means of getting closer to what we already knew and loved: the chapels and frescoes of Italy, the monasteries of Britain (not that we actually traveled; we couldn't afford that). We both wanted libraries more than adventures—we thought libraries *were* adventures.

A year later, as we sat on the saggy futon in our living room after we moved in together, our books stacked and intermingled around us, warmth surged in my chest.

Scouring the academic job listings in the *Chronicle of Higher Education*, he zeroed in on a listing for the University of Northern New York: assistant professor of art history, tenure track. And, glory of glories, an opening for an adjunct professor in the interdisciplinary medieval and early modern program! Sure, not the dreamed-of tenure track, but it was a start, and we could be together. I wasn't even thirty yet, I had plenty of time to find something better. So we both applied, we both got the jobs, we got married at City Hall— much to my parents' disappointment, although we made it up to them later, with a party at their house— and we drove north that summer in a haze of good fortune.

But the fact remained that, at least for now, our professional positions were wildly unequal. What were the gendered ramifications of my adjunct status and his tenure-track position? Was it really fair to position an art-history professor as reaping the benefits of patriarchy? Yes, he taught deep Western canon: the Renaissance, all those Italian guys. But so did I, with my focus on Western Europe, and a central tenet of Western Christianity (the Orthodox Church doesn't profess belief in purgatory). I should have been grateful to have a job, to find a department even bothering to teach medieval studies, to find two positions at a university, even if one was merely adjunct.

But these years as an adjunct were never part of my precise-yet-grand plan. I was supposed to go straight from grad school into a tenure-track position, or at least a full-time one. But as I finished up my dissertation, there were no medieval studies professorships to be found. By the early 2010s, it was becoming more and more common for a retiring professor to be replaced by a handful of adjuncts—no tenure benefits or health insurance for the university to worry about. So the fact that UNNY had positions for both Nick and me was huge, even if mine was just a contract one, renewed yearly, and not yet renewed for next year. If I was offered another yearly contract, should I take it, or should I step back, stay home with the baby, keep searching for something more stable, more permanent?

More than five years, already, of this tenuous in-betweenness. Whenever I remembered just how long I'd been holding in this pattern, my stomach twisted, my head felt heavy with the weight of all this drifting and settling time.

—

I lifted my lips from Nick's curls and said, "Dr. Manheim wants me to teach 'Monks, Monarchs, and Medieval Art' next semester. Apparently, the fact that I'm not an art historian 'tis a mere trifle. Maybe you could reach back into your dusty memories from grad school and give me some ideas?"

Nick yawned and stretched, turned around, took my hand in his. "Christ, that's ridiculous. Why don't they ask a medieval art historian to teach it? There are definitely one or two people in my department who could do it."

"Maybe they already have a full course load. Or maybe they said no, which I can't do, because I don't have tenure. Manheim knows I have to do it. And only three kids will sign up for it, anyway." I sighed, pulled my hair the rest of the way out of my slipping ponytail and wound it back up into a messy bun. "I'll figure it out. At least the class I'm teaching this semester is interesting."

"It's right up your alley—Ye Olden Time Crazy Ladies."

"I believe you mean 'Holy Madness: Religious Women in the Middle Ages.' And you shouldn't say 'crazy.'"

"You're right, my bad. Seriously, it's a great topic. The virgin-whore dichotomy, the limited roles available to women—good stuff."

"As dear old Dr. Manheim said, 'The department is committed to remaining relevant to students and offering them pathways into considerations of the historic oppression of women and women-identifying individuals—as well as how women have protested the aggressions, both micro and macro, they have endured at the hands of patriarchal institutions across the centuries.'"

"You memorized that?"

"I *may* have read the email a hundred times because I couldn't believe the department is finally letting me teach a seminar on a topic this awesome. In the next couple of classes I'm going to introduce the figure of the anchoress, so—what?" I paused when Nick sighed.

"I wish the university would offer a full-time position for you to apply to," he said. "How much longer are they going to string you along like—"

"Look," I interrupted, "if this class goes well, and I get accepted to present at the conference, *then* I can ask Dr. Manheim about my future here, my options, after summer break home with the baby. Who knows, maybe Professor Thaddeus will finally decide to retire by then."

"How old is Thaddeus anyway? He could easily pass for ninety."

I kept talking as I walked into the kitchen to feed Gawain and our other cat, Leonardo. "I have no idea, I just know he's been here forever. The last full-time, tenured medievalist. Anyway, I know this isn't where I thought I'd be—" I peeled back the lid, and as the pungent smell, fish and damp, rushed into my nose, sour liquid surged up my throat, my eyes watered. I closed them, pulled in a long, slow breath, let it go, swallowed. Nick came up behind me and took the can from my hand, and I dropped my hands onto the counter for support just as another wave crested.

I squeezed Nick's arm before I headed back out of the kitchen—slow steps, deep breaths—and dropped down on the living-room sofa. The bile receded, the queasiness dissolved. I was still remembering the fact of this, what was happening in my body, all the time. The knowledge ebbed and flowed, washed over and through me. Us. Endless waves, as I remembered this new fact of my body over and over.

5
———

"PLEASE, MISS, IN HERE," Brother Joseph had said last night, as he stood beside an open door, head bowed. I entered the small room and set down my pack. A pallet, a window, a crucifix on the wall. It felt strange to have a whole room all for myself. I had never slept alone on a pallet before. This one, though simple, looked sturdy. Constructed from wood, it was raised off the ground so that it reached as high as my knees. Although it looked to be comfortable enough, with its stuffed mattress, blanket, and coverlet, I shivered. How would I be warm enough, sleeping all alone, without my sisters curled up beside me?

"Are you afraid?" At first, I thought I had imagined the words, they were whispered so softly. But I looked at Brother Joseph, and he lifted his eyes from the ground, just for a moment. I could see, now that he stood before me, that he was no more than a few years older than me, surely not yet even twenty. Sparse hairs sprouted above his upper lip.

"Yes." The word dry and brittle on my tongue. I should have pretended to be eager to take my place beside the anchoress, but my honest fear pushed the truth out.

"I would be, too." The small kindness of that confession. "I will visit you every day, and I will pray with you. The abbot receives the lady's confession, but I have been chosen to hear yours. Outside of my work in the scriptorium, it will be my highest duty." Brother

Joseph now held my gaze as he spoke, and I saw that he stood very straight, alert to his responsibility.

I did not know what a "scriptorium" was, but I said, "I am grateful, and I am honored that the Lady will instruct me. I know I have much to learn. I hope to be holy and pure like her someday." I pushed these words out of my mouth because I believed they were the right words, the words that should be said. I kept the other words locked in my heart—the words that felt true: *Am I truly meant for this? Why has God brought me here, into this strange stony life? How long will I have to live in that dark little cell? How long can you stay with me each day?*

But I held those words deep inside. I could not utter such things to a man. Instead, I managed to say, "May I ask you a question, please?" When he assented, I continued, "What is she like? Is she—kind?" I felt the childish question slip from my lips before I could stop it.

But Brother Joseph didn't laugh at me. He looked back down toward the floor as he said, "The Lady Adela is not like the rest of us. I sometimes think her eyes see things ours cannot. I bring her meals to her and her eyes are open, she is awake, but she does not acknowledge me, or the food I set before her. Her eyes do not look at me—they look *beyond* me. But she is patient with the many poor folk who come to her for prayers and advice." This answer did not entirely settle me; I noticed that he did not say that Adela was kind.

"She is incredibly strong of spirit, especially for a woman," he continued. "She will not accept extra blankets, and has refused a servant throughout her enclosure thus far, but she finally told the abbot that she wished to have a girl to teach to read and to lead onto a path of devoutness. Abbot Hugh thought this wise, because the girl could also tend to the lady's hearth, and assist with her, ah, bodily needs." Joseph shut his mouth and again looked down; he had spoken quickly, the words pouring out, as if he was unused to conversation.

I thought, *I am not here to learn; I am here to keep the fire burning*

27

and empty pots of piss. I tried to smother this ungrateful thought, to push it down deep, before God might see or hear it.

Perhaps worried that I might pester him with more questions—or aware that he had possibly said more than he should have—Joseph began to step back from the doorway. "I must take leave of you, I have chores to complete before Vespers. I shall bring you your supper tonight."

"Wait, please!" I was surprised at my boldness, the words that rushed out. "Before you go—when the Lady Adela first came to the abbey—when she went into her cell—what was it like?"

"When she was enclosed in the cell, the brothers gathered around the door while the masons stacked the bricks before it, and we recited the prayers for the dead as they worked. Many worshippers and townspeople looked on from the back of the church. That is the standard ritual for anchoresses: because she is dying to the world, her earthly life over, she is buried in her cell—essentially, dead." He must have heard my breath catch in my throat, because he looked up at me as he hurried to add, "But Miss, there will be no such ceremony for you. You are not dying to the world. Lady Adela was chosen by God for her singular path. And you have been chosen to assist her and learn from her—but you will most likely have another life, beyond the cell, someday." He dropped his gaze to the ground again as he said, "Now I truly must go. I will return later with your evening meal."

Most likely?

Joseph closed the door as he left. I sat on the pallet, stared out the single small window. I could see trees. I should have paid more careful attention to the trees all along the path to the abbey. What if I forgot the shapes of their leaves, could no longer remember the sound of the wind in branches? I curled up on the small hard bed, and I whispered the names—*hazel, oak, birch, rowan*—until the soft sound of my voice faded, until I was only forming the names with my mouth, silent, until I succumbed to sleep.

6

—

*W*EDNESDAY AND FRIDAY AFTERNOONS FROM 3:00 TO 6:00 WERE sacrosanct: no student conferences, no teaching, no administrative tasks. Instead, I headed to the university library and settled into the silent, mostly empty, medieval stacks. I heaved open those dense books, and plunged in. My right hand lifted and released the pages, while my left hand hovered at my mouth as I chewed at my thumbnail. The pages smelled like an abandoned room—a fine fog of dust, a sense of undisturbed staleness. I read about ascetics flaying their own backs, I parsed terrified accounts of the plague, the authors convinced that it was a punishment from God: *Sons abandoned fathers, husbands wives, one brother the other, one sister the other. Lamenting our misery, we feared to fly, yet we dared not remain.*

These glimpses of stark emotion, of human reaction, helped me place myself in the twelfth, thirteenth, and fourteenth centuries. These were people longing to understand their world. So I tried to honor, to take seriously, the questions posed by medieval theologians: Did Jesus defecate? Did Mary menstruate? It was a time dictated by the body. Illnesses that are easily treated or long eradicated today felled entire families. Childbirth loomed again and again over exhausted women's days, a mortal threat every time. The limits of the poor body ended many, if not most, lives too soon, in too much pain. So how could God, how could any holy person, be held hostage to the base needs and functions of these sorry contraptions?

Throughout Western Europe during the twelfth century, when the doctrine of purgatory developed and codified, the Church maintained a firm grip on people's daily lives and concerns, and the end of days was eagerly anticipated. At a time when social roles were rigidly delineated, and strictly determined lives from birth to death, purgatory offered a rare universality across classes: everyone needed to pass through purgatory, except the saints, who went straight on up to heaven. And anyone, sinner or priest, peasant or noble, could offer prayers to ensure salvation, for themselves and their loved ones, in the next world. *Purgatory offered degrees of agency, and an opportunity for the marginalized to determine, to a point, the fate of their own souls, and the souls of those who had already died.*

That was true when I wrote it in my dissertation, and it remained accepted by scholars. Still, I wrote that more than five years ago, and I wanted to refine and update my arguments, hone in on the truth, and keep pushing into that question: why did purgatory gain so much prominence, and official Church acceptance, in the twelfth and thirteenth centuries? The concept of purgatory was never fully embraced during the earliest Christian era, nor settled as an undisputed tenet of Christian theology. It's not even named in the Bible; there are references to rituals and acts that fall under the umbrella of purgatory, but that word itself isn't used. Purgatory's position in Christian doctrine reflects its nature: it is neither essential nor discarded, neither fully acknowledged nor utterly rejected. It's an in-between place, its footing in the canon unsure. And yet, during the medieval era, it suddenly gained so much more prominence, not only among theologians and scholars, but among common believers, too. Why?

I kept coming back to the role of the body in medieval Christianity. The physical body as obstacle to purity—but also, conversely, the site of purification, the place that needed to be made clean. I knew that was important, central to my argument, but how? Medieval mystics and saints mortified their flesh, while priests railed against the limitations of our sinful, weak bodies. At the same time, medieval theologians accepted the idea of material continuity—that is, that we all will rise in bodily form at the Final Judgment. Turns out we need these sacks of skin and bone: we use them to carry out our penance in purgatory, and someday, when Jesus comes back, when we all ascend, we will do so as physical creatures, as holy bodies. The body is what lets us perform good deeds, sing songs of praise, build glorious cathedrals—even while it traps the soul on earth, away from God.

I felt my mind circling itself, turning, trying to draw lines from one thematic concern to the next: the role of the body, the role of purgatory, the nature of judgment and afterlife.

I sighed, stretched, and pulled *Holy Enclosed in the Dark* from my tote bag; it had been lurking at the bottom for the last few days, ever since I stole it from the college bookstore. I read: *The tendency of the new forms of monasticism that arose, coalesced, and flourished between the eleventh and fourteenth centuries was away from an intellectualized Christianity, and toward an intensely personal kind of religious experience. This trend helps us to situate and illuminate the rising relative popularity of the figure and role of the anchoress, as the number of women devoting themselves to a locked-away life of prayer sharply rose during these centuries.*

In a way, the life of the anchoress was a straightforward and logical one: enter a cell built into the side of a monastery; let the monks recite the prayer for the dead as they brick over the door; and pray in the dark for the rest of your days. There's an undeniable purity of purpose and existence there: just the body, the prayers it vocalizes, the heart that beats steady, full of nothing but Christian devotion.

I shoved the book back down into my bag, squeezed my eyes shut, rubbed my fists into them, blinked back into the world. I could feel my mind starting to collapse in on itself, the words and theories melting and buzzing, even as my body longed for a nap (even though I'd gotten nine hours of sleep the night before). What if I was studying Hildegard of Bingen, or Julian of Norwich? Or some other woman mystic, or anchoress—someone less well known, or entirely lost to time, but just as devoted, just as devout? Would I keep pushing? What would I write? My own book, maybe, on those strange and long-ago women, who saw a hard and unusual path and started walking, looking straight ahead.

—

I decided, this past summer, that it was time to get pregnant. At thirty-five, I was entering the realm of "advanced maternal age." If I managed to get pregnant in the summer or fall, my due date would align with the end of the spring semester—meaning I would have the summer as a makeshift maternity leave. So I stopped taking the pill, and when my period, almost unnervingly predictable, was three days late, I peed on a plastic stick, and the world grew brighter, but also off-kilter. Tilted. Everyone else was exhaling the same air they had just inhaled, still moving forward in time, while I remained still, held my breath, stared at the black and white bathroom tile, and saw it for the first time.

It had been so easy to ignore those gnawing biological imperatives up until then; there was always another conference; another paper; another class syllabus to write. And I had thought that I would have kids after securing a stable, tenure-track position. But here I was, already halfway through my thirties, and still an adjunct.

So few women, across all the many past centuries, have wielded as much control over their own childbearing as we do now. Medieval women would have been giving birth for a decade at least, probably longer, by this point in their lives. A woman's life was a series of pregnancies, births, and probably a couple of small, early deaths, lives barely begun, or not at all. I envisioned cramped, dark houses overrun with six, seven, eight children—plus the hovering wisps of the two or three who died at birth, or shortly thereafter.

When I called my mom to tell her, of course she cried—she was a crier now. "Your dad would be so happy, Liz," she said. Dad had been dead for five months. The grief was an ache that lived at the base of my lungs. It didn't suffocate me anymore like it had at first, but I still carried it, a dull but insistent weight, all the time, and occasionally, I collapsed beneath it.

What if I had gotten pregnant earlier? Maybe Dad could have at least held the baby. I should have gotten pregnant last year.

Mom continued, "So, what are you thinking about work?"

I'm thinking I want to write a book about weird religious women who lived hundreds of years ago. I'm thinking I'm not where I should be by now. I keep making plans and watching them crumble to dust. Maybe we should have had a real wedding, so Dad could have experienced that, at least. I stole a book and now I'm growing eyeballs and toes and fingers inside me.

"I'm due in April, so the timing isn't perfect, but I think I can manage it. I should be able to teach right up to exams, and then I'm hoping a TA can oversee the exams for me. Maybe I can even grade them myself while I'm home with the baby."

"Hon, you'll have a newborn. You might not have the time or energy to grade papers."

"I just want to do everything I can to make sure that I get offered some classes to teach next September—I want the university to know I'm reliable. I don't want them to think I'm not committed."

"Of course they know you're committed. You work so hard!"

"Until I get a full-time position, and tenure, I can't take anything for granted."

My mom asked a few questions about doctor appointments, and how I was feeling. We drifted away from my job. Well, she did—even before the call ended, I was starting to think about possible grad students who might be able to help me at the end of the spring term. But the religion TAs think my program is mostly historical; the history TAs think it's mostly religious; the literature and gender studies crowds think we're stuffy and conservative. Not sure any of them would be all that eager to help out an adjunct anyway, when they're already assisting with—basically teaching, really—their own courses.

"Liz, did you hear me? I said, I read somewhere that ginger helps with nausea. I think Maddie Smithson's mom posted about it on Facebook. Maddie's pregnant too! Isn't that funny? I think she's working in a hair salon in New London now. Anyway, Maddie's having awful morning sickness, so Patty, her mom—you remember Patty Smithson, don't you?—posted something about ginger candies she found at Trader Joe's that seem to help."

I barely remembered Maddie Smithson. I wondered if, somewhere, Maddie Smithson's mom was telling her that I, too, was pregnant, and if Maddie was also attempting to feign interest in the pregnancy of some woman she barely remembered from her high school.

But my mom was trying, mere months after the slow, painful death of the love of her life: she was keeping tabs on people on Facebook, she was checking in, she was thinking about her pregnant daughter. *The baby will help, she'll be so happy.*

Before we hung up, I thanked Mom for the ginger candy tip. I tried not to think about the quiet and pristine house she lived in, where my brother Jason and I used to leave backpacks and baseball gloves and calculators and crumbs. The dinner she would eat alone that night—no, better, easier, to think ahead to finals, essays to grade, a baby in my lap, a pile of papers on a desk before me. Before us.

—

"Look," said my friend Kat over coffee (decaf tea for me) at Daily Ground, our favorite cafe within walking distance of campus, the next day. "We all know by now that the concept of 'work-life balance' is a patriarchal construct, a second-wave-feminism hold-over, and nearly impossible to achieve on a personal level given the scarcity of public and institutional support for working mothers. It's bullshit." Kat taught nineteenth-century American religious movements: Quakers, Shakers, Mormons, the Second Great Awakening. At the first department cocktail party I attended after being hired, she made a joke about the long-winded Buddhism professor, "Dr. Calder needs to go sit under a tree of enlightenment somewhere far, far away, and stop torturing us with all his mindfulness crap," and I relaxed. I had found my people. Person. But that's enough.

I sighed. "I'm not even sure I would have kept the baby if I had gotten pregnant a month earlier, or later. But, since I'm due in April I figure I can use the summer as a DIY maternity leave. I tried to time it as much as I could to line up with the school-year schedule. April isn't what I'd have chosen ideally, but it's doable." I sounded clinical, cold, but this was the life I knew, the path I knew: take this adjunct position, publish a book, get a tenure-track job, get tenure. I'd been walking this road since grad school—since undergrad, actually. I went straight from college, to grad school, to this job. What will it be like to continue on this route with a baby on my back? Well, no, on my front: I'd seen those ornately looped and knotted back carriers, and I didn't trust them. Or, I didn't trust my own hands to tie every knot tightly enough. I needed a plastic latch, the comforting click of unnatural materials, locking my baby over my heart.

"What does Nick think?" asked Kat.

"He said, 'I am confident that adjuncts have had babies before, at some point, in the history of the modern system of collegiate education.' Entirely reasonable and thoroughly annoying."

You don't understand, I had wanted to say to Nick in that moment. *I have a path laid out here that I'm trying very carefully to walk, to stay focused on, but now there's also this other huge thing that I need to fit somewhere on this path with me. And I know lots of other people have done it, but I haven't, and I like to hold things close, but what if I can't carry all of this?* But I only said, "I'm just worried about how it's all going to play out."

"I know," Nick had replied. "I'm not trying to be facetious. But I think you've planned this as well as you possibly could have. Once you're in the second trimester, we can tell Helen, and start to plan from there." *You mean*, I had thought, *I can tell her. I'll be the one having that conversation, not us.* I wasn't being fair to him. But it was true.

I glanced at my phone. "I have to get going," I said to Kat. "I've got office hours in a little bit. Thanks for discussing the woes of the elder-millennial academic with me."

"Any time," Kat said, raising her compostable cup to me in acknowledgment.

When I left the cafe and got back to campus, I stared at the students passing by, but they didn't see me. They were too busy texting, mesmerized by their cell phones, earbuds shutting out the world beyond their little screens. They didn't perceive their bodies as sites of sin or redemption, only as shells to maintain, to keep attractive, for as long as possible.

Before heading to my office, I turned toward the college bookstore: I would buy two books, I would carry out my penance.

7

WENFAIR ABBEY, ENGLAND, 1370

I NEED TO OPEN THE DOOR. But it is no longer there. How long have I been standing here? My breath rattles harsh in my ears. I hear something else, as well: voices of men, chanting foreign words on the other side of the wall.

—

The same sound as last night, when, alone in that room, late, I bolted up from sleep, into blackness. I wanted to slip back into my dream again. Mother was there. I rested my head in her lap and giggled; she did not have much lap left, she was so round with the baby. A sound from deep within her. A hum, low and constant. At first it soothed me; I closed my eyes against her warmth. She was murmuring something I could not understand but somehow knew to be kind, but then that hum became a burden—it vibrated over me, pushed against me, upon my skin, my tongue, down my throat. My ears ached from it. I reached for her hand, but Mother was gone. No words from her before she disappeared. The hum like a deep angry wind in a storm, or a mean old cur growling. But, everywhere now, it suffocated me. It filled my ears. I was alone.

"Mother!"

I was awake, on that strange pallet, in that unfamiliar room, sitting upright. I did not know if I screamed her name aloud: there was nobody else there to tell me if I had made a sound. A terror sliced me: the humming—I heard it still. But it was no longer so oppressive. I walked over and opened the door, peeked down the long stone hall, and the murmuring grew louder. Finally, I understood: the monks were praying, and their prayers had entered my dreams.

Awake and alone, I could not go back to sleep—the pallet felt so cold, too big, without Anne and Margaret warm alongside me. I decided to rise; I would not waste what remained of my last free night on sleep. I opened the shutters and looked out the window. I wished the sun was up to warm me. I heard, still, the monks praying, and wondered if they ever slept. I stood close to the window, the blanket pulled tight around my shoulders. I watched the stars blinking in the clear dark far above the trees. I looked down the hill, toward the village, silent save for the occasional cow or goat muttering in the dark, the animal sound carried up the hill on the empty cold of night.

I waited for the sun, and when it began to rise before me, I thanked God for this east-facing window. The sky was black, then gray, then pink, then blue. The stars melted into the coming light. On the hill, below the window, I now could see asters, purple and white, wet with morning dew. Farther down, in the village, I heard gates creaking open, and shutters too. From the treetops I began to hear the robins call and chirp, the blackbirds chatter. I was stiff and sore and cold from standing so long at the window, but as I heard and saw the wakening world, I longed to stay there, in that wide and shifting moment, forever.

Soon after the day began, Brother Joseph fetched me from my cell with a knock on the heavy door. "Good morning, Miss. Are you ready? It is time." My head nodded while my insides clenched and tightened. I forced my feet forward. *All shall be well. All shall be well.* The words formed inside me, and I held them in my mouth. With each step, I said them again and again inside myself. *All shall be well. This is for Mother. She is looking down from Heaven. She sees me. She sees me. All shall be well.* And yet my heart fluttered so fast—faster than I had ever felt it before, so hard I worried it might burst through my flesh.

All shall be well. The Lady will be kind. She is holy. She must be kind. She must be.

I followed Brother Joseph down the long hall, across a courtyard, then into the church, up the nave, past the rows of pews, past the altar, to the door of the cell, now fully unbricked and exposed.

Father Everard and Abbot Hugh were already there. Joseph stepped aside, then moved over to stand with the other gathered monks, while the abbot beckoned me up to the door. He intoned, "Glory to the Father, and to the Son, and to the Holy Spirit, As it was in the beginning, and now, and always, and unto ages of ages. *In nomine Patris, et Filii, et Spiritus Sancti.* Amen." He waved his hand over me; the monks behind me echoed, "Amen."

The abbot continued, "Christ Jesus, we entreat the soul of this child to you. Guide her into your light." Again, the monks said, "Amen."

"Elinor," said Abbot Hugh, looking at me, "it is time to join your wise and holy sister, the Lady Adela. Please, enter. You are truly blessed today."

*No, I want my father and mother! My sisters! Please, no, Mother—*I pressed my lips together to hold the words in. My heart still thumped too hard, like a rabbit caught in a trap, terrified, struggling to release itself. I looked to Brother Joseph, who kept his eyes on the ground. I could not move, as if I had rooted where I stood. Father Everard stepped close and put his hand on my shoulder. "It is time, child," he said in a quiet voice, surprising me with how gentle it was. "Fear not, you are blessed. You will not be alone. Step into your new life now."

The hand on my arm pushed me toward the cell. I balked, but the priest's hand was insistent, less gentle now. I stumbled over some stray bricks at my feet, over the threshold, and through the dark doorway. I stood there—here—hoping my eyes would adjust to the weak light before the door shut behind me. The monks began to pray, and the door began to close. I longed to turn and hold it open, but I still felt that I could not will my own feet to do as I wished. I saw her kneeling in the far corner across from me, hands clasped, head bent, folded in on herself. The door closed.

—

Still breathing hard, moments later. Still full of ice. Still here, in this living grave, with this living ghost. The monks still praying beyond the closed door. *What can I offer her? How can I serve her? Will I shrivel up in the dark? Will her holy fire burn me up? Will I be here for the rest of my life? Will I ever feel sun on my skin again?*

8

—

*O*NCE A MONTH, the religious studies department hosted a Friday-evening faculty cocktail hour. Cheap wine, limp Brie, stilted conversation, undercurrents of envy, competition, boredom, judgment. I've attended a few art history events with Nick, and those seemed a bit more glamorous. The wine tended to be better quality, and the art historians—the women in black high-heeled boots (actually, everyone in black everything)—drank it without pause or hesitation.

But over in religious studies, the shoes were flatly practical, the sips more circumspect. Nick had begged off going with me this time. "I'd love to get started on grading some of these half-term essays, do you mind?" I knew it was just an excuse, the exams could wait. But I didn't blame him. Last month he had struggled valiantly to make small talk with the Modern Church History specialist, Dr. Bronman, but found himself, as he put it, "trying not to say anything offensive about how repugnant the modern church is. What could we talk about? Holocaust complicity? Abortion?" He had a hard time seeing the individuals beyond their areas of study in my department, which seems to be an issue with religion scholars in particular. There's always that question, wondered at but generally unspoken by outsiders—at least, the few outsiders who bother to care or wonder, or even know that my field is a viable profession—do you believe? That is, are religion scholars religious? I could see the oddness of what we do: English professors are generally avid readers. Those who teach music play instruments or compose. But there's often little connection between a religion scholar's work and their personal beliefs. Our Hinduism professor was a laid-back Unitarian, and I knew that Dr. Bronman was a congregant at the local, mild Episcopalian church. Sure, I had a moderately scarring Catholic upbringing, but it was hardly a nuns-wielding-rulers nightmare: First Communion, CCD up through eighth grade, Confirmation, and then an announcement in ninth grade to my parents that I was done with church. My mom protested weakly, "Your grandma and grandpa will be so disappointed, it's part of who you are," but even she, by that point, had become pretty easy to convince that French toast and bacon, and the Sunday paper, were more enticing than 9:30 AM Mass.

So my parents were surprised by my choice of vocation. I was home for Christmas during my junior year when I told them I was researching graduate programs in medieval studies. I think my parents had thought that my interest in medieval studies and religion might pass—the temporary interest of a nineteen-year-old. "I didn't realize you were that committed to your major," my mom said.

"Ever since I took 'An Interdisciplinary Approach to the Medieval World,' it's just felt right."

She began to cut up her chicken breast as she continued, "Does that mean you're set on becoming a college professor?"

"I think so," I replied. "It's hard to imagine getting an office job. That just doesn't feel like me."

"But you're not even religious," pointed out my then-fifteen-year-old brother, Jason. "We don't even go to church anymore."

"We go sometimes!" my mom objected. "Once in a while. Holidays."

"Medieval—like, knights and dragons, right?" Jason continued.

"Ye olden days!" said my dad.

I rolled my eyes and said, "I just loved that medieval class so much. Everything was so tangled up together back then: religion and art, literature and prayer, God and architecture—" I paused, my cheeks warm. "I just don't think I'll find anything else I'm more into."

"Our daughter the professor! That's pretty impressive, if you ask me," said my dad. "You have to do something you love—don't give your whole life to some corporation, it'll never love you back, that's for sure." Dad had taken early retirement at IBM—or, more accurately, had been strongly encouraged to do so, with the understanding that, should he stick around and end up laid off, the benefits package wouldn't be as generous. So, after almost thirty years, he left, and the whole plant shut down a couple months later. Almost two thousand people were laid off.

"But I have to ask, who's going to be paying for all this extra school?" Dad asked.

"There are grants, scholarships, loans. I'll figure it out."

It was only last spring, when he was sick—truly sick, when we were beyond the banal phrases, no more "Stop thinking like that," or "Of course you'll get better"—that I really tried to explain it to him. I had been making the nearly two-hour drive back to my parents' house in Connecticut on weekends for several weeks by then, so my mom could run errands but not leave my father alone. He was already beginning the process of retreat into himself that would culminate in his death; he was wrapped in blankets despite the thermostat set to 78, the house silent, no more distracting chatter from the television. He lay back in his recliner with his eyes half-closed, his hand—the skin of it stretched so taut over the bones that it nearly shone, almost translucent—reaching out for mine. Awkwardly, I took it. We weren't an unaffectionate family, but I was a woman in my thirties. When was the last time I had held my dad's hand?

"What do those Middle Ages guys have to say about this? I guess I don't qualify for heaven by their standards since I don't go to church, right?"

"Dad, they also believed that the Jews killed Jesus. They were wrong about a lot of things."

"So why study that stuff? I still don't really get it. Should we have taken you to church more? Maybe you're looking for something we didn't give you."

"No, it's not that. The entire culture was so different than ours. But when I get past all the arcane and bizarre stuff, and really understand what they were thinking, it feels like time collapses, you know? Like I made a connection to something beyond myself." I was embarrassed by my honesty, my fumbling around the heart of my private truth.

Dad squeezed my hand. "That's beautiful, Liz. I'm proud of you."

The cancer pulled him down three weeks later. I wasn't there because it wasn't on a weekend. As an adjunct, I wasn't covered by the university's personal-leave policy.

—

I forced myself back to the present of the party. Ever since Dad died, this happened sometimes: I slipped out of wherever and whenever I was, and instead I was back there, holding his hand in that too-warm house, or staring down into his waxy face in the coffin, wondering who that man was, because it couldn't be Dad. Dad was my *Jeopardy!*-watching partner every weeknight at 7:30 throughout high school; after I graduated from college, he'd call so we could talk about Ken Jennings's winning streak, wondering when the heck he would ever lose. Dad was the guy who decided to train for and run the New York Marathon when I was in high school (he seemed so old at the time, but he was only in his early forties), and who, when I asked him, "What do you think about when you're running for such a long time?" replied, "I was thinking, 'why did I decide to do this?' And 'I hope I don't throw up.'" Dad and I both loathed the same public radio announcer on the local affiliate station; "I don't disagree with the guy," he said, "but he sounds so obnoxious sometimes, so whiny. And always talking about his stupid cat!"

Inconsequential conversations, his taken-for-granted background presence. Sometimes I'd hear that annoying host on public radio and think, *I gotta tell Dad this idiot was talking about his dumb cat again* before I remembered that I couldn't do that anymore. The past was, for just a few moments, more real than the present. No, the past *was* the present.

I brought myself back, and as always, tried to figure out my place: should I try to talk to ancient Professor Thaddeus who, I suspected, still didn't know my name or why I was there? Should I try to ingratiate myself with Dr. Manheim? I piled a paper plate with crackers and grapes (*no wine, is Brie ok? Better skip it, just to be safe*), and then, when I spotted Kat across the room, made my way toward her.

"Glad you came, I wasn't sure if you were feeling up to it. I barely feel up to it, and I'm not even pregnant."

"I wouldn't miss it for the world. The stimulating conversation! The myriad opportunities for professional advancement! But nobody knows I'm pregnant yet, remember?" I had only told Kat because she caught me nibbling Saltines at my desk one day when she came to my office to pick me up for lunch, a meal I was not up to at that particularly nauseous moment. And I didn't really feel like I could afford not to attend—I needed to stay visible, to remind everyone, *look, there's a really dedicated adjunct right here, should Dr. Thaddeus ever finally, actually decide to retire.*

"I don't know how you're going to get through this gathering of great minds without drinking—hi Helen, how are you?" Dr. Manheim, who had just stepped into our general vicinity, smoothly responded, "Very well, thank you, how are you Katherine? It's nice to see you here. And you too of course, Liz. Remind me again, Katherine, what are you teaching this semester?"

"'Religion in America,' the intro course. The one I teach every fall? Decent enrollment this semester, I have twenty-nine students."

"I'm glad we have such an interest, perhaps a few majors will emerge. Excuse me ladies, I need to speak with Dr. Weinstein about his 'Early Modern Jewish History' course next semester."

After she was out of earshot, I said, "Twenty-nine students? I can't imagine."

"Cheer up," replied Kat. "Maybe there'll be a delayed-reaction *Game of Thrones* bump and a bunch of kids will sign up for more medieval stuff next semester."

I rolled my eyes. Comments like that used to get under my skin. I seethed at the limited, clichéd understandings of my field; I hated the Renaissance Faire-belittling of my life's work. The jokes and asides still got to me a little, sometimes. But then again, there was something cozy about being so marginalized. I felt, not an ownership exactly, but a closeness, something protective and proprietary, over the distant world I attempted to enter every day. I connected with those lives in a way so few others got the chance to. Something like a relationship to a husband or partner. Or a child.

It's only in hindsight that we can affix a span of time time with a label and characteristics: the Middle Ages, dark, ignorant, and backward; the Renaissance, bursting with genius and light. In reality, the years just slide into one another, and the people in them keep on thinking and loving and inventing and fighting. We created the Middle Ages—and that term is frowned upon these days, anyway. We create eras unknown to those living in them. But we need these designations and epochs to measure not only the days that have passed, but our own days too. We need to measure and organize time. Otherwise, we'll just be crushed by its unceasing onslaught, won't we?

I studied those distant centuries, and the people who lived them, precisely because they were so far away, but I thought I could bring them closer if I just kept reaching, if I kept reading, moving back, deeper into time. They were aliens to us now, but their hearts once beat like ours.

"Anyway," Kat continued, "lots of students take 'Religion in America' just to fill a gen-ed requirement. They're not exactly beating down the door to sign up for my 'Religion in the Nineteenth-Century American West' class . . . hey, are you feeling ok? I saw you when you came in, and you looked like you were somewhere else."

"I'm fine, I was just zoning out. Shall we get out there and socialize? Just remember, I'm not telling anyone yet." I didn't know how having the baby would affect my standing at UUNY. Technically, legally, it wouldn't, it couldn't. But say I had to miss teaching a class because the baby was sick. Or I had to rearrange my office hours around daycare. I was already so far behind. How would I keep advancing, keep climbing, with a baby in my arms?

"Looks like we have a visitor coming our way, Dr. Clare's heading toward us." Kat waved in his direction.

Timothy Clare was my favorite person in the department after Kat. A fifty-something Christian ethics specialist, he didn't talk down to me, or beyond me, at these functions, just because I was a lowly adjunct. He taught a popular course, "Philosophy of Religion." I assumed it was popular because he was an engaging lecturer—and it probably didn't hurt that it satisfied a graduation requirement.

47

"Here we are, another month, another hopping department get-together," he said by way of greeting.

"Before I forget," I responded, "I wanted to thank you for reminding me, last time we talked, about Jutta of Sponheim. I'm going to use her as an example when my seminar discusses anchoresses this week."

"What's an anchoress?" asked Kat. That was something I respected about Kat: her willingness to admit ignorance. A rare thing among academics, in my experience.

"Women who voluntarily enclosed themselves in a cell attached to or inside a monastery or church," I replied. "They usually spent years there, praying and fasting. Their entire lives, in several cases."

"I'm glad it was helpful," said Dr. Clare, "even though there's not much available on her beyond her relationship with Hildegard of Bingen. Still, she probably gives you a good entry point—her and St. Julian of Norwich. One of my personal favorites, that one."

"All shall be well, and all shall be well, and all manner of things shall be well," I replied, quoting Julian's oft-quoted line.

"I could use a refill, I'll be right back." Kat slipped away to get another drink.

I smiled at Dr. Clare. "I think we might have bored her with our stuffy medieval talk. But yes, I think it'll be great to discuss anchoresses with my students—I'm hoping the extreme nature of their devotion might get a reaction."

"If I can play a small role in the attainment of the holy grail of student engagement, then I'm more than happy to help. Given how interesting they are, and how many themes and contexts they represent, I'm surprised more research attention hasn't been paid to anchoresses, especially when you consider the ramifications of gender in such a constricted, dualistic era."

"Yes, that's exactly what I think! Gender's been explored in terms of medieval culture pretty extensively, of course, but anchoresses are still relatively under-explored. If only I could somehow link them to purgatory, I'd be all set." Dr. Clare smiled but furrowed his brow in confusion, so I elaborated. "Purgatory is my primary research specialty—I just applied to speak on it at the Kingmore Medieval Conference this year."

"I hope it works out—I'm sure it will. Whatever happened to poor old purgatory?"

"It's not important to Catholics anymore, that's true, and there's not that much scholarship on its development, so it's a good topic area for me, at least, for now. Maybe I can eventually do more on anchoresses someday. It would be amazing to have an opportunity to do some research on them."

"It's so much harder for you, your generation, than it was when I was starting out, after grad school. Couldn't you apply for a grant to do some extended, onsite research? I'm sure there must be useful archival material on anchoresses in the UK or Europe."

"That's a good idea, maybe I'll look into something like that at some point . . . but how are your classes going this semester?" The careful dance of academic small talk: now that I had discussed my own classes and research, as well as a recent professional development (well, a hoped-for development, I hadn't been accepted to the conference yet), it would be unseemly not to ask Dr. Clare about his own work.

"A good turnout for 'Philosophy of Religion' again this semester, which is nice, and always a pleasant surprise. I'm enjoying teaching the seminar on the historical Jesus again, too," Tim answered.

I opened my mouth to say something in agreement, but instead a yawn forced its way out. I attempted to catch it, but he noticed. "Am I that boring?" he asked, smiling.

"Of course not, I'm just tired. I think I might need an early night tonight."

"Let me know how it goes in your seminar, Liz, I'm interested to see if you can drum up any interest with your talk on anchoresses. And good luck with the conference!"

I waved to Kat as I walked toward the exit, mimicking an exaggerated yawn, hand over my mouth; she raised her plastic cup in acknowledgment. As I turned away from her and back toward the door, I nearly walked into Dr. Thaddeus. As I apologized, he replied, "That's quite alright, Lily. Are you leaving already?"

"Yes, Dr. Thaddeus, just a bit tired this evening. Enjoy the party, and have a great weekend!" I forced a great big smile on my face, even as I thought, *Five years, and he STILL can't remember my name.*

I walked down the stairs of the otherwise empty humanities building; outside in the dark, huddled bands of students staggered about, giggling into their phones. Sometimes I couldn't believe I wasn't one of them anymore. For a second, I had an urge to approach them, ask which dorm was hosting the kegger tonight, throw back shots with the lacrosse team. But I wasn't a student, I was a pregnant thirty-five-old medieval studies professor. An adjunct, part-time professor. Not that the students would necessarily know, or care, about my status at the university. I was just a teacher, and not young. I remembered when anyone over the age of twenty-nine seemed impossibly ancient, practically another species.

Watching the students lurch from dorm to dorm, shrieking and calling to one another, a hot sour rush of resentment rushed through me. Not at them, but at the thought of all those tenured professors back there at the party. Especially Dr. Thaddeus, the lone medievalist holdout. Which wasn't really fair. Even if one of them were to retire or die, there was no guarantee that a ten-ure-track position would open up. Maybe the department would consolidate, maybe I'd be asked to teach one more course. Maybe the whole MEMS program would be shut down. I was guaranteed nothing.

A cold mist of shame settled over me. The world was burning and crumbling. Why should I be allowed to escape that, to bury my head in ancient books, to teach smaller and smaller numbers of students every year about medieval Christianity, the structural role of monks in medieval society, the churchgoing habits of fif-teenth-century farmers? Who cares?

And yet, Dr. Clare's suggestion was still whispering in my mind. Of course I'd love to go to Europe and study primary texts onsite. But how could I justify a trip to study purgatory? And why would the university, or any grant-giving institution, fund a trip for me to visit anchoritic sites? And now, with the pregnancy, and then the baby . . . I sighed, headed for my bus stop.

Back home, I found Nick in the living room, glass of wine in hand, reading the latest issue of *The New Yorker* on his phone. I climbed onto the couch next to him, stretched out, laid my head in his lap, brought my thumbnail to my mouth. Nick gen-tly tugged my hand away from my teeth. I thought about what Dr. Clare had said. Where did purgatory go? I imagined myself in a church, kneeling at a hard pew, beseeching God to ease my father's burden, to let him climb the mountain and ascend to heaven, to grant him some peace. I dozed off, and while I napped on the couch I dreamed I was riding a bike. A child's red bike, like the one I actually had as a kid. Although in the dream I was fully grown, I somehow fit perfectly. My feet and legs pumped and I moved forward. And my father was there too, watching, supporting me, cheering me on, as I pushed and glided, this small and moving accomplishment.

9

WENFAIR ABBEY, ENGLAND, 1370

*H*ER VOICE IS A SCRATCH, little more than a whisper. "Try to breathe more calm, child. Your eyes will soon learn to see here. You are not being punished. You are here to serve God. This is a holy opportunity. Take comfort in this truth."

I must answer. I force what I think are the right words. "My lady, I am here to serve and assist you. My name is Elinor. I am ready to learn from your holy example." My voice is too loud in my ears, too much for this tight space, although I do not think I am speaking very loud. Mother often told me to speak more softly, but it never felt like a true reprimand. The way she smiled as she said it, called me "little wren," because like that bird I am small and brown-haired, and I sing and chatter. Or I used to. When I heard myself talking too much, too quickly, and apologized, Mother said, "You have a busy head, little wren, that needs to share its thoughts with us. We are blessed to hear them."

The shape in the far corner—not far at all, four or five paces at most—shifts. Lady Adela rises from her knees, and walks over to the small square opening cut into the far wall of the cell, at the level of her eyes. It is covered with a rough hide curtain, but a bit of sun does slip around its edges. Another, even smaller window that I did not notice before is carved below it, close to the ground, into the same wall—I do not think it is much bigger than my hand. As my eyes begin to see more, as she said they would, I note a pallet against one wall, much like the one I slept on last night. And another, identical pallet against the facing wall. A long, narrow window—the squint—is cut into the wall next to me, at the height of my head, and faces into the church. If I look through the squint, there is the altar, there are the tall colored windows, there is Jesus on the Cross in one panel, Mary and the angel in another, aglow with sunlight. There is a bench beneath the squint. An alcove is set into the same wall as the window—a hearth for a small fire, with a chimney leading up behind it. But the hearth holds only a small heap of old ash.

I did not see the anchoress when we came to the abbey last January, at Mother's insistence, to pray to Mary on her feast day for the safe delivery of the baby. Not even a year ago, but already it begins to feel like another life. The abbey church was thick with incense; my head ached with the heavy scent, the haze and musk that did not fully cloak the reek and stench of so many bodies under one roof. The church was full of women, some deep into pregnancy, others still skinny, all whispering their prayers to the Holy Virgin. I recalled Mother kneeling, hands clasped, eyes closed, lips moving furious fast. Father knelt beside Mother but said nothing, merely looked at Mother and then at his hands, back and forth, again and again. He never was very comfortable in churches. Not like Mother, who closed her eyes during every Mass, clasped her hands so tight. Father took a deep breath every time we left after church had ended, pleased to taste fresh air again.

After Mass, Mother had walked up the aisle and knelt before the squint. Margaret, Anne, and I stayed back, in the pew, with Father. Shadow and movement from within the cell. Mother bent her head toward the figure in there, whispered for a few moments, then returned to us, her eyes shining wet. "She is a living saint, truly," said Mother, "and she has heard my prayer."

But now Mother is buried in the ground. Did Adela not pray on her behalf? Did she not think my mother worthy of her prayers? Why hadn't Mother or the baby lived?

Adela walks to the window and beckons me over with a curled finger (*like a witch*, I cannot help but think). I walk the few paces until I stand before her, in the small light leaking around the edges of the curtain.

"You are a rather pretty little thing. What is your age?"

"Twelve years, my lady." I swallow, trying to control my too-quick breath.

"And where are you from?"

I strain to speak above the pounding in my chest. "The village of Fossbury, my lady. My father is a farmer, but he has gone to London to seek better fortunes."

"And your mother?"

"Dead in childbirth, this past spring." The words sting, coarse salt in my mouth.

After Mother died, spring blossomed into summer. The land flowered, the tender green saplings stretched toward the sky, a mockery of the thick death that still hung heavy over our house. My hands pulled at weeds among the squash vines in the garden. The sun was warm on my shoulders. Hands in the dirt, sun on my back—despite my sadness, that day was a sort of grace, I see now. True, after a day of such work I was tired and hot, sore and sweating—but even so, I loved the feel of the fleeting, soothing breezes, how the wind slipped and whispered among the trees. When our chores were finished, my sisters and I ran to the brook in the woods behind our house. I dipped my bare feet in and watched the light gleam and flash on the rushing surface, listened to the bubble and ripple as the water slid over my toes.

But that hot day in the garden, as I knelt on the ground, Father's shadow fell on me as he said, "Father Everard will visit today. The Lady Adela of Wenfair Abbey has made a request."

———

Lady Adela looks at me now, and as my eyes start to accept this lesser light, I can see better. She is not an old woman—I had imagined someone old, with years of wisdom, but she cannot be more than twenty or twenty-five. She could be a bride, or a mother cradling an infant. Her eyes must have been pretty once. They are blue, but dull, like a day of fog and mist. I am not sure how much she truly sees; her clouded eyes seem to gaze elsewhere, past me. "That is very sad indeed. The Lord has cursed us for Eve's transgressions, so pay we must. Should we enter into matrimony and its responsibilities? I have chosen other means of serving. And now you will, too. Do you know your letters? Not Latin, surely, but maybe a bit of English?"

When I shake my head, she continues, "It is no matter. I will teach you myself so that you may read Latin, and thus pray with a true understanding of the words, as befits a devout young woman. That is my belief, at least. There is no reason to shield women from reading if we use it to the benefit of our Lord, to atone for Eve's curse. We will pray together, and I will teach you to read the words of praise that we deliver each day." She pauses and I sense she expects me to respond, so I curtsy and say, "Thank you my lady, it is an honor."

But truly, I have never thought much about reading. Why would I? We are farmers. Not that I don't enjoy tales and songs; indeed, I love to sing, to form the shapes and sounds of words with my mouth, to feel them dance on my tongue. But that is not reading. Reading is for the great and learned, the wealthy and wise. Or, that is what I have always thought. But now that Lady Adela tells me that she will teach me to read, I am curious. How do the words on the page become words I can understand, and then speak with my own lips?

Adela continues, "I pray not only for myself, but for the monks who provide for my needs, and the village people who approach me at this little window, seeking prayers and comfort. And of course my patron, Lord Monmouth."

I know this name. He is a rich and powerful man who owns much of the land around Fossbury and Wenlock. Including the land my father rents—or rented, before he left. The lady's food and care are paid for, and Monmouth's place in Heaven is assured by Adela's prayers and supplications on his behalf.

I wonder what my father told Lord Monmouth—his deputy or underling, more likely—when he left behind the land that the Lord had bequeathed him for a regular fee. Did Father give our plot to a neighbor? Does our garden sit untended, choked with weeds? I do not know, I was not there when Father and my sisters left, and nobody thought to tell me the fate of my home.

"Child—Elinor, yes? I understand this is a strange situation. I have been here many months—years. I pray and the Lord sustains me. But still, it is difficult sometimes. I hope that we might support one another on our shared path toward the holy, and Christ's loving embrace. I hope we might grow to respect one another, to form a bond of trust and affection."

It is far more than "strange!" I want to shout. I cannot imagine feeling affection for this stringy, bony creature, and as I realize this, my guts churn. If I cannot serve her properly, with respect and devotion, surely God will judge me harshly. I must not fail at this trial before it has even truly begun.

I long for no such holy path. I want only a road away from this prison—I want my sisters, our cozy sleeping nook, the warm fields I tended, the cheering brook in the woods—but I swallow my longing and manage to murmur, "Yes, my Lady."

"Because of my weakness as a woman, I am, I must admit, happy to have someone here with me. These many months have been . . . lonely. I have God with me at all times, of course. And there is much that is good about so much isolation. It is peaceful and quiet here, and I am not distracted by chores or wifely duties. The abbot checks on me and visits to discuss our readings and pray. But I began having so many dreams of young girls—for weeks and weeks I dreamed of them, their mouths moving and forming words I could not hear, their hands reaching out to me. I prayed on these visions for many hours. I thought at first this might be nothing more than typical womanly weakness, a longing for a girl-child of my own. Of course, I have put myself on a different path, but that does not mean I must give up the mothering aspect of myself entirely. I realized that this is how God wishes for me to care for a child: by bringing a girl here to me, teaching her, showing her the way. And now, here you are."

Adela smiles at me; her thin lips stretch to show gray teeth, hollowed cheeks. All I feel is ice. I want to scream, "You are not my mother, you never will be! I'm only here because you need someone to empty your chamber pot and tend to your hearth! You had some odd dreams, and now I am stuck here!" Bile rises in my throat. I keep my lips pressed together tight to hold it in, and I say nothing. I wait in the dark. I sense Adela is waiting, too—waiting for me to say something thankful, or kind. But I will not. I cannot. So after a few more moments of silence, Adela says, "You may put your belongings beneath that pallet, it is yours," as she points to the pallet to my right. "There is also a chamber pot for your use underneath it." As I put my sack under the pallet, I note that the cloth cover is stuffed with hay—I smell the familiar, grainy, dusty scent. Our pallets at home were filled with a mixture of hay, wool, and feathers. Far softer, surely, than this pallet; I can see straws of hay poking out here and there.

Adela moves from the corner to the bench beneath the squint, says, "Come, let us pray together."

I kneel next to her on the hard dirt floor, and like her I clasp my hands, rest my elbows on the bench before me. The bench is small, we must be close to both fit—so close that her dress rustles up against me. I cringe but then push myself to stand firm on my knees, on the dirt, my head bent, my hands clinging to one another.

"The light will always come back, Elinor. Remember that—after every night, the light returns in the morning. Much as Christ will return at the end of days, and save us all. Think on that. The fear is Satan, trying to gain a place in your soul, to turn you as dark as this cell. Do not let that happen. When he comes to you, you must pray. Listen to the words, and repeat what I say." She closes her eyes, palms together before her chest, and begins to intone:

"Christ Jesus, I desire heartily ever more to be with thee in mind and will, and to let no earthly thing be so nigh to my heart as thee. May I not dread to die, for I will go to thee. I beseech thee, take me, a sinner, unto thy great mercy and grace, for I love thee with all my heart, with all my mind and with all my might. I love nothing so much on earth as I do thee, my sweet Lord Christ Jesus." As the Lady prays, a stench escapes from her mouth. A sour tang, like rotted meat. I try to settle my shaking body, I try to hear the words she speaks. But all I hear is my own hard heart, still pounding in its cage, rattling my bones.

I can't let the words in. I can only feel the thick stillness of this cell, settling over my flesh, in my mouth. I long to make a fire in the neglected hearth. I want to make something, to tend it and watch it grow. But the lady wants me to pray, so I watch her lips and begin to move my own, copying her movement. Maybe if I mouth the prayers, they will enter me, enter my heart. I do not want to speak the words out into the dark empty space around me; I want to bring them into me. I whisper the prayers, to keep the words warm and close in my mouth. I whisper, "May I not dread to die, for I will go to thee. May I not dread to die, for I will go to thee."

My mother, eyes closed, bloody sheets. Did she dread to die? I begin to feel the words bouncing around in my head: *dread to die, dread to die, dread to die*. They are nothing but sound, rough pebbles on my tongue, empty of meaning. Mother had swelled with child before the last time—I remember once, when I was small like Anne, Mother, sick, heaving into her chamber pot, assuring me that all was well, that it was my baby brother or sister kicking in the womb, that she would be fine—and then, she took to bed, and when she finally rose again, her eyes dull, there was no more talk of a baby. Margaret told me that this happened at least once before as well, when I was even smaller. But Mother spoke with such certainty, this last time: "he is strong, I can feel it."

She was wrong.

I push back the thoughts of Mother and focus on the words coming from Adela's mouth. As she repeats the prayer for the fourth or fifth time, I begin to catch the words, and I let them flow from my mouth, too, and I try to let them live in my heart at the same time. I breathe them, and I believe them. Or, I try to. And then I feel them, just a little, I think. Mind and will. Dread to die. Mercy and grace. Now that I have muttered these words so many times, I begin to feel the shape and heft of each one on my tongue. Something light—grace?—rises to the roof of my mouth. I imagine it resting there. I feel the thumping in my chest, slow, in time with Adela's breath.

I must accept. I must, I must, I must.

I cannot.

Yes, my heart is calmer, but it is not enough. I long to yank at the bricks that block the door. I breathe, I pray. But this prayer is still bitter on my tongue. I long to hold something solid. A hand.

A door somewhere beyond the cell groans open on its hinges, and I hear the shuffling of several feet. Occasional squeaking among the soft steps—I realize these must be the monks in their cowhide sandals. It seems that while my eyes have little to do here in the cell, my ears are sharpened, eager for any detail of sound.

"Terce," Lady Adela says. "Although we are not required to pray the hours with the brothers, it gives a shape to the day that it otherwise lacks here. You are not expected to wake and pray the nighttime offices, but I would like you to join me for the daytime prayers. This will be a way for you to begin to learn and practice your Latin with me. Join me." Adela opens her book of hours— little bigger than her hand, with a hide cover. I have never seen a book so close by. I want to protest—*we were just praying, is that all we shall ever do in here?* But I say nothing, and although I am not eager to pray again, I am curious about the book. Adela opens it and I see that each page is covered in black lines and marks, with colorful little scribbles and drawings along the edges, next to the black marks. I suddenly want very much to touch it. I want to hold the book. I clasp my hands and force them into stillness in my lap.

She continues, "I know this will not make sense, but try to follow along, let the words wash over you." She moves her finger beneath the words as she says them. I want to touch the parchment, trace the inked letters with my finger, but of course I do not. I see a large, rounded shape—a letter—curled and flecked with flowering vines, at the beginning of the first line of words.

"*Beatus vir qui non abiit in consilio impiorum et in via peccatorum non stetit et in cathedra pestilentiae non sedit . . .* " I recognize some of the Latin as she speaks it. The priest spoke in Latin during Mass, and we attended most Sundays (save for when Father was too busy with the harvest and needed us all to stay home and work with him, which always displeased my mother). Here and there, I am able to link a familiar word spoken by Adela with the dark marks on the page, but most of them flow out of reach, beyond my grasp. Adela is not looking at the words: although her finger moves below them, her eyes are closed. I keep looking at the letters, and I hear Adela and the monks outside say *arbor.* I know this is "tree": I see the looping letters on the page, but also, past them, I see the tall and sturdy oak just outside of our house. I know *palea* too: this is "chaff." I see my father, flail in hand, lifting the long staff and bringing the shorter attached pole down on the wheat, or the barley, again and again, the sweat darkening the shoulders of his tunic. I do not understand how I heard *arbor* and *palea* and, somehow, I changed them in my mind to *tree* and *chaff.* I must have heard these Latin words before. Maybe from Father Everard? My mother always said, "Elinor, you have a head made for remembering," because I could list so many kinds of trees, because I was told the name of an herb one time, and I knew it then forever. I can still see a tree atop a hill in my mind's eye; I still see Father hard at work. I try to push these pictures away, I try to focus on the sounds coming out of Adela's mouth, and repeat what I can of them. It does not matter where the words came from; they lodge within me, now.

The monks' voices float into the cell through the squint. I imagine Brother Joseph out there, his kind brown eyes focused on the crucifix over the altar. I imagine those eyes gazing into mine. I feel a heat in my cheeks, and lower, below my belly, as the words of the prayer falter in my mouth, and I breathe in, clasp my hands more tightly, try to catch the current of the prayer again. "*Quoniam novit Dominus viam justorum et iter impiorum peribit.*"

When the prayers end and the monks shuffle off to their tasks, Adela seems to become a different person. She stretches, yawns, and turns toward me, almost as if surprised to see me there. "That was a good beginning. Although we will follow the liturgical hours along with the monks, in between, we will have time for other pursuits. How is your spinning? I see you brought your distaff, as I requested. The monks will give us flax and wool which we may work into clothing for ourselves and for the brothers." This hardly seems enough to fill all the minutes and hours of the day, but I simply nod and say, "Yes, my lady."

"Come, let us work at our spinning now." Adela pulls a long, low trunk away from the foot of her pallet and opens it to show me a trove of wool and flax, many silks. "These were once intended for my dowry, and the household my mother assumed I would one day oversee. Since that was not my path, I brought them here with me—this pallet is my marital bed." She smiles, but I grimace. I hope she did not see the disgust on my face. I do not think she does—I notice that she squeezes her eyes half-shut often, as if straining to see.

We sew in silence, but soon I hear steps—someone is approaching the little window that faces outside, and then the curtain moves aside and eyes peer in at us. Brother Joseph ties the curtain back on a nail as he says, "Good day, my lady, good day, Miss, I have your dinner for you," and pushes a platter and two mugs through the upper window toward us. Ale, cheese, a small loaf of dark bread, and two apples.

I take the platter and hold it toward Adela, who takes only an apple. She sets it on her pallet, then reaches under and pulls out her chamber pot. "Please pass this to the Brother," she says to me. I blush as I reach for the pot and push it through the lower window, the smell of piss unmistakable. I step back as Joseph reaches in for it, eyes downcast, and removes it quickly. "I shall return shortly," he says as he disappears.

"My lady," I manage to say after Joseph has gone and can no longer hear me, "is there no serving woman to see to our dishes and waste? I'm surprised to see a man doing these chores." I am so surprised that I cannot help but ask. I was ready to empty our pots myself, but I was not prepared to hand them to a man, practically a stranger. And certainly not to Brother Joseph. I blush to think of his kind eyes again—which I did not expect to meet over a chamber pot.

"Wenfair is a modest monastery, and the monks perform the duties of the household themselves. The younger ones take on the more menial tasks normally done by women. But there is no shame for them in this work. They are obeying God's will."

I am still thinking on this when Joseph returns with clean chamber pots. I thank him and he says, "It is my honor to be a humble servant. Do you wish to unburden your soul, Miss? Remember, I am here to receive your confession. Adela is a marvel and I have no doubt her light will shine on you, but I am here for your prayers and concerns as well. Please, sit at your bench, I will go into the church and join you, through the squint." He walks away, and I hear the church door opening, closing, steps coming closer, up the central nave, a rustling of robes—he must be sitting on a bench on his side of the wall, as I sit on mine. He sits in sun and air and open space as he wishes, while I sit here in this stony darkness. I glance at Adela—how can I speak with her there, mere paces away? But she is kneeling at her pallet, her apple untouched, her eyes closed, her lips moving, soundless. She is completely in herself.

Joseph peers at me through the squint. I feel that strange heat again, a flush near my belly, as we look directly at one another. I say, "The Lady has been very welcoming. I was scared this morning—it is so small and dark here. But she will help me pray, and learn my letters. I hope I can be worthy of her, of you—of everyone." I pause, feeling the tears rising in my eyes. I beg them not to fall, but they do. "I am sorry," I whisper.

"Oh, Miss, do not cry!" I raise my eyes to Joseph's and again feel a hot rush across the skin of my arms. "It is natural to be frightened. This is a very great change. But try to remember that you are safe, and that you are not alone. God is everywhere." I know he means well, but this is little comfort. I want to say, "I cannot see God anywhere in this dark cold place," but I smile and say, "thank you, Brother," as I wipe my eyes. "I appreciate your concern for me. I am well." He has likely not spoken to a woman or child since joining the abbey. But of course, I am no little child. I am not Anne, clinging to Mother's skirts, singing to her doll. I am nearly a woman. All childishness is long ago and far behind me, on the other side of these walls. I sit up straighter, force my mouth into a wider smile.

Joseph smiles back and says, "Let us not think about confession now. I do not want to overburden you—you've just arrived, I should let you settle in. I will return with your suppers after Vespers. God bless you, Miss. "

I keep looking through the squint as he walks away, watching his shadow recede until it is gone. Adela rises from her bench, and says, as if we were just speaking of it, "When we read earlier, were you able to follow the words of the prayer being spoken as I marked them on the page?"

"Only sometimes, my lady. It moved so quickly, the prayer. But some of the words were familiar, I have heard them in church before." I am still wondering about Vespers—are those the prayers said at the time when I would be eating the evening meal with my family? The dinner was heartier than what I normally ate at home, will supper be as well? I am so greedy—one good meal and already I'm thinking back on our simple farm food with disdain, and thinking ahead to the next time I can stuff my stomach. I should confess this to Brother Joseph. My flesh is weak.

63

Adela beckons me over to her pallet, pats the bedding next to her, and I sit. Her prayer book is in her lap. It is the only lovely thing in the cell. I notice that Adela rubs the edge of her tunic across the brown leather cover, keeping it smooth and free of dirt. Even when she is reciting a prayer by memory, which is often, she holds the little book in her hands, cupping and cradling it in her palms.

Adela opens the book and points at a word. "*Abundantia*," she says, "'abundance.' This first letter, at the beginning of the word, is 'A.'" She takes my pointing finger, places it on the parchment, moves it over the lines of the letter. I shudder and pray she does not notice—her fingers are so cold, mere bones with skin clinging to them. She must not notice my revulsion, because she says, "It makes the 'a' sound, as in 'apple.' Eve accepted the *apple* from the serpent." "Apple," I murmur, the word sweet on my tongue.

"Repeat after me: a, *abundantia*." I do so, and Adela replies, "Good. See the next letter? That is b, it makes the 'buh' sound in aBUHdantia. Repeat it after me."

"*A-BUH-dan-tia*."

As we make our way through the letters, I hold the sound and shape of each one on my tongue. She turns to another word and says, "Can you say this word? Let us make the sounds together: *ann-us*. Year."

I repeat the word, my eyes on the parchment page before me. A year of abundance. A year of apples. I see the tiny orchard behind our house, the six apple trees, the pink blossoms that sprout from the branches in the spring. I saw them last when Mother died. They faded and fell not long after she did.

—

I am still shaping the Latin letters into words in my mouth, with Adela often offering me the proper sounds, when a bell rings somewhere inside the church. "It is the hour of Sext," Adela says, and settles again onto her prayer bench, where I join her. This time we move to another page in her book, and begin to say, along with the monks in the church beyond the wall, "*Deus in adiutorium nostrum.*" I imagine Jesus right here, his feet on the stone floor, smiling at me, standing next to my pallet. No, I do not wish this place for Him. Nor for anyone.

After Sext, I walk over to the window, counting my steps: one. Two. Three. Four. I can cross the cell, from the squint to the far wall with the window, in four steps. I long to see the sun in the sky, so I can know the part of the day we are in. The curtain hangs slack in the still air, and I try to peek around the edges of it. Adela looks over at me and says, "Elinor, you may push the curtain aside and look outside. Do not do so too often. But it is fine to take some air occasionally." I push the rough hide aside, and tilt my face up at a small portion of green and sky.

The sun is high overhead: midday. A path leads away from the window and across a small clearing of grass and clover before it slopes downhill, where there is a stone building, and some sheep munching on the grass around it. The grange. The grass nearer the cell, where the path ends, is patchy, and I wonder if the sheep ever make it up the hill to graze. I hope so. We did not have any sheep ourselves, but we did have a cow and two goats, in addition to our horse Bayard, and our chickens. I liked the goats, Nellie and Jack, especially, although they were loud and silly, pushing their hard heads against my skirts when I fed them.

I will listen for the approach of sheep—I might even share a bit of food with them. I could leave a bite of bread or apple on the window ledge to beckon them. Maybe I could reach out and sink my hand into their wool, or even feel the warm and grainy animal breath on my face.

"My lady, do the sheep often come up the hill? I see they have made a path."

"That is not a sheep path."

I am about to ask who uses this path, but footsteps are coming closer from inside the church, so I drop the curtain as I turn away from the window.

An unfamiliar voice says, "Greetings, Lady Adela. And greetings to you too, Miss Elinor. I hope I find you well?" Abbot Hugh stoops to peer at us through the squint. His eyes sit deep in his face and his hair is gray.

"Yes, sir, thank you," I reply. And then, I cannot help the words, they slip between my teeth: "Sir, that is, Father Abbot, is there any word from my father? Does he plan to visit soon?"

A pause, and then, "No, my child—but you have only just arrived. I'm sure your father recognizes that you are focused at the moment on learning how best you can serve Lady Adela, and does not wish to disturb you at this important time."

Or maybe he is angry with me, still seething over my gall, my cheek, when he told me I would be coming here.

That day in the garden, he told me that I would be going to Wenfair Abbey while he and my sisters left for new ventures in London. But I did not fully understand my fate, not until the night Everard came to visit, and discussed the plan with Father while I tended to supper, my back to both men, my future consigned to a single room with a stranger while I stirred stew in a pot. I said nothing, faced the fire and tended the pottage while the priest explained my fate to my father.

"And all of my daughter's meals will be provided by the abbey?" asked Father. Too obviously more concerned with my bodily needs than spiritual ones.

Father Everard's spine straightened, his voice sharpened at the edges. "Yes, of course. Her meals will be simple but nourishing. Her lodging and care will not be lavish; the Lady Adela has committed herself to an ascetic life. But your daughter will have a roof, a bed, and regular meals."

"For how long does the lady require my daughter's service?" asked my father. My heart chilled to ice inside me as I waited for the answer.

"The Lady Adela has vowed to spend her entire life in the cell. It is . . . not clear how long your daughter's assistance will be required. Adela will surely receive a sign or communication from God instructing her when it is time to release the child. And, of course, should Adela die, your daughter would be released—may God grant the anchoress a long and healthy life, of course."

"Indeed. Of course," replied my father quietly. The priest continued, "God will see your sacrifice. And is this not what your wife, God rest her soul, wanted?"

After the priest left, as we ate, Father said, "Elinor, your mother told me, many times, that a bright spark lives in you. She wanted a different kind of life for you. Not merely washing and cooking and scrubbing." I glanced at Margaret, who kept her eyes down at her bowl, but I saw how her shoulders sagged.

Mother and Father spoke about me like this? When? It could only have been late at night, after all the laboring hours of digging, planting, laundering, stirring, measuring, scrubbing, cooking. Always something to wash, always a need for someone to go to the village well for water. But it seems there were nights when, while I slept alongside my sisters, Mother whispered about me in the dark. Late at night, the fire down to embers and glow, she spoke my name.

"You say Mother wanted more for me than a common life of drudgery—and so you are going to lock me up in a cell with a stranger? Father, please, do not this!" Anne, eyes wide, came over to my side of the table and twined her arms around my neck, buried her face under my chin, and I felt her warm tears slide along my skin as she began to cry.

Margaret said, "Father, Elinor is only twelve, she is too young!" But Father, flashing with fire, cut her off. "Do not speak to me like this, none of you! Elinor, be grateful. It will not be such a hard life. You will be clothed, fed, with a roof over your head. You will spend your days with a noble lady who will teach you well. People visit the Lady Adela's cell to receive her prayers. It will be good for you to be exposed to pious people!"

We were silent, and all I could hear was my own heart throbbing in my chest and ears. I wondered if Father's heart moved like this in him, too. He pushed his bowl aside and stood. "Anne must feed the chickens now, and I must tend to the horse. Elinor, this is what God has brought us. You have no mother, but you will live, safe and warm, with a holy woman who will teach you well, while I seek better fortune in London."

"Why can I not come with you?" I asked.

Father sighed as he said, "Father Everard says this is surely a sign from God. Your mother wanted a religious vocation for you, and now she is gone, bless her soul, and now suddenly the anchoress requests a young woman to join her. The priest says this is the hand of God at work." He walked around to my side of the table and put his hand on my shoulder. "We will visit you when we can, and you will serve and learn from a marvelous, saintly woman. I must believe this would please your mother, and her soul is at rest."

"And one less mouth for you to feed, with me gone. How nice for you!"

Father lifted his hand from my shoulder and I waited for the slap across my cheek. But instead he grabbed Anne's arm and dragged her outside with him. I began to clear the table and wash the dishes with Margaret. We looked at one another, and I wondered if my face was as white as hers.

"I heard them, once," said Margaret, "speaking of you. Mother told Father that she had spoken with the priest. She asked Father Everard to speak to the brothers at Wenfair Abbey. She thought there might be a place for you with the sister-order, at Wilton."

"I don't understand," I replied. "The anchoress's cell is no convent!"

Margaret paused from scrubbing a bowl to tuck a loose strand of hair behind her ear. "When Mother told Father about her idea, he was angry. He said, 'we cannot afford such a thing. As if I could pay a convent dowry!'" She imitated his gruff voice, and I couldn't help but smile, just a little. Until I remembered: there would be no nunnery for me, only a cell in the dark.

"Margaret," I whispered, resting both of my hands on the table before me, "What will I do?" She put a damp hand on my shoulder.

"I think you will have to go to Wenfair. What else *can* you do?"

I imagined stealing away in the night, a loaf of bread and an apple in my sack, running through the woods, toward . . . what? Where might a young woman be safe? What could I do to support myself, to keep myself sheltered and warm, my belly full? A part of me knew the answer to those questions, knew what I would most likely have to do, and another part of me did not want to know.

And now I am here. Perhaps for the rest of my life. I would gladly scrub the house from top to bottom every day, for the rest of my days, if it meant I did not have to be here in this cell.

———

After the abbot takes his leave, there is reading, and there is prayer. The letters in Adela's little book waver and swim before my eyes. Some settle into words that are already becoming familiar, like "Jesu" and "Amen." But most just sit there, meaningless in the dim gray.

My eyes throb, my legs are stiff and cold, so I stand and stretch my arms overhead. I cross the cell: one. Two. Three. Four. But after I have walked back and forth across the cell ten times, I feel my heart begin to rush beneath my flesh, and the air catches and swarms in my throat. I begin instead to walk in small circles, my eyes marking my feet with each step on the hard dirt floor. I let my gaze soften and blur but I keep my head down as I circle. I breathe slow and my eyes flutter.

"Child, you are exhausted. You may rest."

"But, my lady, it is still daylight!" I protest. At home, sleep during daylight would be unthinkable, with so many chores to do.

"These are highly unusual circumstances and you are taxed," says Adela. "You must rest. I—I insist, as your elder." She stumbles over the command, as my mother and father never would. I lay down on my pallet, and it is true, my bones welcome the relief. Adela takes a step toward me, then stops. It is as if she wishes to come close to me, but cannot. She does not move again, so I roll over, my back to her. I stare at the wall. I force myself to imagine a bustling city scene: Anne happily playing with the other city children. Margaret surrounded by new friends, city girls. Maybe a suitor. Father returning home from a good day's work. A happy family, snug in a bright new home. My stomach churns. I cannot see myself in this happy family. I bring a different image into my mind: Mother holding a tiny baby boy, my sisters and I gathered at Mother's feet, Father with his arms wide around all of us. A warm fire crackles and the baby sleeps. Gradually, I drop into the relief of sleep, too.

10

—

STILLBURNE, NEW YORK, 2017

I WOKE UP MONDAY MORNING MORE NERVOUS ABOUT CLASS than usual. That day, I'd introduce the concept of anchoresses to my "Holy Madness" students. I had spent several hours over the weekend rereading the works of St. Julian and Hildegard of Bingen, and a work called the *Ancrene Wisse*, a medieval manual for anchoresses written in the early thirteenth century. It begins with a section devoted to "external rules," followed by seven sections all focused on "internal rules." This makes sense: if your life is lived in a single stone room, you will inevitably turn inward. At least, it's supposed to, for the most part. The writer of the *Ancrene Wisse* exhorted the women to whom he was speaking to aspire to the purest realm of piety, that place of thin air high above the lowly earth, even as they were locked in a dank, dark cell.

An anchoress dedicated herself, her entire existence, to God: she agreed to spend her whole life in a cell built into the side or wall of a church. Men chose that life too, but it seemed to appeal to women in particular during the medieval era, a number of whom gained fame for their extreme piety. The anchoress entered her new little kingdom, and the door was locked behind her forever—or even completely bricked over. All that was left was a small window or two, through which food could be passed, and prayers requested. And that was where she stayed for all of her days and nights. Nothing but four close walls forever, and only the heat of her own pure devotion to keep her warm.

And yet, despite the seeming barrenness of the anchoress's way of life, so much of the *Ancrene Wisse* is made up of admonishments to anchoresses, warning them not to engage in gossip, nor to become overly interested in the daily doings of the local parish village. They should not, the writer instructs, keep valuable possessions, run a school, or send or receive letters. But the fact that he—it was, surely, a he—felt the need to lay out these restrictions suggests that anchoresses were taking part in these less-than-devout pursuits. In their quest to emulate the ancient desert fathers, to live lives of radical piety, did female anchorites actually, paradoxically, find themselves central to the life of the parish—in a way they never could be as regular, working, childbearing wives?

I suspected that the anchoritic life didn't just give women a way to sidestep traditional female roles; it also allowed them to assume a mantle of centrality and importance—of masculinity, in a way—that they never could hope to wear as mere women. The anchoress renounced the sinful, human world, and in doing so, she made herself notable and respectable in that very world, in a way she never could have been otherwise.

There's no point in rejecting the world, if the world doesn't see you doing it.

A solid idea worth pursuing, but not one to dump on the kids first thing. Something I would tackle in a paper, I thought. My mind was already diving into the deep end, eager to swim into heady theoretical waters. But in class I needed to start at the beginning, to make sure that these twenty-first-century kids could at least comprehend the most basic details of an anchoress's existence. I slowed myself down, I started at the beginning, on a Monday afternoon.

A half dozen students shuffled into the sparse classroom. The exterior of the campus buildings looked nice enough—the uniform brick facades either pleasingly cohesive or repetitively oppressive, depending on your perspective, but regardless, a nod to the long-dormant brick industry of the region—but the class-rooms themselves betrayed the limits of a public university budget, with their dingy off-white walls and harsh lighting. An oval table took up most of the small room, and we each sat in a spindly chair. I was at the head of the table, or what passed for the head, and the students faced me in a U-shape, around the curved sides. Windows extended across one wall, giving us a view onto another identical brick building across a small courtyard. I imagined more overly bright classrooms, more dull walls, replicating ad infinitum.

After I had explained what an anchoress was, I continued, "To be clear, this was an option available to both men and women. But why would medieval women, in particular, possibly be drawn to such an intense form of monasticism? Because we do see a significant uptick in anchoresses in the eleventh, twelfth, and thirteenth centuries across Europe, and especially in England. Can we think of any reasons why medieval women might wish to become anchoresses?" I scanned the seminar table as I talked, my eyes pausing on each young face, all of which were turned away from mine: their eyes looked down at notebooks, or at phones hidden poorly under the table, or out the window. Nobody wanted to speak first. This was always the case. It was the wrong kind of silence, the kind that signifies lack of engagement, or caution, or uncertainty, not the comforting quiet of the library, or the shared solitude of two or more minds at peace.

But then, finally, a voice, tentative. A female voice, halting, but still, a voice.

"It was a way to completely escape traditional gender roles, right?" said a student named Emma. She shrugged her shoulders inside her baggy hoodie. "You didn't have to get married, or have kids—you totally denied any typical female role."

"Yes, Emma, exactly," I replied. "Sexuality, childbirth, all of that is taken out of the equation. But then what's left? What I mean is, what would a woman who chose to be an anchoress gain?"

"It's a very performative method of literally embodying devoutness," offered Chris, a nonbinary junior with their gaze focused on grad school, their mouth already comfortable shaping words like "performative." "So, you would gain a lot of respect, probably."

"That's a good point, Chris. These women were simultaneously locked away, but also on display. There was a form of power inherent in the paradoxically highly visible role of an anchoress." The faces looking back at me were confused, lost, so I pulled my language back down from the loftier realms. I tried again. "Although she was locked away in a cell, people traveled to see her, to pray with her, to ask her to pray for them. So, yes, it was a role that got you a lot of respect."

I continued, "I know you're all familiar with Hildegard of Bingen, and her writings from the late 1100s. But I don't think I mentioned that, when Hildegard was a child, around ten years old, she was offered to the Church by her parents as a gift, to be a servant and companion to a woman named Jutta von Sponheim. Jutta was a noblewoman in twelfth-century Germany who decided to become an anchoress, and so she was enclosed in a cell in the church in a town called Disibodenberg. Hildegard joined Jutta in her cell, to both assist her and to learn from her."

"Hildegard is the one we remember now, but at the time, she was just Jutta's assistant and student. Jutta gained fame around the countryside for prophecy and healing, so local people began to visit the church and beseech her through the little window into her cell, just to be near her and receive her blessing. They also came to marvel at her self-abnegation: she eventually refused to eat, she wasted away and her hair fell out, but Hildegard tells us that her emaciated lips continued to whisper the 'Ave Maria' until she died. Just the fact that we have the record of Jutta's feats of piety and devotion, that says a lot about her influence—not much writing in the medieval era was devoted to women's lives and accomplishments." I paused, and saw all the eyes staring back at mine.

"Hold on, Hildegard was just a kid, and she was locked up with this woman? I'm sorry, but that is messed up." This from Emma, indignation leaping from her eyes. A flutter of excitement thrilled up my spine.

"Yes, that's pretty much exactly what happened. It wasn't all that uncommon at the time for children to be offered to churches in some sort of servant capacity. It was considered a way to earn good standing in God's eyes—and, in practical terms, it was one less mouth to feed."

"I don't want to sound judgmental, but I cannot believe that someone could just give their own child away like that—especially if she was going to be locked up forever with someone kind of mentally unstable," Lily, a short pale girl, shrugged as she trailed off.

I replied, "I think that's a very honest response, from our twenty-first-century vantage point. Let's think about this. The anchorite movement grew out of the tradition of the desert fathers and mothers—the very early Christians who wandered in the desert, seeking solitude, to atone and thus connect with God. To the medieval mind, a thousand years later, the closest approximation of that experience was to lock oneself up in a cell. After all, there wasn't any desert available in England or France. So rather than head into the wilderness, they headed into the cell. The result was intended to be the same: isolation, and total focus on prayer and God." I looked around the room, and this time, my eyes locked with others, all turned toward me, engaged. The air felt different than it had a few moments ago: now it was warm and electric.

"Someone like Jutta seems weird to us now because, well, how could anyone think that was a good life?" This from a quiet girl named Maddie, whose long bangs fell into her eyes. I had to lean in to hear her. She continued, "You're alone, cut off from everyone, everything. At least in the desert you had space—the anchoress was in this claustrophobic little room."

"That's true, Maddie. But let's think back to what Emma originally said—that this way of life was also a way to escape

75

traditional gender roles. And Chris's point about embodiment, I think that's really important here. If you escape the body, as a medieval woman, you also escape what was considered a very limited, and limiting, role—women were of course considered inferior to men. When you become an anchoress and escape traditional women's roles, you escape childbirth, sexuality, bodily domination by men—"

"But what do you gain?" asked Emma.

I was homing in, beyond the jargon and abstraction, on a young woman, locked away from the world, for the entirety of her one, specific lifetime. This is what I wanted my students to understand, to feel: the loneliness of belief, and the narrowness of the world for a young woman, and how limited so many short lives were.

The fluorescent bulbs above us hummed. All eyes looked to me, and I had no answer. I pushed them: "Let's think about what Emma asked: what do you gain from a life like that? An anchoress's life, alone in the cell?"

Their eyes looked to one another's, then to mine, helpless. "I can't think of anything good about it," said Lily.

"Maybe," said Emma, "if you're an anchoress, you get to go straight to heaven? You don't have to pass through purgatory like everyone else. You get, like, fast-track entry to heaven."

"OMG, do not pass purgatory, do not collect two hundred dollars. Just collect the glory of God forever and ever. Amen!" said Chris, to appreciative, gentle laughs. I smiled, but under the hot lights sweat trickled down my back. My eyes blinked and watered, my stomach murmured and rolled. *I should probably eat a few crackers*, I thought to myself, as Lily asked, "So, did this happen to lots of kids? I mean, besides Hildegard, did other children get locked up with anchoresses? You mentioned that more women were becoming anchoresses in medieval times—were more children getting enclosed with them, too?"

"It's not clear—we know about Hildegard's experience because she left behind so many of her own writings, and she's a well-known figure, relatively speaking. But there are so few records of medieval anchoresses in general, let alone of any enclosed children—at least, records we know of. My non-answer is, while there could have been more children placed with anchoresses, we don't know for sure."

Ignoring the queasy bubbling in my stomach, I continued, "I think there's a lot to be said about the perceived benefits of a monastic, contemplative life, particularly around direct union with God, and the lack of need for any intermediaries, such as a priest, which could seem especially powerful and appealing to a woman. But," I glanced at the clock, "we should wrap it up. I'll see you next week, same time, same place. This has been really great. Remember, read 'Intersections of Gender and Enclosure in the Middle Ages' before the next class. Good job everyone." I held the tight smile on my face as the kids picked up their backpacks and phones, and shuffled out of the room. Once they were out in the hallway I heard their voices pick up, animated and unburdened, before they receded down the hall and out of the building, toward art or history or literature, down one of many sunlit paths. I sat down and quickly unwrapped a sleeve of Saltines, I answered the demands of my body.

—

Jutta von Sponheim. She's a minor, practically infinitesimal, figure in history—just a footnote, really, in Hildegard of Bingen's biography. In her own life she was highborn, a noblewoman, the daughter of a count, and then an anchoress noted far and wide for her piety. But she's a dusty remnant now, while Hildegard is still read, her biography well known—among academics and medievalists, at least.

Jutta was only one of many anchoresses across Europe in her lifetime, and there were many more across the twelfth, thirteenth, and fourteenth centuries, too. But did any other anchoresses bring girls into their anchorholds with them?

I kept circling back to Jutta, even as I got into bed that night. The idea of willingly locking oneself away, allowing the bricks to be placed over the doorway . . . I tried to imagine it: I sit on the edge of a scratchy pallet, thick stone walls all around me, watching as the doorway to the outside world disappears, and the light with it.

I tried to think of a research angle, so I could write something on anchoritic practices. It wouldn't hurt to get another article published. Before I turned out the light, I reached for the small, thin notebook perched atop the jumble of books on my nightstand and scribbled a few notes: *Female mystics—anchoresses—rejection of the body? Denial of balance, embrace of the extreme. Purity of the extreme devotional act. Performance/performativity of religiosity. Negation of the female body, of biological processes. Subversion of expectation. Power and control. Limited options available to women. Rejection of traditional roles: wife, mother, whore. Children enclosed with anchoresses? Locate more?*

Ideally, if I had institutional backing, that could be a great research project. But instead, in the dark, I turned to wondering if there were any connections to be made between anchoresses and purgatory. If there was some link, maybe I could add it to my presentation at the Medieval Conference, if I got accepted. Maybe I could research Jutta's writings—did she write anything, and if she did, does it still exist? Julian of Norwich might be a better bet, since we have her writings. Did she ever reflect on purgatory?

Too tired to turn the light back on and reach for my notebook, I picked up my iPhone and started typing in Notes: *Anchoress and child helper. Are there more? Inversion/ perversion of motherhood/family/ caretaking? Purgatory of neither "traditional" family nor "traditional" anchoress alone in cell?*

It was so tempting to try to link random and disparate things, just because they happened to exist at the same time—or just because they both happened to interest me. Egotistical, in a way. Why assume there are connections that just happen to benefit me, that work to my advantage, support my interests?

I opened Google on my phone and typed "11 weeks pregnant" and read, "Even though you don't feel it, your baby is now able to kick and turn! Little tooth buds have formed in his mouth. He is preparing for a major growth spurt very soon!" *Or SHE is preparing*, I thought.

Eleven weeks, almost twelve. In a few days I'd enter the second trimester, and it would be time to start telling more people.

As I sank into sleep, my insides fluttered, but it was way too soon to feel the baby. Maybe gas? I nibbled a cracker from the sleeve I kept in the drawer of my nightstand, and sipped a little water. I tried to settle whatever was swirling inside me. The last thoughts always come back to the body.

—

Deepest night. I awoke in the dark, moonlight puddling on the carpet. Something deep and low in me was churning, it bucked and rolled. My feet lurched toward the bathroom. I had no thoughts, I was only the act of seeing: there, in the toilet where I hunched over, blood was coming out of me, dropping thick and placid into the water. So deeply red it was nearly black. It kept coming, it overwhelmed the water in the bowl, turned it all to wet and murky darkness.

I folded over myself, hugging into only myself, all that was left of me, as my new heart sank from sight.

When a sight or a sound/ Holds the soul in its grip,/ We lose all sense that time is ticking.

No. I pushed away Dante's poetry. I heard the rapid breath shuddering up from my lungs, out of my mouth. I shook and shook. I couldn't believe my bones could withstand all this shaking.

I cried Nick's name. When he found me there in the bathroom, I wondered if my face was as white, as stricken, as his. But we said nothing, as he knelt in front of me, as the blood dripped into the bowl.

11

WENFAIR ABBEY, ENGLAND, 1370

I AWAKE FACING THE SAME STONE WALL, to the sound of the same monks' voices. How do they get any work done if they are always praying? That is what my father would say. I still struggle to understand why he put me here. He is not a very devout man. He attends Mass but shifts and twitches throughout, and is always eager to leave as soon as the service has ended, to return home, to his animals and his field. Is he still attending Mass now that it is only him and my sisters? He must be, he must be concerned for their souls. I will know soon enough, I hope. He will visit me, will he not? How long could he possibly leave me here? I try not to think about how long Adela's been here, but I cannot help it: four years. In four years I will be a woman. I could be readying to marry, or married already. Carrying a child.

Or, I could still be here.

—

Did Mother begin to plan for my enclosure during our family visit to the abbey? While she prayed for a safe and healthy pregnancy and birth, was she also imagining another place for me? And would she truly be pleased to know that I am here in this cell?

I remember now: the ride home from the abbey, bumping along the road in our little cart behind old Bayard, who picked his way over the packed snow. Anne dozed in Mother's lap, folded beneath several blankets. Father drove Bayard on, watchful for thieves and bandits, as well as patches of ice. And Mother said to me, "Little wren, although I prayed to the Virgin for a healthy baby, she spoke to me of you. I felt her message to me in my soul: you will take vows and enter a nunnery. Wouldn't that be wonderful?"

"Do you mean I will spend my whole life praying with a bunch of old women?"

Mother laughed. "They are not all old! You only say that because you are a child yourself, you think all adult women are old."

"I am no child, I am twelve!"

"Very well, you wise old woman," she laughed, but the laughter faded from her voice as she said, "But truly, Elinor I do think it might suit you. Your mind twirls and spins so. I hear you talking to yourself in the garden, naming the birds, the trees. You should turn all that focus and attention to godly things." She went on, although she hardly seemed to be speaking to me: "I know we cannot afford it, but I also know what Mary told me as I prayed. The Lord will show a way."

I nodded in agreement, but in truth I was not listening to her. There were puffs of white cloud in the sky, and silvered birch trees along the path. I reached out a hand and dragged my fingers across the white bark, then pulled my hand back in and blew on my fingers to warm them. Mother looked straight ahead, her eyes locked on the road before us, while her body swayed with the creaking wagon, and a small smile rested on her lips.

—

I am fully awake by the time the prayers—Nones, according to Adela—have ended. She is quiet now, kneeling at the bench, eyes closed, mouth whispering. I would recite letters in my head if I knew them more fully. Or maybe I should pray. I need something to say, some words to focus on forming. But of course I do not know my letters, and no prayers rise to my lips. Prayer is not something I do outside of church; on Sundays, we recite the prayers we hear the priest say, and we only speak them when Father Everard tells us to. Religion is much listening, in my experience, much sitting on a cold bench while a man intones ancient words that will save my undeserving soul.

Now, here, I feel wordless, unmoored, floating in a dark sea, yet also, of course, confined, held in place far too tightly. I think again of that sailor in Fossbury, that endless water he spoke of. But I am here in this dry, stone cell. I can cross my whole world in a few paces.

Although I slept at midday—something I have not done before—I do not feel refreshed. I feel as if there is something burdensome on my shoulders. The weight of all this stone, so heavy, so close.

And then, also, a hand—not heavy, but light, nearly nothing. I jerk away on my pallet, and sit up to see Adela, taking a step back, her face an apology. "Elinor, I did not mean to startle you. But I thought you might enjoy looking at my book of hours again— merely for pleasure, you do not need to work on reading and understanding the words. You might find the pictures entertaining—of course, this book is not for mere entertainment. These are prayers of supplication. We must remember our primary duty is, always, to worship God and His Son. But you are a child, and I know children need some time for play and amusement."

I nearly say, "I am not a child!" but I catch the words and hold them back on my tongue. And truly, I cannot deny that the offer is appealing. I take the small book she holds out to me. Although it fits easily in my hands, it has more heft than I thought it would. I open the leather cover. The first page is illustrated with a woman kneeling, head bent, while sun pours in from a window above her, and an angel bearing a trumpet flies over her. The woman is pink-cheeked, white-skinned, small waisted.

Adela leans over and looks at the page. "A flattery by the

limner—that is me, supposedly, graced by God, praised by the angels for my great devotion. Lord Monmouth had this book made for me when I came here." Her cheeks hold no color at all. She turns the page and walks away, leaves me with the book.

The prayers that follow are illustrated with delicate drawings alongside the words, in the blank space at the edges of the pages. The first letter on each page is writ very large, and often wrapped with vines or flowers, or surrounded by small animals. I rub my finger over a tiny dragon curled into the space of a letter with a straight back and a big belly, round as if with child.

The creature's tail droops down the side of the page alongside the words. It is like a whole funny little world, this book. It contains dragons. I trace the lines of the letter and say, "D." Adela turns.

"What did you say?"

"I said 'D,' my lady. That is this letter here, I think." She walks back over to me—three small steps—and looks at where I am pointing. "Yes, that is correct. You do have a quick mind." I feel a warmth rise and bloom on my cheeks. I look to the small letters that follow after the large, illuminated *D*, and I recognize them, I let them form between my lips. *e. u. s.* "Deus. *Day-us.*" I murmur it again and again, the tip of my tongue rises, pushes against the firm ridge behind my teeth, then bounces back down, settles beneath the heavier "uh" sound that follows at the end of the word.

The monks are praying again, so I give the book back to Adela and join her at the bench. I close my eyes and see only roses and flying reptiles. Is this blasphemy? I try to focus on the monks' prayers, and Adela next to me, but I cannot help but see flowering vines before my eyes, rabbits leaping over them, and dragons soaring overhead, shimmering green, fire pouring from their mouths.

12
—

STILLBURNE, NEW YORK, 2017

FOR A LONG TIME IN MEDIEVAL STUDIES, the assumed logic was that, in an age marked by a 30 percent infant mortality rate, wise mothers withheld their love until the threat of early disease or death seemed to have passed. But in recent years, this belief has been challenged, and has lost nearly all its support, based on extant writings and histories. Mothers, even in the fourteenth century, must have ached through pregnancy, groaned through labor, nursed their babies, inhaled the smell of their warm little scalps, gazed at the clichéd miracle of tiny fingers grasping onto one of their own. Why did this love need to be proved by evidence before scholars would accept it? Why would we assume anything other than an early bond, even if it is eventually broken, even if a little ghost floats upward, into the shadows.

—

"We have plenty of time," said Nick, reaching over, placing his hand on my thigh, as he drove me home from the doctor's office the next morning, where the sonogram had showed us what I already knew. There was nothing left for me to do; I would experience some bad cramping, I would bleed a lot more in the next few days, and then it would be done.

"I want to see you again in two weeks," Doctor Anand said.

"You're still in the first trimester, but barely, so I'm a little concerned. Most miscarriages happen in the first eight weeks, and you're at eleven."

"Almost twelve," I said, although I regretted it as soon as the words slipped out—I sounded like a child, petulantly insisting, *not eleven, eleven and a half, almost twelve!*

Dr. Anand looked at me as she replied, "I really am very sorry. An eleven—or twelve—week miscarriage is difficult emotionally, I know. You should expect to bleed quite a bit more over the next few days, until it—the fetus—passes. And let yourself grieve. This is a loss, Liz."

I imagined watching a baby drift away on a little raft, down a stream. Passing by, passing away.

—

"Whenever you want to, if you want to, we can try again," Nick said. "Like the doctor said, miscarriages are really common, one in four pregnancies ends in one. So this doesn't mean we can't get pregnant again."

"But I'm practically in the second trimester! I thought everything was fine. Why wouldn't everything be fine?"

"These things happen. I know that's a massive cliché, but it's true. It's super common. And Dr. Anand doesn't think it signifies anything, that it means anything is wrong. It's just . . ."

"Fate?" I sighed and rubbed my eyes. "I know that's dumb. It's just a random biological thing. Or it's not random—there was something wrong. Something wrong with *me.*"

"Or something *right* with you," Nick replied. "Maybe your body knew that there was something wrong with the pregnancy. Or, maybe it was just a mysterious physical occurrence—"

"Occurrence? Didn't you see all that blood—"

"I'm sorry, that was a stupid word to use, a terrible word. I just mean that we probably can't know what happened. And I know how hard that is for you. For anyone! It's hard for me, too. But obviously, much more for you, this is about you. But you know, it was my baby too—" he stopped, swallowed, glanced over at me before turning back toward the road, and wiping his eye. "Liz, you're right in the middle of all this. It's still happening. Give yourself a break. It's gonna be ok." He wiped his eyes and focused on the road before him. I shifted in my seat, and turned my head so that, as I stared out the window, Nick couldn't see my tears. All the little houses streamed by.

—

At home, there was nothing to do but wait, so that's what I did. I waited for the passing. There was heavy bleeding, sharp spasms deep in my belly, over the course of the rest of the day. I tried to nap but I woke up on fire with it; the throes of the miscarriage were a cruel perversion of labor. I felt my muscles contract and release, as I sat on the toilet and breathed through them, while Nick fluttered, anxious, around me. At one point in the afternoon, lying in bed, I felt a sour wave of nausea rise in me; I barely made it to the bathroom before the vomit poured out. I kept heaving even though I was emptied. Nick half-carried me back to bed where I dozed off until I woke, a couple hours later, to wetness beneath me: I had bled through my pad and my shorts, and the bedsheet was stained bright red. Even if someone tells you there will be a lot of blood, it's still frightening when everything around you turns red.

At dinnertime, I attempted to nibble a couple of Saltines. Two maxi pads stuffed into my underwear.

—

The next day passed in a haze of mindless scrolling on my phone. *The vast majority of miscarriages (also called spontaneous abortions) cannot be prevented; they are random events that are not likely to recur. Up to 70 percent of first-trimester miscarriages, and 20 percent of second-trimester miscarriages, are caused by chromosomal anomalies. Most of the time, a specific cause for miscarriage is not identified.*

None of this was a comfort. I wanted a reason, something to hold on to.

In the second half of the first trimester, the rate of miscarriage seems to be 2 to 4%.

Such a small number. I was—I had been—so close to the second trimester, when I would tell everybody, when my belly would begin to curve, when my energy would come back.

I went to bed early and managed to sleep, thanks to several ibuprofen. I woke near dawn when, finally, the sad and horrible release came: a last rush of liquid, viscous and murky. I stumbled to the bathroom and sank onto the toilet. There was so much of it, which the doctor had warned me about, but even so, it shocked me, the amount of it, the solidness of it. In the midst of all the blood, I felt it—something with more mass, more bloody heft. *Don't look.* But I did. A wet and shining clump. Purple and red. I couldn't bring myself to flush.

I slid off the toilet, and curled on the cool tile of the bathroom floor. The cramps began to ease and fade. Finally I sat up, reached for the cup perched on the sink, took a sip of the ginger ale Nick had put there for me at some point. The walls were off-white, the bathmat overdue for washing. Four walls, so close. I felt my lungs contract, the small space bearing down on my head. I exhaled into a sad and dingy little world.

"Are you ok? Why didn't you wake me up? Oh God—" Nick said as he came into the bathroom. Behind him, the bedroom was lit by the full sun of morning. After he helped me back to bed, he returned to the bathroom, and I heard the toilet flush, again and again.

—

One in four, I reminded myself over and over. I wondered how far back that statistic holds; is that number relevant only in the twenty-first century? Has it held steady for decades?

87

I tried not to think about that other statistic: *In the second half of the first trimester, the rate of miscarriage seems to be 2 to 4%.*

That night, while Nick slept, I typed into the glow of my phone: *medieval miscarriage rates.* But a couple minutes of clicking and skimming revealed nothing. Of course not; what was there to be revealed? Miscarriages have always occurred. Centuries ago, who would even think to keep track of such a thing? Only men—and not many of them—could write. Why would precious time and paper be devoted to tracking something as trivial as the mysterious workings of women's bodies? If you weren't a queen, the contents of your womb were of little importance. And miscarriage, I imagine, was simply one of the many, daily tragedies of medieval life. Why make note of such a common sadness?

I thought back through the last several weeks, I parsed my every little action, I analyzed every bite of cheese, every breathless step up a staircase, every yoga stretch, every sip of tea. No coffee in three weeks, but I did drink one half-cup of strong tea each morning. Otherwise I'd have headaches, and it settled my stomach. It didn't feel indulgent. But maybe it was.

Say I was pregnant in the thirteenth century. If I wasn't a noble, how much would my daily life have changed with pregnancy? Very little, probably. There almost certainly would have been several other mouths to feed, endless rounds of chores to perform. No prenatal vitamins, no medical appointments, no printouts from the doctor, listing all of the foods I shouldn't consume during this special time. I probably would have been drinking beer every day—medieval people considered water dirty and unhealthy, and drank ale and hard cider instead.

And maybe I would have miscarried. Maybe I would have died in childbirth. Maybe I would give birth only to watch the baby die soon after. All of those possibilities were far more likely then, of course.

Every modern convenience at my fingertips, and yet I was emptied, returned to my prior state, the one I had inhabited for thirty-five years, but which was now lacking, desolate, a bleakness at my center.

Maybe I did something for my own pleasure without even fully realizing it. Were my showers too hot? Did I actually eat a bit of Brie, but not even remember now, it was such a casual luxury? I was careful at the last department party, wasn't I?

I put down my phone and settled down in the dark. Not true darkness, of course; the screen was still bright on my nightstand, and the nightlight in the bathroom down the hall glowed.

13

—

*T*HE SMALL LIGHT THAT SLIPS INTO THE CELL EVERY DAY SLIDES from one wall to another, and from ceiling to floor. I keep watch over this light, I mark its movement from the wall above Adela's pallet, across the floor, along the bench beneath the squint, past my own pallet. The light weakens as it nears the far end of the cell, until it is no more than a pale wisp which I press my thumb against, but there is no warmth, only stone. I have been doing this every day all these weeks I have been here: I watch this scrap of sun, I touch this stone. The monks' prayers mark the hours, but I still mark days by the path of the sun, its light and heat. Already I notice that it leaves earlier in the day, and the nights have cooled. Some days ago Joseph brought me a gift of sorts: a bit of flint and steel, and some straw for tinder. Adela, being a noblewoman, does not know how to make a fire. How cold she has surely been. When I first asked if I might make a fire for us, Adela said, "Yes, if you wish—I do not feel the cold myself anymore," but I saw that she wriggled her fingers and pulled her shawl tight around her thin shoulders. In here, every small movement speaks, and the body says what the mouth does not, or cannot.

That first time I stood at the hearth, built into the wall at the height of my shoulders, I struggled to keep the straw aflame. A bit of dried brush, even some twigs or pine needles—I needed something more. I bent and took the edge of my dress in hand, and tore a strip from the hem.

"What are you doing?" asked Adela. She looked up from her prayer book and set it aside as she came over to me.

"I need more tinder to keep a good fire going, my lady," I explained. I struck the flint and steel against one another again and again over the straw and cloth until a spark caught. The cloth took flame, and the strengthening fire spread to the straw.

"Here, might these be useful?" Adela had stepped back over to her pallet, and removed from beneath it several long scraps of clean linen, as wide as my hand. "I can get more from the monks as needed." I thanked her and added one piece to the fire, while I tucked the rest of the cloth pieces in the far corner of the cell, away from the hearth, so they would not catch a stray spark. I then turned my attention back to the fire, and breathed gently on the embers, growing them into flames. Dear lord, I prayed silently, I may not be as holy as Lady Adela, I may struggle here on this path you have put me on, but at least I can make this fire for her. I offer this warmth, amen.

—

I turn at the sound of sandals slapping against hardened earth. It is Brother Joseph, bringing supper after Vespers. His face appears at the window, and then he lifts a platter onto the ledge and pushes it toward me. "Your supper, Miss," he says. More dark bread and cheese, and a small bowl of vegetables in broth. Carrots, onions, a few chunks of beetroot. The last of the autumn harvest. I look at Adela, still kneeling, deep in prayer at her bench, eyes closed. I thank him, and ask, "Will the Lady's food be brought as well?"

Without turning to us, without even opening her eyes, Adela says, "Not now, later. Please eat." Brother Joseph leans forward and whispers, "the Lady has stopped consuming the evening meal. She asked the abbot to no longer bring it to her. She says the hunger sharpens her focus on God, and that if she is to have a fire, finally, as the Abbot has asked her to consider for some time, then she will have to give something else up in return for the warmth. But you may eat—you should. You are not expected to follow the Lady's saintly eating habits."

Because Joseph is near, I try to chew slowly, like a delicate lady, although I long to shove the entire chunk of bread into my mouth, swallow the whole thing all at once. It is good bread, better than what I ate at home. *Home*—the word rises in my thoughts and I think back on my last morning there. I was at our old table, Father and Margaret too, chewing our hard bread in silence, until Anne woke crying— something she had not done since she was a baby, but had begun to do again since Mother died. I rushed up the ladder and pulled her into my lap. "I am here, my sweet. You are safe." She clung to me. We were still up there, rocking and murmuring together, when the priest arrived, and Father opened the door and stepped over the threshold to greet him. Father called to me. "Come, Elinor, it's time."

Anne climbed down from the sleeping platform behind me, and clung to my dress as we left the cottage. I stumbled to a halt, Father kneeling before me in the gray morning. Margaret fussed with my plaits, straightening and smoothing them endlessly, as Father said, "Elinor, listen to the priest. Remember, the Lady Adela is of noble birth. Keep your eyes down, do not speak until spoken to." I said nothing. Father clasped my hand in both of his, and continued, "I will visit you when I can. I know you are frightened, but your mother wanted this, I truly believe that. I know this is a gift from God. I am sure of it," and yet his words wobbled, which was strange indeed. Father's words were always solid, and flowed firm from his mouth. Yet "truly" and "sure" tripped on his teeth.

I looked down at Anne, who said, "Elinor, why must you go away too?" Her words sliced my guts. I knelt down and held her little hands in my own. "I will always be thinking of you and holding you in my prayers. Will you do the same for me, please?" She nodded even as her small chin quivered. I forced myself to smile and not cry. I thought that if I acted devout, full of prayer and unafraid, ready for whatever God offered me, I would start to feel it in my heart. But they were just words. Little corpses in my mouth. I brought her hands to my lips and kissed them, then gently let go. I turned to Margaret, whose eyes shone with tears as she grabbed me close in an embrace and whispered, "Be strong, sister. I love you." She let me go and pulled Anne close.

I walked beside Father to the waiting priest, his hand on my shoulder. But then, as we stood before Father Everard, he knelt again, his arms suddenly hard and fast around me. He wept into my shoulder, he cried, "My child, my child! My dear daughter! I cannot do it, I cannot give her up, I love her too much, I must keep her near me."

I hoped for such a scene, but of course when he looked at me, his eyes were dry. In truth, he merely licked his lips and swallowed hard. "Be good, Elinor. I will visit as soon as I am able."

And then, he released me. The priest and I walked away, into the new, gray day. Anne whimpered. I kept my head up, my eyes locked on the road in front of me. I felt them begin to waver and water, but I told myself, *no, do not cry, not now*, and my eyes remained dry like my father's, and open to the dusty path ahead. I was not a child anymore.

—

"Miss, are you well?" It is Joseph, watching me, as I blink and startle, the memory so sharp I felt myself there, but of course I am here in this cave. I clutch the heel of the bread still. Now I do not nibble, I gnaw and stuff it into my mouth. I seek out every final crumb of cheese; I lift the bowl to my lips and drink down every drop of broth, every scrap of carrot and onion. Brother Joseph's eyes widen as he watches me and says, "I am glad the food pleases you." I wipe my chin with the back of my hand. I set the emptied bowl and platter back on the ledge, and Brother Joseph reaches for them and removes them; I believe he sets them by his side on the ground. I have to imagine the movements of full and free bodies out there now. A turn of a head, maybe a twitch of shoulder. My eyes are learning how an unseen body, chest and belly, legs and feet, move on the other side of the thick stone walls. My ears sharpen, too, alert to every rustle of a robe against legs, every door pushed open or pulled shut.

I remember the taste of the broth on my tongue, I take what small pleasures I can, and hold them very close.

14

STILLBURNE, NEW YORK, 2017

THREE DAYS LATER, I walked slowly from the bus stop to my office at the university, my head bowed, eyes focused on the ground in front of me. Nick had emailed Dr. Manheim when we got home from the doctor. She sent her best wishes, urged me to take care of myself, to take as much time as I needed—and to let her know if I foresaw needing more than a week off. Cancelling my classes one time was not a problem, but more than that and "we can look into making accommodations that will benefit both Liz and her students." I didn't like the sound of that—what "accommodations?" I was finally teaching an advanced seminar. Although I was still just an adjunct, I hoped that the fact that I had been "promoted" to teaching an elective seminar would strengthen my tenure portfolio—if a tenure-track position ever actually opened up. So I told Nick to let her know that I would be back on campus on Monday. I had a student conference scheduled for that afternoon, anyway. "Tell her I'll only need to cancel this Wednesday's 'Essential Texts,' but I'll be able to teach 'Holy Madness' next Tuesday. And tell her I have a student conference on Monday that I won't cancel."

Nick was worried that I was rushing things. He made me eggs and toast for breakfast, he rubbed my back, hugged me tight before I left. I hoped he couldn't sense it in me, that I couldn't stand to be within the walls of our house any longer; they seemed to absorb and reflect all my anguish back at me. I pressed a new clean pad into my underwear, just in case, before I left. I was still spotting and leaking—it wasn't much, but apparently it could last for days.

I turned the knob and the door to my office creaked open— well, it wasn't technically "my" office, it was "our" office. Adjuncts didn't get their own offices. Three desks had been crammed into the room, each one pushed up against an opposite wall, so that when I sat working at my desk, my back was to the door. One of the desks belonged to another MEMS adjunct, a guy who taught on sixteenth- and seventeenth-century philosophical traditions. The third desk theoretically belonged to a graduate English TA studying early modern textuality. The one time I met her she explained that she was interested in "drawing linkages between print technologies of the fifteenth through seventeenth centuries and twenty-first-century social media." But that was a couple months ago, at the beginning of the semester; I hadn't seen her since, and the stack of books on her desk looked untouched, as they had for weeks.

I had a few minutes before my student conference was scheduled to begin, so I picked up my phone and once again went into the r/Miscarriage Reddit I had discovered a couple of days earlier. It was filled with sad and devastated words. *I naturally miscarried too at a little past 8 weeks. Mine stopped growing at 5 weeks. I have my ups and downs emotionally. Husband told me our renter was pregnant (24 years old and first baby) and I started crying. Turns out she would have been a week behind me and will get the Spring baby I wanted so bad. I'm not jealous of her, just sad for myself. My friend blew me off and I suspected its bc she's pregnant. Point blank asked and she admitted it. Then started texting me about how she was scared she was going to m/c. Um, why talk to me about that? Like right now. Because I am the one who actually miscarried not you! IDK, lots of emotions.*

I moved to another open tab on my phone—a Google search for "miscarriage 11 weeks." *After a heartbeat has been detected at the eight-week scan, the chance of a miscarriage drops to only 2%. The chance falls to below 1% after 10 weeks.*

I kept coming back to those two sentences. I whispered, "less than one percent." The words hissed across my tongue, and a sour liquid began to rise in my throat.

There was a knock at the door, and I quickly placed my phone, screen down, on the desk. Spun around in my chair, sat up straight, arranged a tight-lipped smile on my face, said, "Come in." Emma entered, and I told her to have a seat in the chair I had dragged into the office after I found it abandoned in the hallway a few weeks ago.

"I'm so glad you might want to do an honors thesis on anchoresses, and of course I'm happy to be your advisor," I said. True, I technically didn't have a position at the university guaranteed yet next year, when Emma would be writing her senior thesis; my contract was year to year. But the MEMS program was already understaffed, could they really let me go? And, selfishly, I suspected that having a student advisee would strengthen my prospects. *See*, I could say to Dr. Manheim, *there are still students interested in medieval history and culture, interested enough to write a thesis, to consider graduate studies. I'm imparting knowledge to the next generation! I'm valuable! Offer me a full-time position with tenure, please, while you're at it!*

Not that this was about me—this was about Emma and her future. As she explained, "I might want to apply to grad school in medieval studies, so if I can start to research my topic now, I'm hoping I'll be in good shape to write a strong thesis next year." A future in . . . medieval studies? In 2017? Job openings were increasingly rare. Was I being irresponsible, or worse? I didn't even have tenure yet myself, who was I to encourage someone else along this path? Not to mention the minor details of a world on fire, and fascism on the rise.

"Emma, I feel obligated to tell you, there aren't tons of opportunities—professionally, I mean—in this field. I wouldn't want to feel responsible in any way for you ending up like—well, like me." I felt my cheeks warm.

"What? Professor Pace—you've got a great job, don't you?

You're a really good teacher. You make medieval stuff so interesting and, like, *alive*." Emma had wound a red, cable-knit scarf around her neck; she wore a loose gray sweatshirt over leggings.

"Thanks, I'm glad you think I'm a good teacher. I don't want to dissuade you—obviously, I think it's a field worth studying! But I wouldn't want you to think that it's a steady path, so to speak. Who knows what the job market will look like in a few years?" *Hell, I might still be looking for a job, we could be competing for the same openings!*

"I hear you. But I don't even know about grad school or anything like that yet. I get that this might not be the most practical option. But I want to do this project now, at least. Maybe I could focus on a specific anchoress. I've been reading Julian of Norwich. *Revelations of Divine Love.* She talks about God as father, Jesus as mother, the mother-child bond as kind of a stand-in for God's love for us. But, she wasn't a mother or a wife. She lived a totally ascetic life. That might be worth exploring."

The walls all around us were white, but dull, the paint chipped in places. I had no idea when they had last been painted. A thin trace of a crack was just barely visible in the corner, over the door. It crept across a few inches of ceiling. Emma was speaking, but her voice was just sound, no definable words. And then, a high-pitched buzz, a siren-whine rose alongside the sound of her voice, doubled it, shadowed it. *That's weird, what's that buzzing?* I glanced up at the crack in the ceiling, and as I watched, it began to slink forward, splintering its way across the ceiling. A fine dust of drywall drizzled down in its wake. The crack was slithering its way across the ceiling while Emma spoke, and the buzzing grew more insistent in my ears. Faster and faster it barreled across the ceiling; pebble-sized chunks of plaster fell. Sunlight poked through as the crack widened. All I heard was that droning hum, all I saw was blue sky peeking through plaster.

I started to rise from my chair and reach toward Emma, who looked startled and said, "Professor Pace, what are you doing? Are you ok?"

I froze, even as my heart kept pounding, too hard behind my ribs. No whining buzz, no falling plaster. The ceiling had not broken apart, of course. The crack was still a sliver, as it had been when I arrived, just a few inches long, nothing more.

Emma's mouth hung half open. I opened my own dry lips, but it took a moment for any words to come out.

"Sorry, Emma, I thought I heard something but . . . never mind." I sat back down, pushed my hair behind my ears. Sweat damp at my hairline. "Anyway, you've made a good start. Have you read Warren's essay, 'Solitude and Sociability: The World of the Medieval Anchorite'? It'll give you some good starting points. Why don't you read that, and let's plan on meeting again in two weeks to hone your topic. And by the way," I continued, trying to cover the sound of my rapidly beating heart, which I was sure she could hear, "I wasn't trying to tell you not to go into medieval studies. And of course you have time to explore different areas. I just felt like I should say something. Fair warning, you know?" I forced myself to smile again, even as my heart was still pounding so fast and hard, I thought she must be able to see it jumping and straining under my skin.

"I totally get it, and I appreciate it," she replied. "Sounds good about the essay. Thank you so much, again, seriously." She smiled, showing all her straight white teeth, then left. Once she was gone, my office was suddenly a place my body could not bear to be. All those walls. I scrambled out of my chair, down the stairs, through the door, into sunshine. I glanced back at the humanities building. Still standing.

On the way home, my heartbeat gradually calmed. *Take it easy. You're just wiped out. It's been a hard few days, but like Nick said, you can try again. You're fine. A shitty thing happened, but you're ok. You'll be ok. Forget your research today, just go home, lie down, have some tea. Maybe hallucinations are a side effect of miscarriage?* I took my phone out of my bag, opened Google, but found nothing on hallucinating after a miscarriage. With my phone already in my hand, I automatically checked my email.

> Dear Dr. Pace,
>
> I am pleased to inform you that your paper, "The Third Place: Developing a Theology of Purgatory, 1100-1300" has been accepted into the Spring 2018 session of the Kingmore Conference on Medieval Studies. Your work is insightful, and will no doubt be an enriching addition to the Conference. Attached you will find a downloadable pdf comprised of housing forms, FAQs, and the contact information for your session representative. Please note that we kindly ask that you confirm your attendance by replying to this email. I also ask that you fill out the housing form and email it directly to your component representative no later than December 1. We look forward to welcoming you to a stimulating Conference in March.
>
> Congratulations again, and best regards,
>
> Dr. Bernard Apwell
>
> Chair, Kingmore Conference on Medieval Studies, Kingmore College

I stared at the screen in my palm, and tried to remember how exciting this news was. But the words wavered, blurred by the tears filling my eyes.

———

An empty house; Nick was teaching that afternoon. I lowered myself onto a chair by the kitchen table. Too early to make dinner, and the thought of food was horrible, anyway. Leonardo purred around my ankles.

I moved out to the small back deck, just big enough for a table and two chairs, and three pots where I grew herbs, although by this point in the autumn they were long dead. I thought about Julian of Norwich. Julian wasn't even her real name. She's just called that because she was enclosed at St. Julian's Church in Norwich. We don't know who she was, really—not her family, or where she went to school, or her entire life, her first three decades, before she became an anchoress. She isolated herself in her cell and she wrote anonymously. But she was known during her lifetime. Other women came to her, studied under her. Her writings were copied out and carefully preserved by nuns and female scribes. She walked away from the world, and the world came to her doorstep.

I was still sitting there thinking in circles around Julian, the act of cloistering, the push and pull of isolation and recognition, when I heard the door open. "Liz? You home?" called Nick from the kitchen. I didn't respond or even turn around. A moment later I heard the sliding door squeak open, and Nick was standing next to me on the porch. "How are you feeling?"

Without turning to look at him, I replied, "I don't know. I was in a student conference earlier, and I think I had a hallucination. I was suddenly convinced that the building was about to fall down around me. It was literally falling apart. But, it wasn't, of course. So I just came home." I looked up at Nick, and his eyes were full of something new, something unsettled: alarm. "You've been through a lot, babe. I'll make us something to eat, you just take it easy, maybe close your eyes."

I leaned my head back, closed my eyes. The dutiful wife. No, a dutiful wife bears plenty of healthy children for her husband. Of course Nick and I didn't think like that. We were equals—if given the chance, we would coparent, we would embody balance. Our child would be enlightened, surrounded by books, classical music, organic food. But first, I had to bring that child into the world, I had to bring that child home. If I couldn't do that, I couldn't give a child anything else, anything at all. I sat upright and blinked, stood and shook and stretched. *This is stupid. You're being too hard on yourself. You're more than a machine for making babies. And anyway, the doctor said you'd probably be able to get pregnant again. And you have options. There's adoption, all sorts of possibilities.* I reached over and plucked a couple not-completely-brown leaves off the sage plant in one of the pots, inhaled the strong, earthy scent, and dropped them over the side of the deck.

I walked into the kitchen, where Nick was sautéing chicken. I unscrewed the cap of the unopened bottle of red wine on the counter, poured myself a generous glass. Nick raised his eyebrows.

"I can have a glass of wine now. I probably could before, too. I was so careful, and it didn't matter." As we sat down to eat dinner, I said, "My paper was accepted into the conference." I nudged the chicken with my fork, poked at my salad.

"Liz, that's amazing!" Nick moved around to my side of the table, wrapped his arms around me tight. "Damn, this is awesome. You've worked so hard on purgatory for years. Step aside heaven and hell, it's purgatory's time to shine!" He walked over to the counter and poured himself a smaller glass of wine. "Seriously, this is great. Helen is gonna have to do something for you once you deliver your knockout presentation and the publishers come running. Should I come to the conference? Can I cheer? I'll sit in the back and pretend I don't know you." He laughed and took a sip of my wine.

I put a forkful of chicken in my mouth. It tasted sour, but I gagged it down. I shuddered, took a sip of wine. A gulp, actually. "I guess. But I'm thinking of going in some other directions now. Maybe something on anchoresses in the Middle Ages. There was this one, Adela something, in England—I saw her name mentioned in a book." *A stolen book, still sitting in my tote bag.* I walked to the counter, poured more wine into my own suddenly empty glass.

"That's interesting. But it probably makes more sense to focus on the purgatory paper for now, get ready for the conference, right? Maybe a paper on anchoresses after the conference."

"Actually, I'm hoping I can tie anchoresses into what I've already been studying. Because that's what we always do—put each thing into its own tidy little category, right? But that's not how the world is. I've been reading Tertullian, one of the earliest

Christians to write about purgatory—he envisioned it as a realm where each soul receives a sort of preview of their final fate: the wicked are subjected to Hell's punishments briefly, while the good experience bliss, but they need to undergo purification rites to either avoid their fate, or move toward it. But he's mostly remembered now for his misogyny, he's the one who called women the 'devil's gateway.'"

"Sounds like someone could use a few sessions on the couch. 'Devil's gateway'? Paging Dr. Freud!" I didn't acknowledge Nick's joke. Dampness spread in my armpits, across my upper lip.

"Actually, I could tie what Tertullian said in with purgatory, I think. Purgatory is the third place, neither here nor there, in-between, and that's what pregnancy is too, right?"

Nick paused, fork halfway to his mouth. "Liz, what does pregnancy have to do with any of this? First you were talking about anchoresses, then some ancient misogynist."

"No, you don't understand, I can bring it all together. When you're pregnant, you're not a virgin, obviously, but not a mother, exactly. You are, kind of—I was, kind of—but not really.

Pregnancy is an in-between stage. Plus there's the baby's soul: it's not preexistent, but it's not a fully formed singular being either. It's all linked: all this discomfort with in-between stages, this longing to categorize all of existence in dichotomies. But pregnancy and purgatory both exist beyond traditional categories. Pregnancy is a literal embodiment of a purgatorial state. That's really good, isn't it? I'm going to write that down." I got up to grab a notebook from the table in the living room. My legs wobbled beneath me, pinpricks of light winked in front of my eyes.

"But what does any of this have to do with anchoresses?"

I stood still, gripping the back of my chair. "I haven't connected everything yet, but I think I can make everything fit. Anchoresses didn't adhere to any of the typical categorical roles available to women at the time, so they defied categorization, too. They weren't in heaven, or in hell either—they embodied a total reconfiguration of the accepted categories." I breathed hard and shallow. *I'm not making any sense.* I pushed hard against the thought, I swallowed it whole.

"That's all interesting, but honestly? You're reaching. I don't think you'll have an easy time tying all of this together. And your paper was accepted as a study of how the theology of purgatory developed during the twelfth and thirteenth centuries. That's what they'll be expecting you to talk about."

"Oh my god, who cares about purgatory! The country is falling apart, this racist sexist nightmare is our president, what does it even matter?"

"It matters because it's your life's work! Jesus Christ, Liz, when we met, purgatory was the first thing you talked about. You read fucking Dante on the beach! And that's what I love about you." Nick exhaled loudly, rubbed his temples. "Sit down and try to eat something. Please. You're being too hard on yourself. Take it one step at a time. Focus on the conference and your purgatory paper, and then you can expand into other research areas. It's not like you to just drop everything you've worked so hard for."

"Well, maybe I'm sick of doing what I'm supposed to. Where has it gotten me?" I was sweating more; I tasted salt on my lips. The world wavered, all of it: chicken, salad, Nick, walls, kitchen. I blinked. Sweating all over. For just a moment, I saw it: there was a mountain, and at the foot of it, a little cabin or house, but made of stone, with a rounded roof. One wall was cut away so I could see inside. A woman in a long dress, sitting on a chair. Her hands rested on her swollen belly; she stared directly at me. She did not smile, she did not look away. I stared right back.

And then the darkness dragged me down.

15

---

*N*IGHT HERE IS TOO DARK. At home, the night was often tempered with a single candle, offering Mother a small light by which to scrub the last stubborn pots. Or the final embers lingering in the hearth as I sank into sleep. That was a warm darkness, heated at its soft edges.

But the struggling light given off by the weak fire I poke and tend without end is nothing against the black walls of this place. The close walls loom over me, so it truly does feel like all is black, everywhere, no beginning and no end—like God. I know this creeps close to blasphemy: comparing the vastness of God to this endless, cold darkness, and in God's holy house, while supposedly serving a holy woman. And yet why do I speak of endlessness, when I am contained in such a tight place? It may be that all this darkness, this lack of light and air, tests my mind. It may be *this* is my test: I must not succumb to the blackness. I bring my hand close to my face: I sense the shape of my palm, my own breath on it. Here. Living flesh. Here.

I sleep, I think, because then I wake to more dark. Sleep again, and wake to constant dark. My body cannot rest, it seems, in so much stillness. I need the sighs of settling cows, or the whispering crackles of a low fire. I slip back down into sleep, but wake again—this time, to something else in the dark: a voice whispering "Lady? My Lady, please, I beseech you." The words scratch the air, and Adela stirs and stumbles to the outside-facing window. There is movement on the other side, a gray shape distinct against the darkness of the sleeping world. I do not move on my pallet, but I listen.

"Yes, I am here, I shall pray for you," Adela whispers, settling herself on the bench.

"My Lady, if you please—I do not know what to do, where else to go. I have sinned terribly, but my father cannot find out, he shall beat me to death. My Lady, I am a horrible sinner before Christ, but please, I need help."

I am still cobwebbed with the last threads of sleep, but I hear that the voice is young and full of terror.

"You are not married, I presume?"

"No, my Lady. He assured me that he would marry me—he swore it! But now he will not speak to me, he does not meet my eyes, he walks right past me as if I were a stranger."

"You committed a great and terrible sin, child. You were consumed with lust and succumbed to the flesh. I will pray for your soul now. And I will entreat the Virgin to watch over you." Lady Adela begins to intone, "Hail Mary, full of grace—"

"My Lady, I thank you very much for your prayers. I am in need of them, I know I have been weak, and I pray that Jesus and the Virgin will take pity on me. But also, Lady, might you be able to help me with . . ." And here, her voice drifts to nothingness.

Adela's voice is ice. "What, exactly, do you ask of me? I offer my prayers for your soul, in the hopes that it will not be consigned to the fires of Hell. What other assistance do you seek?"

"My Lady, please, I do not mean to offend you. I am most honored by your prayers. I thought you might also be able to pray that the baby might go away? Or, maybe, you might even know of a remedy, something I might do—"

"How dare you? You come to me and wake me in the middle

of the night, I pray for your endangered soul, and you now ask me for—what? Potions and spells? I am no witch!" Adela rises now, her hands on the ledge as she spits the words. "You dare speak of these things in a consecrated church? I am a Christian, I have given everything to Christ—"

"Apologies, apologies, my lady! I should not have asked. I am a fool. Please, forgive me, lady. I—I thank you for your prayers, I should go." As she scuttles off, Adela sighs, leans forward, and calls out into the night air in a harsh whisper, "Child, wait, come back." As the girl returns, Adela, her voice now worn and tired, whispers, "Go to the midwife Alice. Now. Wake her, and tell her I sent you. Do not wait for daylight. She will help you, and you will not have to pay. May God bless you."

"Thank you, my Lady. You are truly holy. I will pray for you every day for the rest of my life. I know my prayers are not as powerful as yours, but even so I will do it, I swear." And she is gone.

I roll over, sit up on my pallet, and pull my knees to my chest, as Adela sighs and leans back into the cell and against the wall. She seems to shrink as she closes her eyes, opens them again, and her eyes meet mine. Questions flicker in my mind but do not reach my tongue. Her shoulders sag as she says, in a voice hardly more than a whisper, "These girls, their lives will be ruined if they bear such ill-gotten babies. Because of Eve, these bodies of ours are contraptions seemingly intended to trick and condemn us at every step. When these girls come to me—yes, she is merely one of many—I am so angry at their stupidity, at how easily they swallow the smooth words of men."

I am not sure that Adela is speaking to me as she continues, "Some of these girls can't bring themselves to do what they know they need to do, they need to hear me tell them to go to the midwife. Or, they cannot pay. So, I give them permission to do what they already know they must. If need be, I pay for it. But I pray for them, their souls, and those unborn little souls too. God understands. Does He not? He must."

I want to ask, "What can the midwife do for them that you

cannot?" but I hold my tongue. As my father said, it is not my place to speak unless spoken to, and I do not believe Adela is truly talking to me.

She lies back down on her pallet, and I do the same. I try to think about my body as a curse, as something outside of my true self, something working against my true self, at all times, by its very nature. I know that what Eve did condemned us all to blood and pain. But Eve did not speak sweet lies to that girl, and then ignore her in her misery. And neither did Adela. She prayed for that girl, and she sent her off to yet another woman who would help her body, while Adela attended to her soul.

—

I sleep again, then wake to less dark. A lighter black, if that is possible, coming from the outside-facing window. Not yet gray, but not darkest black, either. I wish there were more words for black. Maybe I might create them myself in the time to come, as I become more familiar with the many shades. Is this blasphemy? Could a girl make words?

I watch from my pallet as the wall grows grayer, until the light stops shifting and settles into a weak white. It feels odd to lie still, to hear no animal sounds close by, no smells from a bubbling pot, no snores from a sister beside me. I roll over and see that Adela is kneeling at the corner altar. Her pallet looks firm and untouched. Has she been awake for hours? Ashamed now of my own sloth, I sit up, stretch, and walk over to join her. I hear the low murmur of Lauds, as the monks recite their dawn prayers. I close my eyes and will the sound to shape into words in my ears. "*Verumtamen ipse refugium meum et salutare, et defensione mea; Me vehementer movet, non potest.*" I manage to understand the last part, about "not being greatly moved," which seems a mockery. Where could I possibly move?

Adela says and does nothing to acknowledge me. Her eyes are shut tight, her mouth moving along with the monks' words.

I shape the words in my own mouth, too, but my thoughts keep wandering away before I reach the end of the phrase, every time. "*Verumtamen ipse refugium—*" I picture Anne waking in our bed, her braid loose, hair knotted, while Margaret washes the dishes, alone.

"*Verumtamen ipse refugium meum et salutare, et defensione mea*"— How will I fill the days? Will more troubled women come in the night? Does the Father Abbot know about them? Should I tell Brother Joseph about them? No, it is not my place. Adela seems willing to meet with them, and that is her decision.

"Me vehementer movet, non potest"—Mother. You were wrong. I am not special. I am just a girl.

I AWOKE IN MY BED, with no idea how I got there. The blinds were drawn down across the window, but one slat had come loose, and dangled, crooked, letting in a trickle of light.

The door creaked open. Nick, with a glass of water, his phone tucked between his shoulder and neck. "She's awake. Yes, it was only a few seconds, she's alert now."

Nick handed me the water while continuing to talk to my doctor, assuring her that he would keep an eye on me and that I would stay in bed for the rest of the day. Nick hung up and turned to me, all beseeching eyes and worried smile, as he said, "It's ok. Nothing, none of this, is your fault. I mean, I don't even have to say that. Why did I say that? Forget it. How are you feeling?"

I heard him, but also, I didn't. I thanked him for the water, took a sip, asked for some toast. He backed out of the room, didn't close the door all the way behind him. I could hear him talking to my mom now, assuring her that I was fine.

There were several books stacked on my nightstand. I reached for *The Birth of Purgatory* by Jacques Le Goff. It's a foundational text for my work; Post-It notes poke from nearly half its pages. I flipped to one of the yellow tabs, and read what I had underlined: *The dead exist only through and for the living.* The living remember the dead, pray for them, light candles for them, support their progress toward heaven. Or not.

Maybe, I thought, *this isn't going to work.*

I imagined a young woman, feverish lips moving but making no sound, trapped in her stone cage: *Blessed art thou among women, and blessed is the fruit of thy womb.*

And then I pictured a mountain, just like Dante wrote it: yearning souls praying their way upwards, enduring their tests, accepting their sentences, but also buoyed and lifted by the prayers of those left behind in the living world, always moving, looking ahead, looking up. Bodies turning away, toward peace in another realm.

Jutta of Sponheim—and so many other women full of yearning, their names long disappeared to dust—tried to pray her way to transcendence, but her body anchored her to the world. She was probably stabbed by hunger, smothered by fatigue. She may have been holy, but she also probably stank, her body weakened and decaying in her holy prison, her hair dropping from her skull in clumps and tangles, her teeth rotting down to stumps.

I thought about how we long for judgment, the comfort of believing that someone will measure the weight of our time on earth, recognize what we have and have not done, mark our place. Give form to the chaos of our days. Tell us what we need to do, what purifying fire we need to walk through, and we'll do it, we'll come out clean and unscathed on the other side.

I thought about Margery Kempe, medieval mystic and saint who lived through fourteen pregnancies, although several of her children died at birth or soon after. She believed that God wanted her to be a pilgrim, so she left her family and spent the last decades of her life making pilgrimages to the shrines and holy sites of Christianity, including Jerusalem. How did a medieval women manage to live outside the designated roles, to literally keep moving past and beyond categories?

I thought, too, of Tertullian, sitting at his desk in Carthage, when it was still part of the Roman Empire, only a couple hundred years after the death of Christ. He looked up at me, his lips moved, and somewhere in me I heard the words *in thy body is uncleanness and infirmity.* In my head I responded to him, *Why are you here? Fuck off,* and he was gone.

Next in my mind I saw a woman in a long and dragging skirt, hunched over, an anchor on her shoulders. According to the author of the *Ancrene Wisse,* that how-to manual for female anchorites, an anchoress is called by that name because she holds steady the church "as an anchor under the ship." Her mission is to protect the church so that "storms and waves do not overturn it." It's more likely that the terms "anchorite" and "anchoress" were simply derived from the Greek verb, *anachorein,* which means to withdraw, as if into a desert.

So, not oceans, not ships battered by waves and storms, but the opposite: a dry place of sand and thirst.

I've never been to the desert.

Next I saw Jutta, or some long-ago holy woman like her, kneeling on the stone floor of her cell, but then the stone faded, the walls crumbled, and she rested in the sand that now surrounded her. Jutta, or whoever she was, prayed in the desert, the sun on her neck, her words mingled with sand, grit in her teeth. I could not hear her, but I remembered something Hildegard of Bingen wrote: *My new song must float like a feather on the breath of God.*

I remembered then that, last night, I dreamed I was standing in a desert, but there was a fortress in front of me, built of sand. I could hear scraping and muttering from within its walls; eventually, I understood that it was my father, trapped inside. I tried to dig my way through the sandy wall to him, but the sand didn't give, didn't fall away. I walked around the structure, looking for a way in, but there was no door, nothing but smooth sand all the way around, seamless and whole.

I put down my book. I shifted in bed, reached out, grasped the broken slat of the blind, and yanked hard. It came away in my hand. A band of sunlight stretched across my body.

I looked over at the pile of books on my nightstand. About five books down, creased and smudged, was my old copy of Dante's *Purgatorio*—not the newest translation I spotted in the college bookstore a few weeks ago, but the classic translation, still respected fifty years after its publication. I opened it and read: *like one who will not stop but moves along his path, no matter what he sees, if he is goaded by necessity, we made our way into the narrow gap and, one behind the other, took the stairs so straight that climbers there must separate.*

"What are you reading?" Nick was standing in the door, holding a plate of toast, which he placed on the nightstand next to me.

"A classic throwback," I replied, showing him the cover. I struggled to sit up and he said, "I'm making soup, I'll bring you some when it's ready, ok? Butternut squash, your favorite."

"Thanks—that sounds good. But wait, don't go yet." He sat on the edge of the bed, placed his hand over mine, and remained silent, looking at me.

"I'm sorry for acting so crazy. I don't know, ever since Dad died, I just feel like the carpet's been pulled out from under me, you know? Like I'm just totally knocked off course. And now, all this, too." I waved my hands over my stomach.

"You're too hard on yourself. It's not your fault the academic market sucks. And you're still grieving, babe." He leaned over and kissed my forehead. "I'm gonna get you some soup."

I smiled and squeezed his hand before he left. I looked back down at the page, and read again: *one who will not stop but moves / along his path, no matter what he sees.* And then I was walking up an endless set of stone stairs myself, cut deep into the side of the mountain. Before me walked a tiny translucent thing, its feet barely touching the stone. Not that it really had feet. It had a lightness, a glow. It danced and flickered. It rose rapidly, practically skipping up the incline, and I breathed hard, I couldn't keep up.

This mountain is so formed/ that it is always wearisome/ when one begins the ascent,/ but becomes easier the higher/one climbs.

I exhaled, and that small shadow was carried aloft on my breath, it mingled together with my hot air, and evaporated.

Maybe I would never get a good job. No tenure. Nothing is promised or guaranteed. Maybe I should just follow whatever

113

multiple, meandering paths I want to, find some small measure of joy. Or, not even joy. Contentment. Knowledge that I'm doing something I'm good at, something that makes my mind shift, expand, and leap.

A hum at my side; it was Gawain, purring. I reached my hand into his fur, felt his flesh rise and fall beneath mine.

Contact. The living thing.

I stood up, went to the window, raised the blinds. I blinked, my head dizzy with sun. The walls were not tumbling down. But also, they were not suffocating me. Stand up, move forward.

—

Of course, it didn't end there. It wasn't as if I simply stood up, stretched, smiled in the sunshine, and made peace with the miscarriage. What kind of story would that be? Not a very believable one.

But here is what I did do: I did walk downstairs, with small, careful steps, to the kitchen, where I found Nick stirring the warming pot of soup. It smelled like comfort and my stomach rumbled. He turned and smiled, although worry still lingered in his eyes.

As I sat at the table, I reached for my laptop on the kitchen table, and automatically flipped it open, checked my email. The message from Dr. Apwell was still there, unanswered, inviting me to the Conference on Medieval Studies.

Nick was at my side, bowl of soup in hand. "You could email him back right now, to let him know you're coming. If you want."

"Yeah, you're right, I should," I replied. But my fingers didn't do anything. I stared into the soup, stirred the orange warmth a bit with the spoon.

"I get it, this maybe doesn't seem as important now. But you worked hard for this, Liz. Your work on purgatory is groundbreaking, it's important— "

"Important? It's another tiny academic paper on another tiny pointless topic. Nobody even cares, or will ever read it, except for a few other medievalists."

"Liz, our work isn't going to get major news coverage, obviously. We're not gonna blow up on Twitter. But that doesn't mean it's not important. Every time you come home from the library, I swear to God, you've got a glow. You love your work. Just like me. We're preserving ways of being in the world. No, really, we are. I know, your colleagues know. The conference is still a few months away. Maybe you'll feel different about it by then. Just RSVP to confirm that you're going, ok? I'm worried that, in a few weeks or months, you'd regret not going."

Nick was right; who was I to throw away this opportunity? All those ideas about following different and random paths already felt beyond my grasp, fantastical ghosts conjured up by another mind. So I typed:

> *Dear Dr. Apwell, Thank you so much. I'm honored and delighted that my paper has been accepted, and I look forward to taking part in the 2018 Kingmore Conference on Medieval Studies. I will fill out the housing form and submit it directly to my component representative.*
> *With best regards,*
> *Elizabeth Pace*

This was supposed to be a big deal. The next step. So why did it feel like a dead end?

I couldn't change my conference topic. I had been accepted for my research on the codification of purgatory during the twelfth and thirteenth centuries. Better to hunker down and plow forward. Onward, upward, etc.

But first, Instagram. Maybe it would help to dull my brain with grumpy cat memes, and home videos of doped-up kids on the way home from the dentist. But the ceaseless feed of unnecessary information did nothing to distract my brain. I couldn't shake what I had expressed to Nick: the meaninglessness of what

I was doing. Plenty of academics I know have had to struggle with similar feelings, especially those working in the humanities: *does it really matter if I write the definitive article on the cultural role of eighteenth-century French courtesans? I've devoted my life to proposing a radical rethinking of the ramifications of a fully engaged Kantian ethics . . . but what impact could it possibly have on the world?* I think that most of us have been there, except for the truly egomaniacal. And now, the emptiness I was feeling had spread, it seemed, from my brain, throughout my body, right into my bones.

I put down my phone. I needed something else in my brain, a new pointless path to follow, more meaningless knots to untangle. No, that's not fair, not meaningless—small, perhaps, or overlooked or under-explored, but that could be enough, I thought to myself, as I blew on the hot soup and carefully sipped it, trying to fill my body again—failing probably, but still, it tasted good.

17

—

THE DAYS ARE ROUND AND RETURNING, each one falling into the black mouth of the next night. Without my regular chores, I feel myself floating: no daily tasks to busy my body, to hold me to ground. The hours of prayer marked by the monks—I know them now: Matins, Lauds, Prime, Terce, Sext, Nones, Vespers, Compline—are regular, but slippery and passing. I try to grab onto the prayerful hours, but they slip away in a chorus of male voices. I've begun to hear the separate tones within the whole: I can pick out two or three pleasant, strong voices in the collective, but there are also one or two that do not follow the line of the tune, that pitch and sway. There is at least one that struggles with the lowest sounds, and often squeaks in a way that makes me want to laugh, although I do not. I call him Mouse although I've never seen him.

Today at Terce, I hum along with Mouse and all the other monks, and I understand much of what we are saying. The Latin sounds shift into English in my mind: "May mind and tongue made strong in love / Your praise throughout the world proclaim / And may that love within our hearts / Set fire to others with its flame." I do not know how this happens, but now I hear the words and understand them. *Fire*. I glance at the small glow in the hearth, and long for a great flame to rise and heat this place as I shiver.

My cold fingers struggle to thread my needle, as I sew a button back onto my other dress. My mother's thimble cradles my thumb while I work. After she died, it sat untouched in her sewing basket, until I left for the abbey. I see my mother's smiling face while I mouth the words of the hymn. *My mind and tongue made strong in love.* I wish that were true. I do not feel strong, I think because the foundation of my days has been so weakened. I used to mark days by work: the morning chores, the afternoon chores. Market day, laundry day. Although each day ended where it had begun, in our loft bed, I still felt that I was moving forward through time and the world. I ended each day tired, sometimes very hungry, sometimes a little sore, but at least I knew which weeds I had pulled, what wool I had carded. I knew that the seeds I patted into the dirt would become plants, then food. The chicks would become chickens and give us eggs.

But here, I fall asleep and wake in the same drizzle of weak light. I kneel to pray and rise to read. I do not help sustain a household, I do not grow or fix or make. My body walks in circles, through shades of gray, my thoughts and footsteps intruded on or accompanied by the rising chants of male voices. Many times a day, into and through the night, the same men's voices can be heard from the church, reciting the same prayers as the day before. *And may that love within our hearts / Set fire to others with its flame.* I sigh and move to hearth, and gently turn the thin layer of ash, in the hope of encouraging a bit more warmth.

There are long dark spaces of silence at night, between the times of prayer, and those black empty times are when the women come. They do not come every night, or even most nights, I think, but they do come. Men never come to Adela for nighttime beseeching—at least I have never seen one. They do not have to, I suppose—they can carry their sins in the daylight, right up to the priest, to the confessional. Women can and should do that too, certainly—but these nighttime women need a different kind of absolution. So much of what these women seek requires other forms of help: I understand now that what they usually need are herbs of some kind, or the experienced hands of a midwife—often, both together. Oftentimes they are like the unseen girl who came that first night, many weeks ago, who needed something to end the life in her womb, but was too afraid to go to the midwife for help, or simply unable to pay for her services. So, that girl, and many more like her, come to Adela instead.

But tonight the voice at the window is not girlish. I wake to see Adela huddled at the opening in the wall, patting the hand that rests on the ledge. She says, "Your husband should not hurt you this way."

"It is his right and duty, my lady, I understand that he can do what he wishes with me. I am his wife, and if this is how he finds his pleasure—"

"Yes, husbands may beat their wives and lay with them whenever they wish. But we might pray that he loses his desire to treat you so roughly. I see no harm in that. Let us pray." Adela bows her head, and I see the shape outside the window do the same.

The woman departs, murmuring her gratitude for Adela's prayers. Adela pats the hand before it withdraws. She is still standing there, her palm on the empty ledge, as I drift into sleep.

—

My dreams are muddles of male faces: Brother Joseph, Father Everard, Abbot Hugh—and an unfamiliar face, formless, but somehow my dreaming self still know it to be male. It smiles and its teeth shine huge and sharp. It laughs and I wake up sweating, the damp immediately cooling on my skin.

—

In the morning, Adela speaks to me after she finishes her prayers, although she continues to face the wall.

"Your sleep is disturbed, child. I heard you muttering and whimpering last night—many of these last nights, in fact. Come," she instructs, craning her neck to face me, placing her hand on the low kneeling bench next to her. "Pray with me."

"Yes, my lady." I unbend my stiff limbs and settle next to her. She begins: "O Jesus, let me never forget thy bitter Passion that thou has suffered for my transgression. Grant that I may love thee so that the wisdom of the world may go clean from me. I burningly desire to come to see thy face in whom is all my comfort and my solace."

As she begins the prayer again, I join her. We recite this prayer every day, we have been for many weeks now, I think. I do not know the number of days, but some are colder, some are darker. All I know are shades of light and degrees of warmth, not numbers. On the sunniest days, I can make out the Lady's features clearly. I can see that her eyes sit deep in her skin, which is stretched tight across her cheeks. Her lips are thin. Her teeth seem too large by comparison. Yesterday there was good sun, and I saw her pressing a finger against one of her upper teeth, wiggling it under the slight pressure. She stopped when she saw me looking.

I grow so tired of this prayer. Father Everard is wise. Abbot Hugh is wise. I know they would say they are concerned with God's wisdom, the only true wisdom. But there is wisdom in how the apple tree grows and fruits from a tiny seed, too.

Our prayers are finally finished. Adela takes a deep breath, stands up. I gather up the courage to ask, "My Lady, why must we pray for release from the wisdom of the world? Is wisdom not a good thing?"

She sighs, looks down at her hands, as she says, "Little good comes from this world. This earthly realm was born of sin, and is marked by suffering and death. This world offers only false comfort and empty promises. Yes, even for me," she says—she must see the doubt creeping into my face. "Before the Lord called me to enclosure, I was a mare dressed in fine silks, nothing more. I was expected to marry well and produce children. Produce *sons*."

"You did not—you do not—want to be a mother?" The words slip out of my mouth before I can catch them.

"Elinor, think back on that poor girl who came to me many nights ago. That is the world for women. Men make or break us as they fancy, in a moment of passion, whether they intend to or not. Some lure us with sweet words—and some do not even bother, taking what they wish and ignoring our screams of protest." Her voice has risen on these last few words, and she stops speaking, but I feel the anger left behind, thick in the space between us, but then she suddenly stoops, her body wracked with hacking coughs. She coughs and coughs and when she finally she stops, she rubs at her eyes, and says in a tired voice, "And of course some men say they act from a place of love, but it matters not—let us speak on this no further. Please check on the fire, and then continue with your sewing." She kneels on the bench and squeezes her eyes shut, begins whispering rapid prayers.

I say nothing more. She did not address whether or not she wanted to be a mother.

18

STILLBURNE, NEW YORK, 2017

I WAS SITTING IN MY USUAL SPOT AT THE SCRATCHED-UP TABLE AS MY seminar students arrived for the last week of classes for the semester. I smiled and nodded as they entered, but didn't say anything until everyone had shown up and settled into their chairs, which squealed as they were dragged by the settling bodies across the old linoleum. I greeted them, apologizing for having cancelled classes the week before due to illness. I had wondered if any of them would question me, ask where I'd been or what was wrong, but nobody did. A few were still sliding their phones into vibrate mode while I was speaking. Others were pulling out pens and notebooks. A couple of the girls smiled politely. They were still young, at least by today's standards. I barely existed beyond the confines of this classroom, as far as they were concerned.

I continued, "I'd like to ease us back into our earlier discussion, from a couple weeks ago, and maybe see where else it might lead us now, or what issues or questions, if any, have been raised for you during my little leave of absence. Does everyone remember what we were saying about anchoresses?" More nods, and eyes looking to mine from all around the table.

"Great. But just to quickly recap, we've been discussing women who chafed at the limited roles available to them and used their religious practice to determine new paths and ways of being for themselves. I'm not saying these women weren't truly motivated by Christian devotion, but they were clearly also women who didn't want to accept any of the few roles available to them, so they felt a need to create new roles for themselves. Whether we're discussing an elderly queen mother, such as Elinor of Aquitaine, who joined a monastery and became something of a recluse in her final years, or Hildegard of Bingen, who embraced the traditionally masculine roles of healer, writer, mystic, and theologian, we've seen how a small number of women were able to either expand beyond the limitations of traditional female roles, or else create entirely new, perhaps ungendered, spaces for themselves."

"But," interjected Chris, who wore glittery blue eyeshadow in the same shade as the new streak of blue in their blond hair, "anchoresses weren't creating entirely new roles, were they? I mean, there were male hermits and anchorites, too."

"Absolutely," I replied. "But what's notable, and germane to our discussion, is the fact that women in particular embraced the anchoress role during the medieval centuries." I licked my lips and reached back to tighten my low ponytail as I felt my hair begin to slip free. "The option was certainly available to men too—but the records available to us indicate that there was a significant uptick in the number of women choosing to become anchoresses in the eleventh, twelfth, and thirteenth centuries. And it's primarily anchoresses whose words and lives remain known to us now, which suggests they were famous enough in their own lives to be written about, and their own writings were considered valuable enough to copy and preserve."

"Professor Pace?" It was Emma, my honors thesis student. I pushed away my memory of our conference, that crumbling ceiling in my office. "Remember I mentioned to you that I've been reading Julian's *Revelations of Divine Love*? I was really struck by one of the visions she describes having—the one about a hazelnut?"

"Oh yes, that's a beautiful piece of writing. Do you have it with you? Could you read it aloud to us?"

She pulled a library book from her backpack and began, "He showed me a little thing, a hazelnut, lying in the palm of my hand, it seemed, and it was as round as any ball. I looked thereupon with the eye of my understanding, and I thought, What may this be? And it was answered generally thus: 'It is all that is made. I wondered how it could last, for I thought it might suddenly fall to nothing for little cause. And I was answered: 'It lasts and ever shall, for God loves it; and so everything has its beginning by the love of God. In this little thing I saw three properties; the first is that God made it; the second is that God loves it; and the third is that God keeps it."

She closed the book, but her words lingered. Softly, I said, "So often, medieval people get a bad rap. We think of them as ignorant, dirty, and obsessed with punishment, hell, suffering. But this passage was written by a women who had seen her home town of Norwich ravaged by the plague. When she was probably only five or six years old, she saw bodies piled up in the street, because there weren't enough living people left to bury them properly. She barely survived a debilitating illness herself in the prime of her life. And after that, she decided to lock herself in a cell for the rest of her life. But here, she isn't bemoaning the earthly realm, or castigating herself or humankind. Instead, she turns her focus to a humble object of nature: a hazelnut. And God tells her it's a product and manifestation of divine love. God made it; God loves it; and God 'keeps' it, which here means 'protects' it. Such a simple message—but in that very simplicity, utterly radical."

Katrina said, "I was raised Catholic, and I don't think I ever heard anything like this in church! Maybe if I had, I would've kept going." Laughs and smiles all around, including from me.

"I agree with you there, Katrina," I said. "But whether we're Christian or not, whether we follow a different faith tradition or none at all, I think these are words nearly anyone can find some comfort in."

"I identify as an atheist," said Chris, "but I respect that she uses the image of a hazelnut—something concrete, from nature. Even if you don't believe in 'God'," they wiggled their fingers in air quotes, "you can agree, I think, that there's something amazing and awe-inspiring about the natural world. At least, before we entirely destroy it." Earnest heads nodded in agreement all around the table.

I knew we were veering away from the safe, flat land of scholarship, and edging toward the cliffs of personal experience and sincere belief—something potentially dicey in all disciplines, especially so in religious studies. I had taught other classes, mostly when I first began teaching, when I let the conversation get away from me; I'd watched as students indulged in personal memories, and we'd drifted into the realm of pop psychology, sharing long-ago traumas of Sunday school and awkward bar mitzvahs. When that used to happen, I was ashamed and embarrassed, because it wasn't scholarly, it wasn't cool and clinical; too personal, too close for my comfort. But now, this time, I let it go. Let them connect. It was enough.

"But isn't it kind of weird," ventured Chloe, who hadn't spoken all semester, "that on the one hand, she was praising this humble example from nature—but on the other hand, she cut herself off entirely from nature? I mean, she was able to see God in a tiny hazelnut, which is beautiful—but she locked herself away from the world. Doesn't that seem totally contradictory?" She pushed her large glasses back up the bridge of her nose, as I sensed ripples of surprise around the table.

"Chloe," I responded, "that's a very insightful question. You should speak up more often!" She blushed, but then a small warm smile spread across her face. I continued, "I don't have a definite answer, of course, but I would suggest that Julian saw the earthly world as a distraction. Perhaps she could only recognize and acknowledge the holiness inherent in every small thing by stepping away from it all, by giving herself the stark space of her cell in which to look back on and appreciate the world she left behind."

Katrina replied, "That's so sad! It's like she didn't trust herself. Like, she knew God was everywhere in the world, but still, she couldn't devote herself to him *and* stay in that world. Like the fact of God being everywhere, in everything, was too much for her, or something."

"Maybe," said Emma, "she just felt like being an anchoress was something she had to do. Like that was the life she had to live."

"That's a perfect place to end for today, Emma," I replied. "I have to say, guys, this has been a fantastic conversation. I know this is strange stuff—anchoresses, mystical writings from hundreds of years ago. But I feel like we got a little closer to those long-ago people today."

And then they were gone for another day—except for Emma, who lingered at her seat, slowly shrugging her backpack over her shoulder before walking up to me. "What's up, Emma? Shall we schedule another conference to go over your thesis more?" I asked.

"Sure, that sounds good. To be honest, after you mentioned it in our conference, I did start to have doubts about this— like, medieval studies? Really? With everything going on in the world?"

"I know what you mean. Like I said, I can't tell you that it's a field with great job prospects. I'm headed to the library, would you like to walk with me?"

"Sure, I'm going to a meeting near there anyway, at the student center—Climate Action Now. That's what I mean—here I am, studying these people who lived hundreds of years ago, and the planet might not even be livable by the time I'm an adult."

"I get it, Emma. You don't have to make any decisions yet. Why don't we meet next week, and in the meantime, you keep reading, and together we can keep thinking and talking our way through it? If you don't end up doing an honors project with me, no problem. I'm just glad you're interested, and thinking about what we're doing in class this semester seriously."

We said goodbye in front of the library and I headed in. I hadn't been there in two weeks, but given how often I normally went, it felt much longer. Once I was in the medieval history section, I located the shelves devoted to Christianity. Julian's

Revelations of Divine Love, and Hildegard of Bingen's *Know the Ways*, *Book of Life's Merits*, and *Book of Divine Works*. The visionary writings of two long-ago women, the fire of their mystical devotion tamped down into antiquated English, but still, the embers glowed, even now, in the twenty-first century. I just had to cup my hands around the flame, give it a little protection and a little air, and I'd receive warmth in return. Wouldn't I?

I stacked several volumes on the table in front of me, but I didn't actually open any of them. I just sat there, soaking up the silence, and thinking about Julian. And Hildegard. And poor Jutta too, remembered now only in relationship to another, her own words buried with her bones centuries ago. They all felt certain that they were living the life they had to. Or maybe they weren't certain at all: there must have been dark days, in the cell, no light anywhere, the bread stale or moldy, when all they longed for was a glimpse of another face, the touch of another hand. But even so, they stuck with it, they stayed locked in their devoted realms, behind stone. Or, in Jutta's case at least, she forced another face into that cell alongside her.

I can read any of these books. I can buy myself a cup of coffee. I can have a child. Or not. When I want to. For the most part. But we're still stuck with these bodies, all these centuries later.

I looked around at the stacks, I let my gaze wander across the accumulated words and wisdom. My god, I loved being there. Nick was right about that. But after several quiet minutes—five? ten?—my body began to protest, gently. My lower back ached, and I still felt weak all over. It was time to leave. It was late afternoon by then, the day was easing over into night, over the bridge of dusk. The students were finishing their classes for the day, heading into lacrosse practice, laboratory time, studio hours, or simply dinner and then studying. The regular rhythms of their lives, for just the few enclosed years of college, before their next paths widened out before them.

As I walked down the stairs, out of the library, I reminded myself: Hildegard and Jutta and Julian, and all the unnamed others like them, the mystics and martyrs, the nuns and anchoresses, they were just women. Strong and devout, yes, and perhaps marked with what we would call a kind of lunacy now, single-minded to the point of deprivation and exhaustion. They followed the path they had chosen, no matter where it led, no matter how faded it grew, or tangled and overgrown. But that was just one path, walked by other women long ago.

My legs carried me down the stairs. Leaning into the door, I pushed my way out, into the late day. I saw the sun, still lingering in the sky. I tried to feel its last, lingering warmth, which of course I'd be able to feel again tomorrow, and the tomorrow after that. Even at this late point in the day, it reached me all the way down here on the ground. I closed my eyes and imagined a new possibility, a new warmth in my belly, maybe, someday.

19

—

WENFAIR ABBEY, ENGLAND, 1370

ANOTHER MORNING, icy stone, poor light—even less than when I arrived, for we are in deep winter now. The constant damp along the walls has stilled to frost. I curl my stiff and freezing fingers, watch my breath puff into a small cloud before my face, briefly, before it disappears. I sleep in all my clothing, but these thick walls seem to absorb the winter chill and hold it close. I rise and smooth my pallet, tuck my hair up under my cap. Brother Joseph brings our morning ale, which I drink after I pass our chamber pots to him, through the low window. The shame and strangeness of our little ritual sting less now. There is a comfort to its regularity, in fact—the small acts lend some shape to these cramped and frozen days.

I long to ask Adela what Christmas will be like tomorrow, but I am afraid to know the answer. Indeed, I am afraid I already know the answer: it will be like all the days: moments of prayer only interrupted by sewing and prayer and reading.

Nothing like Christmas at home. Mother would prepare a feast of ham and black pudding. My sisters and I would have decorated the house with holly, boxwood, yew—whatever greenery we could gather. The Yule log would be set to burning for the whole twelve days of Christmas. Father was less burdened, as farm work slowed, even for the small farmers like him. His shoulders eased and he sat before the fire, tending the log and soaking up the warmth. We were together, and the house smelled of the forest, pine and sap, despite the bleak bare winter outside. Mother wove new scarves and hats for all of us. Father would have received a loaf of good bread and bacon from Lord Monmouth for all of us to share.

And now, what would Mother and Father think to see me here, warming my fingers with my own breath, tending a weak fire, while a sick-looking woman prays and prays just steps away from me? And what would they think to see me reading—and not merely reading, but loving to do so? It heats me like nothing else. Adela is generous with her book of hours, and has made it clear that I am welcome to it whenever we are not praying or sewing. Every day, in the time between our main midday meal and the afternoon prayers at Nones, I read. I feel, strangely, that it is something I have always known how to do, in some deep-rooted way. That it is a coming home of sorts. I move my eyes over the parchment and the letters fall into neat and clear arrangements.

Adela has said, more than once, "You read so well, Elinor. Were you truly unable to read at all before you came to me? God has clearly gifted you with this ability, rare indeed in a girl. He is truly wondrous in his benevolence." And it is true—I never feel closer to God than when I am reading. That is probably a blasphemy so I do not tell anyone—what if I were forbidden to read any longer? I cannot truly see the evil in this feeling; as Adela says, God has given me this ability, and I feel so warm and alive when I take in the words on the page. I can almost forget about the stone walls, the chilled air, how my toes ache from the cold, and Adela's coughing fits, which have not only continued, but which grow in strength and number by the day.

I especially love to read the *Magnificat*, the song of Mary: "My soul doth magnify the Lord, and my spirit hath rejoiced in God my Savior, for He hath regarded the lowliness of his handmaiden, for behold, from henceforth, all generations shall call me blessed." Mary is secure in God's love, and in the knowledge that she will be remembered forever because of her son.

Who will remember me? Could my soul magnify the Lord?

I rise and peek through the squint into the church, decorated for Christmas with more candles than usual, and fresh fir boughs around the altar. I breathe in deep to catch some of their wild scent.

Some of the monks are there, kneeling on the benches before the altar, deep in prayer. I do not know their names, but I have caught glimpses of most of them before, either passing by the outside window, or at prayer through the squint. I do not see the one I call Mouse, but there is Gray Hair, Skinny Bird, Moo Cow (for his loud and low chanting), and Stub Toe (he is younger, probably close in age to Joseph, and seems to manage to trip nearly every time he walks up the aisle toward the altar). As I watch, I hear the sound of someone coming up to the window behind me—I know the light steps of Joseph, bringing our supper.

Tonight's meal is heartier than usual, with an extra hunk of bread, more cheese, and even a portion of meat. My nose fills with the smell of pork and my stomach flips. "A Christmas Eve treat, Miss," says Brother Joseph as he hands me my plate. "And there will be a midnight Mass open to all tonight; traditionally, the townsfolk attend, so you will hear more people in the church than usual."

As I nibble on my pork, my eyes begin to water, I am so overwhelmed by the rich taste. Adela nibbles on bread and cheese for a change—"My weak body needs a bit of extra nourishment, I think, to be able to attend the Mass tonight." The word "attend" pokes at me. We will not be choosing to sit in the pews in the church, we will be merely peering through a small opening in the wall, into the church. Still, I am excited at the thought of more bodies out there, and new voices mingling with those of the monks.

I drift in light sleep until Adela nudges me awake in the dark. My nose fills with the hazy, woozy smell of incense. I peer through the squint. Most of the pews are full of townspeople, many with eyes closed, some staring around the church, gaping at the high vaulted ceiling, the stained-glass windows dappled and twinkling in the candlelight.

Abbot Hugh stands at the front of the church, his back to the pews, his words directed toward the crucifix above the altar. He prays in Latin, of course—and I understand what he says. "*Populus qui ambulabat in tenebris, vidit lucem magnam; habitantibus in regione tenebrarum, lux orta est eis.*" The prayer dances around my ears and I whisper the words again to myself: "those who lived in a land of deep darkness—on them light has shined." The words are both a comfort and a cruelty.

The children in the pews lean against their parents, many of them deeply asleep. Men and women rub their eyes and try to hide their yawns. The cows must be milked and the eggs must be gathered, regardless of the birth of Christ. The sagged and bent bodies in the church reflect this truth. What I would give to be like them—aching down to my very bones, fighting to keep my eyes open, exhausted after a day of tossing feed to chickens, sewing holes in worn-out clothing that must last at least another season, stirring the massive pot of stew at the hearth. "The people who walked in darkness"—oh, to walk! Suddenly I can see it—the door to the cell opening, and standing there, with her arms open, is Mary, or is it Mother, she is waiting for me, beckoning me into the light. I move my feet across the hard floor and go to her. She is lit from within and smells sweet, of chamomile. She smiles without speaking but somehow she is saying the words "*Apparuit enim gratia Dei omnibus salutem afferens.*" I stumble and begin to fall toward her, I open my arms—

"Elinor!" It is Adela, and I wake on her shoulder. "Careful, you fell over. Are you well?"

"Yes, my lady, I am sorry. It must be the incense, the late hour—"

"And no doubt you are overcome by the joy of the occasion. Also, child, your Latin is nearly flawless. *Apparuit enim gratia Dei omnibus salutem afferens!*" I repeat the prayer back to her, but now it feels like a taunt in my mouth. Is this salvation?

I focus again on the abbot, as he speaks of miracles, the birth of a baby boy, a holy and chosen woman.

20

KINGMORE, PENNSYLVANIA, 2018

"*P*ACE. First name Elizabeth."

The graduate student overseeing the registration table—mid-twenties, skinny jeans on skinny legs, remnants of adolescent acne scars—smiled up at me as he handed me my badge. *Elizabeth Pace, University of Northern New York.* I checked the details on the first page of the informational packet he handed me: as I had been informed, my presentation would be at 11 in Conference Room 1A on Tuesday. Opening convocation tomorrow, Monday, at 9 AM by Dr. Apwell in Tunney Hall.

The passageways of Kingmore College hummed and bubbled with reunions and meetings of minds. *I haven't seen you since the Articulating Medieval Art conference in Boston! . . . Yes, the book's in proofs now, we finally settled on a title*—Heavenly Time: Clockmaking in Medieval Islamic Societies . . . *I'm looking forward to the talk on vernacular literature in medieval Spain, will I see you there?* We were finally standing in the sunlight, no longer scurrying in the dusty shadows of academia, the musty corners of medieval studies. Our life's work wasn't met with indifference or ignorance; here, it was easy to feel vibrant about one's career, passionate about one's scholarship, like the heady first days of graduate school all over again.

The Medieval Christianity component of the conference was overseen by Megan Dean, a professor at UPenn. I had emailed her the draft of my presentation; four days later, I had received an email in response:

> Dear Dr. Pace,
>
> Many thanks for sending me the draft of your presentation "The Third Place: Developing a Theology of Purgatory, 1100–1300" for the upcoming KCMS. This is a sorely neglected topic, so we're very pleased to offer you a platform for discussing the conception and evolution of purgatory. I agree that it is worth attempting to determine why, precisely, this theological concept gained more prominence in the twelfth and thirteenth centuries, culminating eventually in its codification at the Council of Lyons in 1439. What you present here is sound; I would only suggest that you perhaps devote more space to Aquinas. As it stands, I don't think his centrality in the development of the theology of purgatory is adequately expressed. If you'd like, we can discuss Aquinas further over email. But otherwise, this is admirable work. I look forward to attending your presentation at the conference, and wish you the best of luck.
>
> Best regards,
>
> Dr. Megan Dean
>
> University of Pennsylvania
>
> Component Representative, Kingmore Conference on Medieval Studies

It was a relief to know that my presentation was basically on solid ground. I had pulled back; I had paused at the edge of the known with my sturdy dissertation in hand. More Aquinas? Sure, why not?

I thought again about a line from my dissertation: *A number of political, economic, social, and cultural developments in the West during the twelfth century contributed indirectly to the codification of a theology of purgatory during that time period.* People in the 1100s and 1200s were gradually moving to cities in greater numbers. They worked and sweated and agonized and died. They buried babies in the cold ground. They wanted answers. They needed reasons. And so the theologians and poets, Thomas Aquinas and Dante and others, devised an orderly world beyond this one. While the Church maintained a firm grip on people's daily lives and concerns, a rise in more earthly interests is discernible during that time as well. We think of medieval people as hopelessly stuck in their ironclad roles, their lives of drudgery. Of course there was grinding poverty, there was the backbreaking work carried out by the many peasants and serfs. But the rise of cities led also to the rise of trade guilds. Merchants, carpenters, blacksmiths, bakers: people found new jobs and roles, they found new places in their communities. They joined organizations with fellow artisans, they perfected their crafts. They bought and sold, they apprenticed and professionalized. They focused on the world around them. They enjoyed the results of their choices and efforts. They understood the roles they played in society, they wondered what roles they might play in the afterlife, what they might do to earn and keep and better their lives to come.

135

And here I was, presenting my single piece of the complex puzzle in this field where the primary sources have been disintegrating and fading for centuries, and have already been pored over by generations of previous scholars. But I could add the polish and gleam of my insight. I could add my piece to the greater design.

God, I had pictured all of this so differently: me presenting some innovative theory, backed by my thought-provoking findings, resting my hand on my gently swelling belly while I spoke to the assembled crowd of colleagues.

After picking up my registration materials, I thumbed through the program, scanning to see which presentations I wanted to attend. *Illustrating Female Poetic Agency in the Work of Marie de France?* Or perhaps *Castles for Capitalists: Medievalist Houses, Robber Barons, and the Aesthetics of the Feudal State?* How about *Reading Augustine in Conversation with Derrida: Translation and Transference?* And then my eye was drawn to this: *European Anchoresses and the Conduct of the Self.* I continued reading the thumbnail description of the lecture: *Dr. Sloane Lanham, author of* Holy Enclosed in the Dark: Anchoresses in France and Italy, 1100–1400 *(Princeton University Press) will discuss the fraught relationship between the anchoress and her own enclosed body, illuminating key concepts relating to medieval constructions of femininity and the performance of piety.* The photo next to the description of the lecture was her author photo. From her book. The one still in my tote bag. The one I stole.

The next morning, I settled myself into the auditorium ten minutes early for Sloane's presentation, opened up Instagram on my phone, and found a post by someone named @theladymedievalist: a photo of Dr. Lanham hugging a middle-aged blonde woman draped in flowing black pants and matching cardigan, captioned *So excited to be back at #kingmore for the #medieval conference! Especially thrilled to get to see this gorgeous and super smart gal again. You're gonna rock tomorrow @sloanestudies!*

And there she was, approaching the podium. I quickly closed the app and put my phone back in my bag. Her nearly black hair was pulled back into a just-messy-enough bun, and she put on a pair of thick, black-rimmed glasses at the beginning of her talk, as she thanked us all for coming. Were they the same glasses from her book jacket photo? I visualized a shelf in a sleek, uncluttered office, identical black-framed glasses, one pair after another, lined up neatly, stretching the length of the sunlit room, the walls all painted white.

I forced myself back, to Dr. Lanham's words. "At first glance, anchoresses seem to be intent on obliterating the self; they commit themselves to an existence purely devoted to an external God. They direct their focus and attention, their prayers and devotion, to God in heaven, utterly forsaking any attention to their own physical comfort. And yet, paradoxically, their exalted positioning as anchoress is essentially, and I would argue inextricably, intertwined with their physical presence in the cell. In their ostentatious denial of the self, they are, paradoxically, locating

136

the essential nature of that very self: the core of that self is abnegation, and without that physical debasement, the anchoress has no self at all. The anchoress's self *is* that refusal and rejection. The world held at a distance while also invited to peer through the window. In that place of tension—in that female body, both subverted and centered—*this* is where the self is to be located."

She spoke clearly and convincingly on the inherently performative aspect of the anchoress, how her role was entirely reliant on the body she sought to hide away from the world, to punish and debase. At the end of the presentation, there were several questions. And after the question-and-answer session, four or five people approached her to offer congratulations and further comments, while the other thirty or so people filed out, moving on to the next round of lectures. I picked up my phone, thought about trying to snap a quick photo of myself with Sloane in the background, lost my nerve. As the last person moved away from her and she began to put her papers back into her sleek leather satchel, I walked up to her and said, "Professor Lanham, I'm so sorry to bother you, I just wanted to let you know I really enjoyed that. My name is Liz Pace, I taught a seminar on anchoresses last semester. Well, they're one of the categories we covered, the course was called 'Holy Madness: Religious Women in the Middle Ages.' We focused a lot on anchoresses. Your talk was just wonderful, I was so excited to see that you would be presenting here.'" The words poured out quickly, but at least I didn't say the rest of the sentences that formed in my head, too: *Your book. I stole it. It sits in the bottom of my tote bag all the time, I am afraid to look at it. But it never leaves me. I carry it around everywhere. It's in my bag right now. I have no idea why I did it.*

She replied, "Thank you so much! Please, call me Sloane. Liz, right? That sounds like a great course. Where do you teach?"

"University of Northern New York, in Stillburne, it's upstate, not too far from Albany. You're in New Hampshire, right?" As if I didn't know.

"Yeah, Wolverton College. You have a decent MEMS program at Northern New York, don't you? I remember meeting the director here once . . ."

"Dr. Manheim?"

"Yes! She made quite the impression, with that hair!" Sloane tossed her head, flinging her own sleek hair back behind her shoulder.

"That's definitely her . . . she can be a bit much, but she does do a lot to maintain the program. I'm just an adjunct, I owe her a lot." *Why are you defending Dr. Manheim? Sloane doesn't care, she barely knows her!*

"We don't even have a full medieval studies program. Wolverton just offers an interdisciplinary 'Medieval History, Literature, and Religion' course that is tag-team-taught by me, an English professor, and a philosophy professor. And then I teach 'Here Be Dragons: Monsters in the Bible.' I think the department felt the need to spice things up for the 'Game of Thrones' generation."

"Ah yes, come for the dragons, stay for the foundational literature of the Western religious tradition!" Sloane laughed, and I continued, "Seriously, though, I thought what you were saying about anchoresses and the need to create a new kind of feminine self was, well, revelatory."

"I know the topic of female mystics and the denial of the body is old news—you know, *Holy Feast, Holy Fast*, second-wave feminism—but I'm interested in contextualizing the anchoress as a member of a community, as counterintuitive as that might seem. And, the anchoress brings in the angle of the common person's experience a bit more. Not that anchoresses were generally representative of the lower classes—but lots of them were 'regular' noblewomen at least, or from families of well-off merchants or burghers. We can't all be Theresa of Avila!"

I was a part of the .00001% of the world's population who would even consider that a joke, much less laugh out loud at it.

Sloane continued, "But also, we need to consider this intense strain of competitiveness, I think, which is generally frowned on in women. Anchoresses could pray the hardest, fast the longest, you know?"

"There's a power of a kind in all that self-abnegation," I replied.

"Would you like to have dinner tonight with me and my friend Jasmine? There's a good Indian place within walking distance of campus. Not many other culinary options in Kingmore as far as I can tell, but it sure beats the school cafeteria. And Jasmine is amazing, she's delivering a talk tomorrow afternoon on 'Teaching Medieval Studies in an Era of White Supremacy.'"

We agreed to meet at seven. It was a relief not to have to face the cafeteria on my own, which would surely be a sad and anxiety-inducing reopening of long-ago junior-high wounds. During the conference, given that the school was on spring break, the attendees slept in college dorm rooms and ate in the cafeterias. Middle-aged men contorted themselves to fit into twin beds; women in their forties and fifties jostled one another at the mirrors in the shared bathrooms. Everyone forced themselves to act like this was a wacky and fun experience. I suspected that conferences in the STEM disciplines didn't put those professors in dorms, though.

I met Sloane at the campus gates, and as we set out on the ten-minute walk downtown, we chatted about the usual safe topics: weather, our trips to the conference. "I almost didn't make it," Sloane said. "My kid came down with a fever the night before my flight and I felt weird leaving Sheila—my partner—alone to deal with it. But Maggie—my daughter—didn't seem that bad the next morning, so I just packed my mom guilt in my suitcase with my lecture notes and headed out." She smiled, but I saw the guilt she was carrying, nestled in the corners of her eyes. "Do you have kids, Liz?"

"No, not yet." My heart skittered for just a moment, but the words poured out smoothly.

Sloane smiled again and changed the subject to a movie she

139

had seen recently and liked. I had seen it when it came out last year: two young men, Italy, the early 80s, first love. "What I wouldn't give to visit Italy again!" said Sloane. "Even just for work."

"There must been some Italian anchoresses you could research, right?" I said.

"Yeah, there are. I went to a couple anchoritic sites for my research for my book. I felt like I couldn't write about those women without seeing for myself where they stayed. Maybe that sounds a little basic, but there's a lot to be said for direct, on-site research, rather than just relying on books—don't tell anyone I insulted books!" She laughed and continued, "Don't think I'll be traveling for work or research anytime soon though, I've got a full teaching load in the fall, and this summer I'm going to be splitting childcare for Maggie with my wife—she's only two, so summer camp isn't an option yet. And daycare is ridiculously expensive." We had reached the restaurant. As she opened the door for me, Sloane said, "Sorry, I'm talking way too much about my kid!"

"No, you're not! It must be a lot," I replied, stepping over the threshold.

Sloane approached another woman around our age, tapped her on the shoulder, and when she turned, gave her a hug. "Liz, this is Jasmine Lewis, she's the assistant director of the Medievalist POC Association. Like I mentioned, she's delivering a lecture on Wednesday, right Jasmine?"

"Yeah, but it got moved to Williams Auditorium."

"That's the biggest venue on campus. Impressive!" I said as we headed toward our table.

Sloane turned toward the waiter who had just approached and, after asking me if I was ok with white wine, ordered a bottle of Sauvignon Blanc for the table.

"I'm speaking tomorrow, in just one of the regular conference rooms, as planned!" I said, smiling. *Why do that? Why turn every possible opportunity into one of self-deprecation?*

"She's going to be talking on purgatory," Sloane interjected. "I feel like there should be more work on purgatory. There's the idea of individual and communal responsibility for one's fate in the afterlife—this idea that you can pray on someone else's behalf, offer indulgences to help yourself out or a loved one—"

"It's like a proto-capitalistic mindset, isn't it?" continued Jasmine. "If I pay enough money, I'll get to heaven."

"Totally," I said. "If I work hard at these prayers and these pilgrimages, if I do these things, I'll be safe. It's sort of touching, this idea that all it takes are very concrete actions, following the right steps, to keep you and everyone you love safe, for all eternity." Nobody else spoke, so I added, "Say what you will about downsides like plagues and massive inequality, there's something to be said for an orderly world, and a sense of meaning and progression, as opposed to, well, the chaos that is 2018."

Jasmine laughed. "Only Trump could make the fourteenth century look like a pleasant time to be alive. Screw these incels decking themselves out in their Celtic crosses and carrying their cute little English heraldic crests on shields to their racist rallies." Jasmine sighed and took a sip of wine.

I had thought about this before of course, and thought about my own complicity. After all, the image of the purgatorial penitent was, generally, white. And those women who enclosed themselves? White. I was focused on Western Europe and Britain. But we knew that the idea of a homogenous and entirely white medieval Western Europe was false. There was travel and trade across continents and national boundaries. Yes, most peasants stayed close to where they were born for most of their lives, but there were also traders and pilgrims, explorers and dignitaries, crossing countries and regions.

I told Jasmine I'd be at her talk, and she replied, "Thanks, Liz. I'm excited about it, but I'm worried some of the older crowd might just write it off as woke shit."

"No way, lots of people will be there, it's such an important topic," said Sloane.

Over saag paneer and samosas, we griped and gossiped. The professors well past retirement age clinging to their positions, locking new and recent PhDs out of the job markets. The infamous, aging Chaucer scholar who lavished deeply inappropriate attention on the youngest female scholars at the conference every year. The embarrassing musicologist who wore long skirts and played her lute—an actual *lute*—in the courtyard at lunchtime.

"OK, so tomorrow at 11, right Liz?" Jasmine asked.

"Yes," I said, and I felt the floor of my stomach drop. "But please don't feel like you have to come!"

"Of course I'll be there!" said Jasmine. "Like Sloane said, there's so little work on purgatory. I'm honestly interested. Why is that? Why isn't there more work on or interest in purgatory?"

"That's a good question. I've been focusing on how and why it came into being—but what about why it faded away? I know that's outside the bounds of medieval studies, but now you've got me wondering."

What happened? Where did purgatory go? A new path of research to follow who knows where. Never mind that this topic was far beyond the confines of my professional position. I wasn't supposed to expand outward in my studies; if I wanted to advance, I needed to burrow inward, deeper down into the ancient texts, closer and closer to the source. Backward and inward, not outward and forward.

Honestly, I didn't really care what had happened to purgatory. I was still thinking about what Sloane had said about on-site research, and someplace stone and ancient, and the idea of actually being there, in my body. I didn't want to drag myself up purgatory's dry mountain. I wanted to cross an ocean. I sipped my wine and felt it slide down my throat, I imagined it joining with my bloodstream, the rivers inside me, my living, liquid body, which I wanted to carry across the world, water across water.

21

—

WENFAIR ABBEY, ENGLAND, 1371

ADELA SAYS, after our morning prayers, "Today shall be busy, I expect a line of prayerful women at the window."

Christmas has come and gone—the day itself was fairly muted. The monks were in the church praying most of the day, and my supper again included meat—and again Adela took none. Christmas morning, after her prayers, she presented me with gifts: a rosary of my own, and a wool blanket. She must have seen the surprise on my face because she said, "I sent word to my mother, asking her to have these sent for you." The rosary was a leather cord strung with carved wooden beads, with a wooden cross dangling from the center. And the blanket, thick and warm, was certainly welcome; I keep the fire going at all hours, but even so, the walls seem to absorb the winter chill and hold it—and me—in a tight embrace at all times. As I said "thank you, my lady" my breath rose before me, ice-white.

No word from Father that day. I should not have been surprised or disappointed; I could see out the window that a great deal of snow covered the ground, as high as a man's knee. The roads would not be easy to travel. Still, I had wished to see him. I also hoped Father knew to give Anne a new doll or some such small plaything. I thought of them on Christmas morning— without Mother there to sing hymns, without me there to play with Anne and her new toy, what had their holiday been like?

"Why shall today be busy, my lady?" I ask, and she replies, "Today is the eighth day of January, the Solemnity of Mary." I feel my insides drop to my feet, while at the same time, something hot and watery rises in my throat. But Adela does not sense my distress as she continues, "On this day, we honor Mary as the mother of Christ, and women who wish to bear children, or hope for a safe pregnancy and birth, seek the Virgin's intervention." So, unlike those nighttime women, the women who want to be with child do not come at night; they pray in the light of day. Like my mother did.

"I know this feast day. My mother and I, my family, we were here, last winter. She prayed, I think, to you."

Adela looks closely at me. "And your mother died in child-birth, yes?"

"She lost too much blood, and the baby was very small. That is what the midwife said."

Adela sighs and closes her eyes. "I am sorry, Elinor. Did she light a candle and pray at the side altar, or did she speak to me directly?"

"We all prayed and lit candles. And she did speak with you. I was right out there," I wave my hand toward the church. I feel tears rise and rush down my cheeks, I cannot stop them. "She prayed and prayed and she was so good! She didn't do anything wrong!" I turn away but of course there is nowhere I can go. I crumple to the hard dirt floor, my back against the cold wall, and continue, "She was good, and she died, and the baby died, and Father made me come here, and I cannot brush Anne's hair and sing to her when she is frightened in the night, and Margaret said she heard Mother and Father talking, they said I was special, but I am not, I am cold, I am alone—" I cannot breathe, and I cannot see for all these tears that blind me.

Adela sucks in her breath sharply between her teeth and stands frozen, her hands hanging awkward before her, as if she wants to touch me but cannot. She turns away toward her altar, kneels, gets back up, walks toward the window, but then comes back again and kneels in front of me. Her hands clasped tight in her lap, she says, "Elinor, of course your mother was not at fault. If anyone is to blame, it is me. I do not know why my prayers for her did so little. I wish I could understand God's ways. I wish—no. Wishing is a silly, childish thing. Elinor." She reaches out, takes my hands in her freezing, scrawny ones. "I truly am very sorry about your mother. She must have been a good person, to have raised such a strong and smart girl as you. I will keep your mother in my prayers. And I swear to you, she is in a far better place than we are. She basks in the love of Christ and his mother, I am sure of it." I pull my hands away as I lean forward toward her, wrap my arms around her thin body, and, still crying, lay my head in her lap. She whispers, "Dear Jesus, what have I done?"

22

KINGMORE, PENNSYLVANIA, 2018

I WOKE UP EARLY THE DAY OF MY PRESENTATION. I tried to sit and breathe and be still for a few moments, but my brain was already pinging and reverberating. *Focus. It's going to be fine. It's totally normal to be nervous. Maybe try some yoga.* I breathed deeply and slowly, I listened to the air filling my lungs and leaving again. In downward dog, I looked back between my legs, at the plaster wall of my temporary dorm room. How many kids had slept in this room, had had sex in this room, had gotten stoned in this room? *Focus. Breathe.* I tried to move consciously for another few minutes, bending myself into the angles of warrior, triangle, tree, but I finally succumbed to child's pose. Then I stood up, and faced my day.

I arrived at my assigned lecture room at 10:45. People were already beginning to wander in, which seemed like a good sign. I walked to the podium at the front of the room at precisely 11. I quickly scanned the room; there were about thirty people in attendance—a very respectable number, considering that there were three other talks going on at the same time, as well as a performance of troubadour lyric poetry. My stomach fluttered; I had never addressed such a large group before.

"Thank you so much for coming to my talk, 'The Third Place: Theories and Theology of Purgatory from 1100 to 1300.' I'm so honored to be speaking at this year's conference on what

I consider to be a surprisingly neglected topic within medieval Christianity studies. I hope that by the end of our time together today, I'll have shed some light on this overlooked corner of medieval studies, and if I can inspire anyone to join me and dig deeper into the origins of purgatory, well, then I'll consider this presentation a success."

Someone in the audience coughed. I saw Sloane and Jasmine slip into the back row.

"Purgatory's theoretical and theological origins can be traced back to the earliest Christian writers and thinkers: for example, the third-century martyr Perpetua wrote about the process the soul underwent of being cleansed of sin after death. She also noted that this process occurred in a specific place. The early Church fathers Tertullian and Origen also referred to a place where souls ascended after death to atone for their sins before moving onward to Heaven. But it was medieval theologians who first codified a theological doctrine of purgatory; this process was completed at the Second Council of Lyons in 1274. But of course it was Dante who did so much, perhaps the most of all, to bring purgatory to the forefront of Christian thought. He gave us the first detailed, richly imagined map of purgatory as a physical mountain, which souls climbed during their process of atonement."

I presented my findings; I made my case. I systematically built my own mountain of theory and evidence, starting from the foundation of my dissertation. I noted that the social, cultural, political, and economic upheaval of the twelfth and thirteenth centuries indirectly supported the increased need for a theology of purgatory. During that period, individual agency was honored and prized; a single lowly Christian could influence the fate of a beloved, departed soul; a prayer said on earth could lift that soul higher up the mountain, closer to God.

"What I personally find so fascinating and confounding about the increased medieval prominence of purgatory is how it illustrates—indeed, embodies—the tension of the body-mind duality. The medieval relationship to the physical body was a conflicted

147

one, of course. But, whether intentional on the part of theologians or not, purgatory, it seems to me, values and honors the body in a way so little medieval theology does otherwise. The afflictions of purgatory are, in many cases, physical ones: the soul is subjected to cleansing fire as it trudges up the mountain. And down below, in the earthly realm, living loved ones knelt, hands clasped in prayer, lips beseeching for the dearly departed, supporting the soul in purgatory in its climb toward glory. How would we pray without lips, breath, a beating heart? And how could we climb the mountain without our lowly feet? Purgatory offered a degree of power to the devout body—something rare and beautiful indeed during the turbulent medieval era."

—

So, was it a success? By the modest standards of academia, I suppose so. Nobody stood up and shouted, "You don't know what you're talking about, you fraud!" Nobody walked out or laughed inappropriately. People didn't check their phones (too much) or doze off. The q-and-a session at the end was reasonably interactive: I fielded about half a dozen questions that asked for fine-tuning or clarification of certain points. I was surprised when Sloane raised her hand to ask a question.

"A wonderful presentation, Dr. Pace, very informative. It seems to me that purgatory does, as you noted, bring to the fore the overriding concern with the dichotomy of body and mind, the earthly realm and the heavenly one. My own research focuses primarily on women and the bodily and cultural impacts of enclosure, specifically the enclosure of the female anchorite. I wonder, do you see purgatory in any way as a gendered category? That is, how might men and women visualize and perform purgatory differently, if they do at all?"

"Thank you, that's an insightful question, and you've touched on a topic that's near and dear to my heart—and yours, I'm sure, given your own wonderful lecture yesterday. I've been thinking about this quite a bit, trying to tease out the ramifications of a gendered approach to purgatory and purgatorial practices. I think it's safe to say that, generally speaking, the body was a far more problematic site for medieval women than men—but that is probably a statement that could apply to women well beyond the medieval era." Sloane and a few other women smiled.

"Women, of course," I continued, "were encouraged to view their bodies as sources—really, *the* source—of sin. Let's not forget Tertullian's description of women as 'the devil's gateway.' But also, the small amount of agency available to women was located in their bodies: as queens, they could achieve meaning through their bodies by bearing royal heirs, especially sons. And other women could assert themselves by entering nunneries or monasteries—the power of refusing the body. It was women, especially, who prayed in order to assist and advance their loved ones in purgatory. There's a type of power, or at least independent agency, there: the power to affect, and change for the better, the status of others. The female body may have betrayed us all, led humans to the fallen state of original sin, but in the centuries to follow, female bodies could perform the devotions necessary for souls in purgatory. It might be useful to posit the biologically female body as a purgatorial state, in and of itself: both less-than and exalted, site of death and site of life."

And then it was done. As the attendees filed out, Sloane and Jasmine walked up to me. "Great job! The female body as a purgatorial state—that's so cool," said Jasmine.

"Thanks! It just came to me now."

Sloane said, "Let me buy you a drink tonight. A group of people are going to a pub in town—Duck McGee's, 8pm."

"Duck McGee's?"

Sloane rolled her eyes. "I didn't name the place. See you there?"

Jasmine looked at me closely for a few seconds, then continued, "Are you ok? You look a little pale. But also flushed, if that's possible—white all over except your cheeks are really pink."

"I'm fine. Probably adrenaline or nerves. I'm going to gather up my stuff here, you go ahead. I'll see you tonight." Sloane and Jasmine left, and I peeked in my tote; I had been so aware of Sloane's stolen book in my bag the whole time we were talking. I needed to make sure it hadn't somehow been visible to them, but it was still hidden in the bottom of the bag.

I was still peering at the book when an unfamiliar voice said, "Dr. Pace? I'm Lucinda Chen. I enjoyed your talk very much. I'm an editor at New England University Press. I work on our religious studies and medieval studies lists." A thirtysomething woman in a gray corduroy skirt and black turtleneck. "If you're thinking of expanding your research into a book, I'd love to read a proposal." She handed me her card as she continued, "Here's my contact info. Please do feel free to reach out anytime."

I thanked Ms. Chen, and after she left, I sat down in the nearest seat in the front row and reminded myself that this was what I wanted. This was what I'd been working toward for years.

I thought about the library back at school, those endless rows of books. The campus bookstore, all that bright light bearing down on those spines. Even my own desk, in the corner of the kitchen—a small tower of books next to my laptop, another pile precarious on the floor.

When I was a kid, I read everything, all the time. I read the cereal box at breakfast. I read during dinner, or tried to—I would put an open book on my lap beneath the table, and glance down to sneak in some reading while eating, until my mom or dad told me to stop.

And now, someone was asking *me* to make a book. To put *my* words, *my* name, on one of those shelves. To write my way into the mystery of purgatory: where it came from, who dreamed it up, and why.

A book would be a huge boost toward a job. The tenure track, the right path, within my grasp. Ascending the mountain. I had been walking this path and it was leading right where I had always hoped and thought it would.

I didn't want to go to a bar called Duck McGee's with a bunch of academics. I didn't even want to sit next to Sloane—not with her stolen book in my bag on the floor, a scarlet accusation lurking next to my feet. I liked Sloane, I liked Jasmine, and I was flattered by Lucinda's attention. Kind and intelligent women, all of them.

I walked up to the stage, to the podium where I had just spoken. I placed my stolen copy of *Holy Enclosed in the Dark* there. I didn't need it anymore. I never did. I needed my own words, my own steps, my own body.

I walked out the door, back to my dorm room, thinking about what Sloane had said: "I couldn't write about those women without really seeing and feeling for myself where they stayed." The body. My father's body, collapsing in on itself, turning on itself. My own body, creating, rejecting, releasing. And those women, across Europe, forcing their singular and specific bodies to bend to darkness and enclosure, choosing a kind of purgatory, placing themselves in a cramped place of penance. One of them, maybe some of them, placing a child there with them.

Those women plunging themselves into intense and abject prayer and devotion—not the fires of purgatory, not the mountains, but stone, low ceilings, darkness, little light.

The words rose up in my mind: *The purgatorial body. The female body as a state of purgatory. Anchoress as embodying purgatory.* I quickly typed into the Notes app on my phone.

I wasn't trapped. I wasn't bent or broken. My body could carry me wherever I wanted. It was the twenty-first century. I didn't have a full-time, stable job. And I didn't have kids. What was I waiting for? What was I doing?

I opened my laptop, went online, and began searching for flights to England.

23

―

*T*HIS MORNING FEELS SOMEHOW DIFFERENT THAN ALL THE OTHERS before it, although it is marked by the same intoned prayers of the monks, the same view of Adela, as she is every morning, already at her bench, deep into her prayers. I fell asleep last night with her seated next to my pallet, her hand on my head, softly brushing the hair away from my face with her fingers. She has done this for many nights now, ever since that January feast day of Mary.

She did indeed receive many women at the squint that day. I knelt alongside her and prayed, my voice echoing and braiding around hers and the voices of those women, all of us together a chorus of longing and supplication. I lost count of how many women there were, and as I confessed later to Brother Joseph, I did not always pray with my whole heart for each and every one of them—at times, I was distracted by the ache in my knees from that hard bench, or the rumble in my stomach, dreaming already of supper.

I could not help but remember myself out there, on the other side of the squint, back in the pews, while Mother waited in last year's long line of women eager for Adela's blessing. I thought of reaching backward through time to say to myself, *you will soon be on the other side of the cell wall. There is much grief coming your way, and your life will become nothing familiar to you.*

Adela devoted herself fully to each and every supplicant,

gazed into the eyes of every woman who approached her: the nervous young one who looked to be only a few years older than me, who whispered, "My lady, please, I only ask that it not hurt too much." The one who carried a baby in her arms, balanced over her large belly, as she murmured to Adela, "I pray that the Holy Mother might look on me, a poor sinner, with kindness, and bring me a healthy boy, as my husband says, if I bear him one more girl, he shall toss it to the wolves." To each of them, and all the others, Adela offered fervent prayers for safety and ease, for health and comfort. She looked into their eyes, then squeezed her own shut, mouthing passionate pleas to the Virgin.

And now this morning, some weeks later, there she sits, stick-straight once again at her prayer bench. I woke up at the first glimmer of slightest light; how long has she already been awake? I sometimes think she never sleeps at all.

But this is the difference of this morning: my belly feels like there is something in there with claws. Something scratches at me from behind my skin. When I crouch to use my chamber pot, fear seizes my throat: there is blood coming out of me from between my legs. Am I dying? Dear Lord, will I die in this cell?

"Are you crying, child?"

"It is nothing, my lady, Just a pain in my belly. And blood." I cannot help it, the sobs leap from my mouth, I cry and cry. My worst fear. I will die here. I must be even more sinful than I knew.

Adela reaches behind her pallet and pulls out a strip of old cloth—the same linen she gave me for tinder for the fire. "Here, put this between your legs. I have more for when it is full. And if you need it, I'll ask the brothers for more."

I turn my back and fumble with the grayish scrap—my fingers are clumsy and slow in this cold, and resist my mind's bidding—but soon I am able to wind it around and between my legs. I don't hear Adela approach, but then her hand is on my back.

"This happens to all women. It means that you are now able to bear children. You are marked by Eve. This is the blood of our womanly sin. It will come at intervals throughout your childbearing years, for a few days each time, until you are an old woman of forty or fifty."

"It happens to you, too?"

"It did, but no longer. My menses ceased months ago. It is a sign that God is pleased with me. He has released me from this female curse." Self-satisfaction flickers across her face—I see it slip to the surface for a moment before she pushes it back down. "But I should not boast. This moment comes to all girls, as it came to me. It is not pleasant, but you need not be afraid." Her hand moves up and down my back, kneads my skin in circles, and I loosen there. I sigh and settle under her hand.

"The pain will subside, and you will become used to this. Lay down, try to rest. I will ask Joseph to bring us a steady supply of heated stones for your bed. I can tell him it is merely because we are chilled by these last days of winter, but the warmth will help with the cramping as well." With my eyes closed, Adela's hand becomes my mother's.

No, that's not true. Adela's hand is all bone, nothing like hers was. I cannot trick myself into believing that simply because I want to. I am no child. But it is a kindness, and I am grateful for it, in this half-lit place.

—

The night women keep coming with their requests and prayers, despite the lingering winter's cold, their feet leaving prints in the old brown and gray snow in the morning. The women who yearn for a child came in the light of day after Christmas, but in the dark come those who, also through tears, long for an empty womb instead. I wish God could move the babies from the reluctant bellies to the ones filled only with longing. Sometimes I hear them speaking quietly with Adela in the dark. In the mornings when Adela seems more fatigued than usual, I suspect she was awakened by nighttime visitors that I did not hear.

Such as this morning, for purple furrows sit beneath Adela's eyes. "My lady," I ask, "did you not sleep well?"

"No, I am afraid not. We had another visitor last night. Another foolish girl who believed a man's false promises. And now her belly swells, and the man, of course, will not acknowledge her, will not even meet her eye. So I instructed her to ingest a mixture of pennyroyal, rue, and sage."

"My Lady, I did not know that you—that is, I thought you sent them to the midwife, or offered prayers. I thought—"

"You thought that I am a pious and pure soul who prays and fasts in her dark little cloister. That is what I try to be, but I am a mere woman, no matter how much I pray, until God chooses to release me from this world." She shakes her head, looks into my eyes as she says, "You are a woman now, Elinor, it is time you begin to learn of womanly things. There are ways to rid a woman of a child in the belly. There are plants that can bring this about. Some girls cannot wait for prayers, or cannot risk going to the midwife. She might be missed at home, or spotted by prying eyes." Adela looks down at her hands, clasped in her lap, and says in a gentler voice, "I am still a woman, too, Elinor. I am still here, on earth, in this body. I may not want to be, but I am. I cannot help but feel something for these girls. I pray every day that the Lord will not judge me too harshly for my weakness in wanting to help them."

"Lady, it is not weakness, I cannot believe that. You act from love, and Jesus is a loving god. Or, even if what you are doing angers him, surely Mary understands, she would tell her son not to judge you harshly."

Adela looks up at me. "You have such faith, Elinor. Thank you. For being here." Her arm reaches out and I take the little claw she holds toward me. A hot rush of anger nearly forces me to snap, "I hardly had a choice or say in the matter!" But her cold hand, so fragile in mine, cools my brief rage, so that I merely force a smile and hold her hand gently, afraid it will crumble in my grasp like an eggshell.

155

Later, I form the words, soundlessly, between my lips: "pennyroyal, rue, sage." I cannot write words, but hopefully I can make my mouth remember them. They are a different kind of prayer, a different kind of hope and beseeching. As Adela says, I am a woman now, I must learn of womanly things.

24

—

*F*LYING OVER THE OCEAN, **on my way to a tiny dark place.** Sloane was right; the books get you only so far. Sometimes, you need to touch the stone, walk the hallways, shut the door behind you. The books, and my brain, had done their job, now my feet needed to do their part. My body carried over the water, from one landmass to another. I told myself I was leaving my own small past behind, while the whole great expanse of the historical past—its records and buildings, its art and writing—was still before me, still to come.

—

At Kingmore, at the conference, at the bar (yes, I went, it would have been rude not to), I told Sloane that her words had nudged me into action. "I've been thinking about what you said about direct, on-site research, and now I'm wondering about the gendered connections between purgatory and the body, too. This idea of the female body and a state of in-betweenness—I can't articulate it yet, but I there's something there."

"That's great, Liz! Just keep your hands off my Italian anchoresses, if you don't mind." She laughed and smiled, but I heard it, the possessiveness, maybe even a little fear, insecurity, in the way her lips dropped the smile so quickly, how she looked down at the table, not at me. *Those crumbs are mine.* I didn't tell her I'd already bought tickets to England. And I certainly didn't tell her that I had looked at tickets to Italy, but they were more expensive, and there were no flights that aligned smoothly with the dates of summer break, when I wanted to travel. "I'm joking!" she continued. "Gender and purgatory sounds like such an intriguing path of study. Hey, do you wanna go to Jasmine's lecture with me tomorrow?"

Jasmine's talk was great: a thorough and convincing argument for medieval Europe as a place of cross-cultural exchange, and cities that were homes to diverse populations—"but cities which were still, of course, hotbeds of virulent antisemitism and misogyny, and general fear of the other. In teaching medieval studies to twenty-first-century students, we best serve them by presenting the era in all its honest messiness: 'medieval' means more than white, and more than European. There was no medieval world, per se, but rather medieval worlds, which cross-pollinated and communicated, in ways both beneficial and harmful, to the many diverse populations of the time."

Fluid worlds, porous places.

—

Back home in Stillburne after the conference, the spring semester soon ended as it always did, in a rush of final exams, piles of final papers to be graded, the drudgery of logging final grades. I had managed to get through "Monks, Monarchs, and Medieval Art" reasonably well, I thought, although I had missed teaching "Holy Madness." But my ongoing conferences with Emma throughout the semester had kept the anchoresses in my life. "I'm gonna do it," she had said. "I want both. The past and the future. I can't stop thinking about Julian of Norwich, all those other anchoresses."

I smiled as I replied, "Emma, I think it's wonderful. Let's get to work." I sent her home for the summer with a list of recommended reading that would be useful before she began her independent study in earnest in the fall. Would I be here in September to guide her? For the last three years, my contract had been renewed in the summer, after the end of the semester and graduation were behind us. I still wasn't sure encouraging her on this path was absolutely the right thing to do. But I couldn't bring myself to talk her out of it, to crush her delicate hope already.

—

It was the Tuesday after Memorial Day, an overnight flight from Albany to Heathrow, a train from the airport to the town of Wenfair, then a taxi to the abbey. "Please be careful, Liz," my mom had said on the phone the night before.

"Mom, I'm 35 years old! It's a direct flight, and the UK has a great train system. I won't even have to do any driving on the wrong side of the road! This is important to me. It's the first thing I've felt excited about in a long time."

"Honey, I know it's been . . . well, it's been a shitty year, hasn't it?"

I laughed. "Mother, I'm shocked! Such language! But yeah. Really, really shitty."

"Except for your conference, of course. That went well."

I thought about Ms. Chen, the New England Press editor. The book idea I'd left behind. The actual book—Sloane's book—that I'd left behind. "It did. But this trip is different. It isn't the expected thing. I don't have to go on this trip, but I want to. I want to see these places I read and write about. I haven't traveled abroad in years. There's always something—work, a paper, the pregnancy . . . Dad. But right now, at this moment, I feel like I have a little space. It feels right."

"That makes sense. Those reasons aren't shitty at all!" I laughed again as Mom continued, "But I still wish Nick was going with you. I can't help it. I know you're an independent woman, but you're also my little girl."

Truthfully, I would have preferred if Nick came, too. But he had a paper to polish before submission to a notable journal. And we couldn't afford a second plane ticket anyway. After Kingmore, I had approached Dr. Manheim with the idea of developing an advanced seminar on anchorites and hermits. When I mentioned my (self-funded) research trip, she gave me the go-ahead to devise a sample syllabus, which she would review it over the summer. So, maybe, in a year, I'd be teaching that course—maybe, even, as a full-time professor?

—

The train pulled into the Wenfair station. About twenty thousand residents, in the southeastern part of the country, near Reading, and home to an abbey that dated to the tenth century (although little of the original structure remained), which had housed an anchorite in an extant cell. Wenfair offered a number of retreats on its website—"Contemplative Hiking Weekend," "The Wisdom of the Desert: Ancient Teachings and their Relevance Today"— and offered "simple accommodations to anyone, from all religious or spiritual backgrounds—or none at all!—seeking to replenish and reinvigorate."

An imposing, sprawling stone building, fronted by a massive tower with a large rectangular window, loomed over the village below. The taxi driver maneuvered up the small road that turned to gravel and narrowed as we got closer to the abbey, and pulled into a small parking lot with half a dozen spaces. After I got out and paid, I walked up a path past a few benches until I reached the entrance, where a heavy wooden door greeted me.

When I lifted and released the substantial brass knocker, I felt it reverberate against the wood, and I imagined the wave of sound continuing to roll down a long stone passageway, a hallway flanked by soaring stained-glass windows, perhaps incense wafting from thuribles hung from chains along the hall.

A tall, lean, almost gaunt monk, probably in his fifties, opened the door for me.

"Welcome, are you Elizabeth Pace?" he asked.

"Yes," I replied. "Thank you so much for allowing me to visit."

"We are happy to do so. I am Brother Sebastian. Please, let me assist you with your luggage. Kindly follow me; I'll show you to your room. The abbot invites you to join him for a cup of tea in his office, but thought you might wish, first, to rest or freshen up after your travels. He'll fetch you in an hour."

As soon as I stepped inside, I felt the coolness of the air, despite the summer heat outside. We continued down the hall until we came to another door; this one opened out onto a small courtyard. I walked across the stone path that ran across the center of the yard until we entered a more modern building. Here the walls were plaster, and I noticed radiators along the walls. We turned a corner and Sebastian stopped at a door on the left, which he held open for me.

A twin bed on a metal frame; a large wooden crucifix on the wall overhead. A small desk, with a chair and a lamp, against the wall to my left. Against the opposite wall there stood a small wash-basin—no faucet, just a large ceramic pitcher full of water on the small shelf next to it—and a floor lamp. The walls painted a dingy white—not the exposed stone I had romantically expected, but there were thick wood beams that looked old crossing the ceiling. I could touch them with my arm outstretched, given how low the ceiling was.

A well-lit cell with solid walls that smelled only, faintly, of soapy lemon—and, Sebastian informed me, a full, modern bath-room down the hall.

After Sebastian left, I peeked in the closet: two towels, two washcloths, a spare set of sheets. All faded white, all threadbare. I unpacked and hung up my pants, straightened out my shirts and sweaters, washed my hands, brushed my teeth, combed my hair. I looked out the single window, to the right of the bed. From up here on the third floor, I could see the village of Wenfair below, as well as a glimpse of an herb garden if I tilted my head to look nearly straight down: I saw mounds of tiny white flowers, and fuzzy leaves of what I was pretty sure was sage.

I walked to the door and opened it when I heard a knock. An older man with white hair, wearing a tunic similar to Brother Sebastian's, said, "I'm Abbot Michael. I believe we have exchanged emails these past few weeks."

I followed Michael to his office, down a further hallway which opened onto another, smaller courtyard before we entered a smaller stone building, turned down yet another hallway. As if he knew what I was thinking, Michael said, "Because the abbey is so old, it is something of a mishmash. The entrance building and the chapel—with the attached anchorite cell—are partly original structures, but the rest of the buildings have been built over the centuries. The guest quarters date to the sixteenth century, originally, but were quite damaged in the air raids during World War II. We like to say that here at Wenfair you're in the fourteenth century until you turn a corner, and suddenly it's the nineteenth. Or, in our case, we're in the fifteenth at the moment." He held open the door to his office, which managed to be quite dark despite the tall window dominating much of one wall. Two other walls were covered by bookcases. Above the door there hung a large crucifix. The abbot's desk faced it. He gestured toward an armchair before his desk, and as I sat down, I imagined staring at that tortured body every day. Even with my back to it, I sensed the weight of that agony behind me.

After offering me tea and inquiring about my trip, Michael said, "so, you are interested in anchoresses. And you study purgatory, yes? How interesting. May I ask what stirred your interest in such women? Of course, you're a scholar, but outside academia, so few people have even heard of anchorites."

I was about to launch into the expected professional-chitchat routine: my longtime work in medieval religion, especially in relation to women of the era; how the anchoress models and mirrors a unique pathway for women in a regimented, highly structured era; how I recently heard Dr. Sloane Lanham speak intriguingly on the topic at a recent conference. But I stopped up that stream of words in my mouth, and allowed myself instead to say, "I don't really know, to be honest. But I keep circling back to them. I've spent years writing about medieval conceptions of purgatory, and at first I thought I could somehow weave the two topics together. I tried to rewrite my research, I thought I could even present about the two topics together at this conference I spoke at a few months ago, but that didn't work out. I do think there's something interesting about the anchorite's cell as a purgatorial state, but I haven't parsed that out fully yet. I had a miscarriage, too, and I'm not sure if that has anything to do with this. Lots of women have miscarriages. This was my first one, and I'll probably get pregnant eventually, it's fine, although it's not common to have one at the end of the first trimester, when I did. It's so hard to make things fit. I pushed away my interest in medieval gender and anchoresses, for so long, and I just don't want to anymore. The idea of sitting in the dark, where these women lived—I know it's not necessary, but it feels critical somehow. I want to tell my students about them, so that they aren't completely forgotten." I paused to take a breath and, embarrassed at the words I had just spewed at this man, I said, "I'm sorry, I must sound ridiculous. I do have a professional and academic interest in anchoresses, but it's more than that. It's personal, too."

The abbot set his teacup down and said, "Dr. Pace, I think that sounds entirely reasonable. Honorable, even." He was so calm, so unsurprised, no hint of shock—for a moment I longed to confess my dumb crime, from months ago, to him: *Bless me Father for I have sinned. It's been fifteen years, at least, proably more like twenty, since my last confession. I stole a book from the campus bookstore. I went back and bought two more books to make up for it. Then I left the stolen book at a conference and hopefully someone else took it and is enjoying it. That's good enough, right?*

Michael picked his cup back up and took a sip. I did too, and washed the unsaid words away. Michael continued, "The records are spotty, as I'm sure you can imagine, but we know that at least four women stayed here in the cell in the thirteenth and four-teenth centuries. In my opinion, one of our anchoresses, Adela Webster of Kirkby, is an especially interesting case. She was here in the fourteenth century, and she was famed for being especially rigorous in her asceticism. Apparently she ate little or nothing—at least, according to the writings about her that survive—and she could have married a very wealthy nobleman if she had wished. And she had a child, a girl, brought to live with her in the cell."

"Like when Hildegard of Bingen was enclosed with Jutta of Sponheim?" The walls seemed to unsettle, just slightly, around me—the stone seemed to quiver, but it was only me, my blood racing, my heart rushing.

"Yes, precisely. Although bringing a young girl to live with an anchoress seems incomprehensible to us now, in some ways it offered the young woman some benefits—"

"—she learned to read and maybe write, which would have been unusual at the time of course, and she avoided an early mar-riage and thus the dangers of giving birth early and often. I'm sorry, I interrupted you," I said, before continuing, "I'd love to learn more about the girl who was enclosed here. Is there any-thing in your library holdings about her?"

"You're more than welcome to explore our archives, but I'm afraid you won't find much. The only mention of a girl in the cell appears, just once, in a later record. Any contemporaneous record of her from her time here is lost, if it ever existed. Not even her name is known."

"Not even her name?" A ghost girl, unnamed, locked away, hovering behind me like a shadow.

—

That night I joined Father Michael at a small table in the corner of the dining hall for an early and simple dinner of vegetable stew, while the other monks sat at long tables and benches, assiduously keeping their eyes on their food. "When," he asked, "would you like to see Adela's cell?"

"As soon as possible, please," I answered without hesitation.

"In that case, I'll send Sebastian for you in the morning, after Terce, which is—

"Nine in the morning."

Michael smiled. "Most of our visitors are not so attuned to the monastic way of life. They're mostly frazzled, artistic types seeking peace and quiet, a break from the pressures of modern life. Often they tell me they are 'spiritual but not religious,' but I must confess to not entirely understanding what that means. I think it means they know God exists, but they perhaps don't quite know how to reach Him. But, we are happy to share our beautiful, blessed home with such seekers—and the income does help maintain the place."

"You called it 'Adela's cell,' is that because she was the last person to live there?"

"No, we think there were at least a couple more anchoresses after her. I didn't even realize I called it her cell. But I suppose I do tend to think of it as Adela's cell. I've read about her extreme ascetic devotion, and the thought of the girl with her—it's hard to shake. At any rate, please join us in the dining hall at seven in the morning for breakfast, and then Sebastian will fetch you from your room afterwards, as soon as the morning prayers are complete. You're more than welcome to explore our grounds while you wait, if you wish."

I thanked Michael and we finished our stew in silence. A girl, trapped in the dark. What would she have thought of someone like Adela? Would the girl consider her a saint? Or, would she be afraid of Adela, think her insane?

How cold that little girl must have been.

25

"TODAY IS THE DAY OF LORD MONMOUTH'S VISIT." Adela had received the letter announcing his impending arrival some days ago—and had reminded me of it several times since. Even so, she said yet again, "I've had a letter from Lord Monmouth. He will visit today. As my patron, it is his right to be reassured that I am being treated adequately by the Abbey, and fulfilling my duties." No morning greeting, not even a turn of her head to face me. "Please see that the cell is clean and orderly before his arrival."

What happened to the woman who spoke to me of the distasteful ways of men and this world, who showed me such compassion when I bled for the first time? Now I think she must truly be mad. The floor is mere dirt; if I sweep, it will only resettle into another dusty pattern. All of my clothing fits into a small chest which fits into the space beneath my pallet. Adela's clothing— no more than a couple of singlets and gowns—is tucked under her own pallet. What am I to do, dust the prayer benches, fluff our pallets? Not knowing what else to do, I do precisely that. It takes but minutes.

Prayers, reading, sewing, more prayers, and then the cloth at the window flutters; it is Brother Joseph with dinner. I reach for my bread and cheese and nibble. I force myself to feel gratitude: *Lord, thank you for this bread and cheese.* Adela picks up her prayer book and begins to read while I eat. I can hear her insides growling, an anguish of hunger, from across the cell.

Joseph has just left with the remnants of my morning meal when we hear the church door open, and then the thud and clatter of many feet. And then, a voice.

"I will see her now, Brother."

And then, something I have never seen: Lady Adela, full of grace, her eyes nearly always cast downward or beseeching upwards, springs across the cell in two light, quick steps, as she calls out, "Lord Monmouth, I am here, please approach." Her words are dignified, but he cannot see what I can: her flushed cheeks, her eyes gleaming, her hands shaking the dust from her gown then smoothing it out, tucking lank hair back under her wimple.

A hand pushes the cloth aside, and a male face peers in. Like Adela's, it is not old; his hair and mustache are both brown with no hints of gray. "Adela, is that you?" The eyes glance toward me and I drop my head, attempt a graceless bow. I long to ask, *do you know my father? Do you know the land of yours he farmed? Who tends the garden now?* but I say no such foolish thing. Lord Monmouth surely has so much land, he cares little for the fate of one family plot. He probably does not even know that my family left; surely he has people who oversee his vast holdings for him.

"I see your handmaiden has arrived. Do you find her acceptable?"

"Yes, Lord, she is a dutiful servant and a devout child. Elinor, please return to your devotional reading while I converse with Lord Monmouth." I had not been reading, I had been cleaning, or attempting to do so, again. But I sit down on my pallet, taking the prayer book from her outstretched hand, and face the wall, while I listen to their hushed words. How can I not, in that cramped space?

"My lady, you look even more diminished than when I saw you last. The abbot tells me you do not eat more than a single

167

meal a day. You are a noblewoman, you must care better for yourself." I wonder what he would say if he could see her clearly, in a sharper light. He does not see her bald patches beneath her wimple, which I glance at when she takes it off to shake out her thinning hair and readjust the headpiece, or her gray teeth behind her thin lips, which I see when she whispers over the rosary clasped tight in her skinny fingers

"I am fine, Robert." I note her use of his familiar, Christian name. But she seems unaware of what she has said. As if she has said the name many times before.

"Adela," he says, the name more a sigh than a word. "I must ask, again . . . must you continue with this? Nobody doubts your piety. You will ascend straight to the right hand of Christ, I am sure of it. You will sit upon his throne, a queen in heaven."

"That is blasphemous. Only saints ascend directly to the heavenly realm; I will pass through purgatory and endure my trials first, like any humble Christian."

"Well, who can know what will be, what the path in the world after this one looks like. I cannot believe that you, of all us poor mortals, will face more suffering in the next life. You have already endured—are enduring—so much. Too much, I fear."

Even from across the cell, I can sense Adela hardening, sitting up straighter. "Please, my Lord, do not speak to me this way. I am forever grateful for your support and care of me, and I pray for your soul every day. But I am mere flesh, weak and evil and womanly, and I must suffer, as Christ suffered for me, for all of us."

"You have suffered enough hardship already. I do not blame you for . . . what happened. We have prayed endlessly for God's forgiveness." Here his voice drops to a whisper. "It was a moment of weakness born of—deep affection. I know you endured so much anguish—what happened to the baby—and, nearly, you—"

Adela's voice is far away and formal. "Lord Monmouth, I thank you as always for your concern and support. I am provided for. My heart is at peace, for I know this is where I am meant to be. Let us not question the Lord's mysterious ways. He has called me, and I have answered. And I will continue to answer him for all the days of my life."

"Very well, as you wish. Adela, I must tell you something else. I am a father now. Christine has borne me a son. A healthy and strong babe. Surely this means God's grace shines on me? I waited for you, I thought this—interest—of yours would pass, but I could wait no longer, given the need for me to marry and then secure an heir."

"I am well aware of the pressures you face as a man of your position, my Lord," Adela replies, the words dropping like daggers from her mouth. "I assure you, as my patron, this enclosure is no mere passing fancy. I am pleased for you and the duchess. It does seem that you are in God's favor. I will continue on my own path toward His benevolence. And now," she leans back into the dimness of the cell, "I must bid you farewell. We shall be called to prayer soon. And I am teaching the child her letters, we have much to do."

Lord Monmouth sighs, places a hand on the edge of the squint, and looks past Adela to me. I glance up, drawn by the sensation of his eyes on me, but quickly look down again when our eyes met. But not before seeing that he is indeed handsome, with those clear deep brown eyes and his thick hair to his shoulders. "How old is that child? She is nearly of marriageable age, is she not? I wanted to grant your request. I thought, Adela will have some company, a friendship, in that dark little cell. But now that I see her, I think that child should be with her family. It is not right."

I let myself imagine Lord Monmouth striding over to the door, yanking it open—never mind the bricks blocking it—and me rushing through it, and there, waiting for me, stands Joseph, smiling at me—

Blushing, I exhale and push that silliness aside as Lord Monmouth speaks to Adela, his concern for my well-being seemingly passing. "Adela, God has smiled on me, and you are clearly beloved by him. I married Christine because I must secure the family name and holdings. Christine is good and kind, but she is not you. But someday, when at last we both leave this world for the next, I believe it is you and I who will be reunited—"

"Lord Monmouth, please, I must insist that you say no more. Even if God favors it, we must not chance to incur his wrath again by saying such things! Again, I bid you good day." Adela stands, steps back into the darkness.

I hear Lord Monmouth sigh again. As he stands, he says, in a louder and more formal tone, "I will gladly continue to pay for your place and comfort here at the Abbey, my lady. Should you require anything at all, please have me informed me at once." His hand lingers on the ledge of the squint, but then disappears, and I hear him walk away. I imagine walking the length of the monastery too, past the rows of pews, toward the thick wooden doors I entered through those months ago. I press my dirty nails into my palms, thinking about those solid doors giving way as I push, and then step into world.

I force my eyes onto the page in front of me, and whisper the words that slowly form between my teeth, as I string the sounds together: "My God, have regard to help me. I have many thoughts and great fears afflicting my soul. How will I pass through unhurt? How will I break them to pieces?" I manage to read to the end of the question, but no answer is written there. Still, I do like the feel of the words as I make them on my tongue. I just wish this writer had received an answer from God, and shared it, here, with me.

26

WENFAIR ABBEY, ENGLAND, 2018

I DIDN'T REALIZE HOW DARK IT WOULD BE. It was just a little cloudy outside, but in that cell, it felt like an autumn evening, when the warmth of the day dissipates as soon as the sun goes down. Although, there were no seasonal signifiers at all; it could have been any season, any year, outside of time. A present marked only by absence. There was no past or future, only the dark, and the walls.

The abbot was standing outside the cell, in the yard, having walked out there after closing the door to the cell behind me. When I commented on the darkness to him through the small upper window, my words felt insubstantial against all that stone, silly and small, not up to the task of filling the space. A space both so shrunken, yet expansive.

"Yes," he replied, "no matter how light it is outside, the cell remains dim, because there are only the two small windows to the outside, and the squint, over there, across from the windows, in the other wall. They simply don't allow much sun to get in. We do not know if the cell was purposefully built that way, at a particularly sunless angle, or if it's merely an accident of design and construction—although I suspect the former. In addition, the windows would have been covered with a cloth, probably an animal hide, even thicker than the curtain we've added. The cell is always quite dark. Just imagine it at night."

I shuddered, imagining myself here, alone, within these walls, in the middle of a winter night. In a world with no cars whooshing past on highways, or trains whistling and humming by on tracks. No artificial, but comforting, companionship from a tv or a podcast. No glow from a charging computer or phone, the microwave, the nightlight in the hallway.

I touched the stone wall to my right, let my fingers slide along the cool, bumpy surface. Then, just a few steps across the cell, to the far wall, and I peered out of the crude little squint. I looked into the church: a dozen rows of silent pews, and along one wall, a long wrought-iron stand holding dozens of votive candles, about a quarter of which were lit. I moved back toward the window, so that I could see Michael out there.

"I didn't realize just how small it is in here. Two people living together, day in and day out, for months. Even though I've read so much about anchorites, being here, I feel it really sinking in, what it must have been like—as much as I can, knowing that I can step outside whenever I want."

"Yes, and the door would have been bricked over during the years that Adela resided here," Michael said.

Remembering the rack of votives along the side of the church, I asked, "Do people come often and light the prayer candles?"

"A few times a week, mostly tourists," he replied.

The air was so heavy that I could practically taste it, thick and mossy, settling between all my paltry words. I needed to push through it, to offer something like light.

"That seems like a more reasonable amount of devotion to the Lord to me. Just light a candle and say a prayer. This literal imprisonment is so extreme. But I suppose there's an allure to transcending the ordinary, isn't there?"

"Ordinary devotion," he said.

"That's a lovely phrase. Is it from the New Testament?"

Michael stepped up close to the window, so I could see that he was smiling as he said, "No, it's not in the Bible. A child psychologist named D. W. Winnicott coined the phrase; he meant that an infant would thrive as long as it receives 'ordinary devotion' from its mother. We don't need to give extraordinary care, we don't need to contort ourselves to meet impossible demands—or to lock ourselves up and starve ourselves. Our ordinary, loving care is enough."

"Abbot, that's beautiful. Inspiring."

"I suppose it is, isn't it? My father was a child psychologist in the '50s and '60s, and Dad was influenced by him, so the phrase must have imprinted on my psyche. Just now, when you were speaking, it came to me."

I sat in the cell for a few more moments, in my ordinary body, in silence. I tried to feel some vestige of holiness in that small cold cell, but I felt no devotion, no yearning. It was only a carved-out place, empty at its core.

—

173

That evening, after dinner and Vespers, I asked Michael if I might visit the cell again, to get a sense of what it was like at night. He agreed, and I stepped from the pleasantly cool dimming of an English summer evening into the cell's stony black. Behind me, Michael closed the door, and panic fluttered in my stomach, rose up through my lungs and throat. I placed one hand over the other. *You are here, this is you.* I closed my eyes and my breath slowed, my skin cooled. I floated, formless. Everything obliterated, including that nameless girl who sat here centuries ago. I breathed in through my nose, out through my mouth, and now felt grounded, enclosed—no, embraced—but also, somehow, expansive, as I stood where, hundreds of years earlier, other women, and at least one girl, had stood as well.

"Professor Pace? Is everything all right? Do you need some light?" Michael called from outside the cell. I wasn't sure how long I had been quiet. Seconds? Minutes?

"No, no light. I'm fine. Please step away and leave me alone here for a few minutes." An alien, commanding voice rose from my lips.

"Yes, of course. I'll head toward the back of the church. I will come back in five minutes. But I suspect even that might feel like a very long time in there. If it becomes too much, please just call out through the window and I will immediately open the door."

—

I was alone. I held my hands up before my face, I could see them in the small light, but just barely. I was breathing, and that was all I was. I walked carefully and slowly across the floor, my hands held out in front of me, until my palms pressed up against the stone wall. I held them there, moved them over the ungiving rock. And then, I couldn't help it: I took my phone from my pocket and turned on the flashlight. I moved the unnatural light across the wall before me, gazing at the rough-hewn blocks of stone, the crevices between them— and, down near my knees, several silvery, spidery, vertical lines scratched into the rock. I traced my fingers along them, and turned off the flashlight.

I inhaled, closed my eyes, thought of my father. Not at the end, closed in on himself, his body struggling to preserve itself, but before all that. Sitting in his favorite recliner, reading the newspaper, lowering it as he looked up at me and said, "Hey kiddo, what's up?" An utterly normal, random, inconsequential memory.

I squatted and peered at those lines traced across the stone. I remembered that day in my office, with Emma, that crack in the ceiling seeming to lengthen and widen above us. These lines were each no more than a few inches long, and stretched down to the bottom of the wall. They huddled there, one after another after another, repeating, going nowhere.

After what must surely have been two or three minutes (but then again, I'm not sure at all), I thought I heard someone speaking. Asking me something. Michael? No, it sounded more like a woman's voice. Not possible. I must have imagined it. I could barely hear it: the stone kept the words from forming clearly, the wall between the voice and me blurred and muffled whatever was being said. I was tired, probably still jet-lagged, and adjusting to the murky cell. I was sure it was imaginary. I didn't answer. Instead, I sat down on the small stone bench beneath the squint, and closed my eyes again.

I wasn't sure if the unintelligible words were spoken into the air around me, or only lived in my mind.

There was no differentiation between the dark of the cell and the dark of my body. There was no in-between. I felt the black emptiness surround me and hold me. I felt a cool and melting embrace. I let myself be darkness, be breath, be un-body. I felt formless, but also, like something new, small and fishlike, promised and promising. A line from *Purgatorio* rose before and within me: *Once my beating heart brought me back/ To myself, the woman I'd found earlier by herself/ Was over me, saying, "Hold on to me, hold on."*

*S*HE WOBBLES OVER TO ME, as I sit reading on my pallet again, moving my lips to shape and sound each letter. She places a hand on my arm and murmurs, "I am pleased to see you reading, Elinor. May I join you? Would you read to me?" I nod and she settles next to me. "*Ave Maria gratia plena Dominus tecum.*" Mary was just a young virgin, told that she must birth and care for and raise up a holy creature. Did she wonder why she was chosen? Did she resist her fate, even for a moment?

Adela smiles and says, "Elinor, your reading is like music, so smooth and pleasant to hear." Her breath smells more strongly than ever of decay; I press my lips shut against the gamy reek. Her smile fades as she continues, "I sometimes wonder what the Holy Virgin thought when the angel told her his Good News. As a daughter of Eve, she knew her body to be the source of all sin. And yet here was a messenger of God, telling her that, through her body, mankind would be saved." She sighed and looked down at her hands, clasped in her bony lap. "This is the cell, Elinor. Nobody else can see that, it seems. 'Why lock yourself away, why imprison yourself?' they all say, but this"—she pressed the thumb of her left hand down on her right palm, the flesh whitening under the pressure of her finger—"*This* is the prison. I am already in a cage. I am already tethered in place like a beast. I am *not* merely this body." Here, her eyes latch onto mine. "I am a humble servant of God, a lowly woman, but I am more than that, also. I know my place—it is not here, in this skin. It is with my Lord. This body keeps me from Him. It is because of this body that I am cold and alone in the dark, unable to feel my love's embrace. Oh, to be loved by God like Mary!"

She is breathing hard now, a rasp and rattle in her chest. I do not feel the same kind of revulsion toward my body that she does. My hands tug weeds from the ground, making space for beans to root and sprout. My legs chase Anne and other children around the village square on market day, my ears full of their shrieks and giggles. My mouth makes the words I read, lifts them off the page, into the dark air around me.

And then my mouth offers these words to her: "I am sure that God looks on you with love, my lady. Your devotion is extraordinary. Everyone can see it. You parents must have been so pleased when you told them you wished to take vows and enter the convent, and then become an anchoress." In truth, I suspect her parents were unhappy with her decision; a noble daughter would be expected to marry well, to the benefit of the whole family. But I am curious about her past. As the visit from Lord Monmouth helped me realize, she had a life outside of this cell, too.

Adela sighs and smiles a smile with no true mirth in it. "No, they were not pleased. My father raged about alliances and lineages, and my mother wailed at the prospect of no little grandchildren to fuss over." She pauses, looks down at her hands, clasps them tightly together, and then continues, "But soon after I announced my desire to take the veil, Mother found the servants letting out my dresses. She saw my rounded belly, and I confessed—" she looks up at me, then back down at her hands— "our sin. My weakness. My sin. I was sent to a far-off nunnery to hide my shame. At that time, the plague was tearing through the land— Mother used the stench and threat of relentless death as an excuse to hurry me away to the safety of isolation. And then, there was so much pain, and so much blood—" Her voice trembles on that word, and I see her fists are closed tight, her nails pressed into the flesh of her palms. She takes a breath and continues, "God spoke to me again, he told me to offer myself for enclosure at the abbey when I was . . . well again. He let me live, to atone. I was sinful, and God in his endless benevolence set me on this path toward redemption. The nunnery was no longer enough. I had done and seen . . . too much. I needed to offer more of myself to God's mercy."

Adela gazes toward the window, which she rarely does—she refuses herself even that glimpse of light, that occasional breeze. I am not sure what she is looking at, but I suspect it is something I cannot see, something that is not out there at all, but lodged deep in her instead. Her body so near to mine, and yet it feels like she is not here at all. I grasp her hand. "If it pleases you, my Lady," I say, "I would pray with you."

A smile, then, in that sunken face. We kneel on the hard small bench at the altar. "O Jesus, let me never forget thy bitter Passion that thou has suffered for my transgression. Grant that I may love thee so that the wisdom of the world may go clean from me. I burningly desire to come to see thy face in whom is all my comfort and my solace."

Adela is marked by the world too, as much as she may long to hold it away, to keep it at an arm's length.

After we have recited the prayer many times, Adela sighs and wipes a hand across her brow. "Elinor, I'm sorry. My burdens are not yours. I know this is a very hard place for someone so young, away from your family. But I hope that you might also see the gift you have been given—the gift of release from female obligation. Here, you may read and pray, with none of your worldly duties or chores."

Adela in her dirt-dragged skirts, her eyes struggling to see in the gray light. Her hollow cheeks, gray teeth. I feel something warm rising from my heart: tenderness. Tenderness for this strange and struggling woman who truly believes she is offering me a gift with this enclosed life. She is a holy noblewoman, I am nothing like her. But she is also made of flesh that longs and loves and needs and wants. Like me.

I say nothing, but I smile, and Adela says, "I am suddenly feeling quite weak. A bit more rest this morning might help."

She returns to her pallet and turns her back to me. I crane my neck to look through the squint, into the church. I see the statue of Mary. Light trickles through the windows above and behind her. I imagine curling up in a dusty pool of it, like a cat. I think about climbing up and somehow squeezing through the squint, into the church, walking up the aisle, pushing open those heavy church doors. Feeling wind like warm breath on my skin. All that sky.

I know this world is a pale shell of heaven, that it is nothing compared to the eternal kingdom that awaits. But I cannot let it go. I turn away from the squint and go to the window. When I push aside the hide curtain and stand on my toes, so I can place my cheek on the ledge, so, the sun lands on my face, my weak sinful skin.

I cannot love Adela's gift.

She is asleep again when Brother Joseph visits me after Vespers; he often checks in with me before retiring for the night. It is not often that Adela is already asleep, but that is the case more often of late.

"She seems unwell, Brother. She is so thin, and her skin has an unnatural pallor." I hear something new and sure in my voice. I do not whisper or hold back the words I truly wish to say. I look into the monk's eyes as I speak.

Brother Joseph glances around behind him in the church, then turns back to me and says, her voice quiet, "Miss, she is dying. I have heard Abbot Hugh discussing the matter with some of the other monks. They say the Lady is ascending to a new level of devotion."

Joseph takes his leave of me, and I turn to the hearth, poking at the ash to uncover a few more embers. Winter begins to finally thaw, and give way to spring. Might the increasing warmth and sun of the new season help heal Adela? The thought of her dying sits like a black rock in my stomach. Yes, my time here would end, but so would my time with *her*. It is the idea of the loss of Adela that darkens my heart. I pick up my rosary, her Christmas gift to me, and pray, working and worrying my fingers over the wooden beads.

28

—

*T*HERE WAS NOTHING FOR ME THERE IN THAT CELL. **Not that I actually** expected a grand moment of insight or salvation in the darkness. I couldn't manage to understand how a person could think to find God in such a place. Why would God want someone to starve themselves, locked away? What was the point? And to bring a child into it— although of course, medieval conceptions of child- hood didn't align with ours. Say this girl was twelve or thirteen. That would have been considered the cusp of womanhood. If anything, she would have been a valuable resource, extra hands in the kitchen, or on the farm. If a family gave their child up to a monastery, it was because they were either very wealthy, or des- titute, desperate for a pressure release, one less mouth to feed. Which was she? What was her story? Buried for centuries, that story, and probably too deeply to unearth now.

I imagined speaking to that girl, trying to understand her own understanding of her experience: *Were you scared? Did you miss your parents? Were you mad at them? Why did they do this to you? Did you wonder why God put you in the cell with Adela? Did she seem like a saint to you, or were you afraid of her? What was she like?* So many questions, but of course that girl, whoever she was, would never answer.

I never prayed. I wasn't religious. I suppose I prayed when Dad was sick; "please" repeated over and over. But that was all, until, in that little stone room, these words rose in my mind and they were, indeed a prayer: *I hope she found some peace. Then, and now, too. Whatever that means. If that's possible.*

It was time to go. I didn't belong there. I stepped across the ancient hard-packed floor, and pushed against the closed door (no handle or knob on the interior side), the wood cold beneath my hands. It didn't move and a wave of fear rolled in my stomach: *I'm trapped here, I can't get out.* I pushed again, and the door didn't budge beneath my flattened palms. I leaned against it, trying to push my way back out into the world. Wait, what was I doing? All I had to do was go to the squint, call out to Michael that I was ready to leave. But suddenly that small window seemed far away. It didn't make sense, but I wanted to keep my hands on the door. I wanted that solid, firm wood under my palms. I was still standing there several seconds later, my hands pushing into the door, when it began to open from the outside, and there was Michael.

"It's quite intense to be in there with the door closed. Hardly anybody ever does that. I tried it once myself and I've no desire to do it again."

I stepped out of the cell as I replied, "It doesn't sound like that big a deal—just sitting in a dark little room for ten minutes. But I felt so . . . disoriented. Like I was floating—but also stuck, like I couldn't move. Which I know doesn't make any sense."

"I understand. You feel both disembodied, but also acutely aware of the fact of being trapped."

"Yeah, I think that's it: knowing that you can't leave, that the door is locked from the outside."

"Not only is there no knob or handle on the inside, but remember, the door would have been bricked over from the outside after the anchoress was enclosed."

"And the burial rites were said over her before she entered the cell. Would that have been done for the girl, too, when she arrived?" I wondered.

"I suspect not, but I don't think anyone has carried out extensive research on the girl, ever. There could be something on her in our archives—nobody has turned anything up yet, but I don't think anyone has looked very closely. You should feel free to access all of our holdings if you'd like to try and learn more about her, Dr. Pace."

I thanked him as I looked back into the cell and said, "How strange our world would seem to medieval people. A supermarket, electricity, all of it."

The abbot nodded and smiled. "Yes, even here in the monastery, where we live in a way that is closer to how people lived centuries ago, it's hard to imagine the mindset of people then. Enclosure seems drastic, even to us. And the idea of enclosing a child . . . I'm interested to see if you do find anything more about her in our archives. It would be wonderful to know more about her. Our holdings are quite modest, though, so it's perhaps best not to get your hopes up too much. Our librarian, Brother Andrew, will assist you."

The duties of the anchoress's child assistant. It was a good topic for a paper, maybe a book, but it was more than that, too. I would open the door. I would bring a child out of the darkness, into the light. Or, I would try to, at least.

The abbot walked me back to my room. I sat on the bed and looked toward the window.

The final lines of Dante's *Inferno* arose in my mind: *we came to a round opening/ Through which I saw some of the beautiful things/ That come with Heaven. And we walked out/ to once again catch sight of the stars.* That's where that book, full of the horror and despair of hell, ends. It's where the ascent, the striving, the work to come, begins.

183

29

WENFAIR ABBEY, ENGLAND, 1371

A KNOCK AT THE WINDOW. A slight rapping, but in the cold silence of my night, it is like the earth itself is shaking.

Adela wheezes and snores in the corner, asleep in the heart of the dark, prayerless hours. No blanket: she lies curled on her pallet like a field mouse. I am always cold, all the way through to the bones of my fingers and toes, and all winter I wore my Christmas blanket over both my dresses, and both of my pairs of tights. Even though the earth has woken from its winter sleep, the nights retain a sharp chill edge. How does she do it? Her flesh has a bluish hue all over. I walk over to Adela's pallet and pull her single blanket up over her body. She mutters and grasps at it in her sleep.

The monks said their bedtime prayers long ago. At least an hour or two until they shuffle back in for Matins. The hours of the liturgy are so familiar to me now, they are like breathing. I forget to remember them, but they are always there, they keep me going. Otherwise, there is only dark, and then a little light, and then a bit more.

Another knock, and then an aged voice, full of cracks and creases, whispers, "My lady Adela, pray, wake, I beseech you. I require your prayers, my lady." A woman's voice. I'm reluctant to wake Adela; it is surely better for her to rest.

I walk over to the window. I leave the curtain in place so I remain unseen. I respond, pushing my voice down into what I hope is an adult register, "I am here. You may speak."

Moonlight seeps around the corners of the rough curtain, and the woman shuffles closer to the window. Although I cannot see her, I know that she is old: she moves slowly, leans toward the window, but her head barely reaches it. Her voice is faded and wrinkled, as her skin surely must be. She murmurs, "Thank you, gracious lady. I know it is a strange time to visit, but I also know my days are few, and my sins weigh heavy on my old bones."

"It is no trouble; I welcome all visitors and supplicants at all times. But, if it is confession you seek, why do you not simply go to the local parish priest, or the brothers here at the abbey?" I am certain God will strike me down dead at any moment for my transgression.

"Those feebleminded *men?*" she nearly spits the word. "They don't understand women's troubles. Men who hide themselves away in their comfortable churches, telling us women we are so dirty and full of sin. What do they know of the world?"

This all sounds very disrespectful to me, even blasphemous perhaps, but I simply reply, "You say you are heavy with sin."

"Yes, my lady, it's true. But I had my reasons. Men would not understand, but I know you do, for you are a woman too, a wise and holy one."

I am too far into my falsehood now to find a way out, so I burrow deeper into it. "Begin, then. I am listening. Confess."

"Bless me, Lady, for I have sinned terribly. It was so many years ago, but I still remember the pain of bringing her into the world. They all hurt, of course—my first four children were each an agony as they slid from me. But the fifth, she was the worst. I thought it was because she knew I didn't want her, so she hurt me the most as she was born. Once she was out, I ordered the midwife away. I didn't look at her, I didn't touch her. No, that's not true, I did. I picked her up, I took her to the basin of water the midwife had used to wash me, and I pushed her under the bloody water. She was too small to fight. She left so quick. It was the right thing to do—my husband spent all he earned at the tavern, and four little mouths already, always crying, always wanting, always dirty and hungry. I couldn't do it—I couldn't care for another, couldn't face it. Another demanding mouth. Too many already. I dried her, screamed for the midwife, who never accused me of anything. But I think she knew. She looked in my eyes, just for a moment, and she understood. Do you understand too, my lady? The world does not need another girl. Another life of drudgery and pain, birth and death. Men don't understand. But I know you do, my lady. I did the right thing, but I know it was wrong. Does that make sense? It was wrong, but for this world, it was right. But I am sorry, truly I am." Her words have poured out faster and faster, and now she is crying, the words nearly drowned by her wet sniffles and hiccups.

"Hush now, mother. I understand. That is, God understands. We do the best we can. We are weak and feeble. I . . . I forgive you. That is, God will forgive you, I believe." I grasp for the right words. I've heard Adela talk with these women so many times. But most of them required something direct: an herbal tincture, a specific prayer directed to a certain saint. They want Adela's prayers, but they also want medicines to take away what they do not want. This old woman doesn't seem to want anything like that. It is all already done. I think she merely needs to speak, to release what she did into the air, into my waiting ears.

I hear her still sniffling outside the window, and then a harsh, hacking cough that goes on too long. A watery cough, boggy with sick. When the coughing finally eases, she says, "Thank you, my lady, God bless you. I knew you would understand. And God too."

"Even so, you must pray on this further. Pray to the Virgin Mary, and I believe she will bring peace to your troubled heart."

"You are a saint, my lady, truly. Thank you, thank you." She shuffles away, still murmuring her gratitude.

After she is gone, a dread cold covers me. What have I done? I had no right to deceive that crone, to pretend to such holiness.

I stumble over to the bench beneath the squint, kneel and whisper, "Bless me, O Father, for I have sinned. I beseech your forgiveness for my transgressions. I have indulged in the sins of pride, and deception. Forgive me. Forgive me."

A small weight on my shoulder nearly causes my flesh to jump right off my bones. It is Satan's claw, I'm sure of it! I shudder and turn—and Adela stands there, slight in her threadbare gown, yet it is definitely her, not the devil: her pale flesh, her skinny arms, her dirty feet. She is looking at me so fully, so deeply. As if she could see into my very soul.

"Elinor, I am so pleased that your desire for forgiveness for your sins has led you to awaken and beseech God even in the darkness of night, while the rest of the world sleeps. Including me! You have inspired me with your devotion. May I pray alongside you?"

"Yes, my lady, of course." My blood roars and crashes, I am overfull of heat in my chest. I am sweating, sticky with shame and terror. First I lied to an old woman, and now Adela believes that I have merely awoken to pray in the middle of the night because of my great piety! She is inspired by my devotion to God! I imagine a furious man, his face looming down at me from the clouds, twisted with rage at my wickedness. I am surely bound for hell now.

She kneels next to me, and something in her shifts. She turns and looks at me, truly *looks* at me, as she places her hand on my shoulder again and says, "I know it has been very hard for you, these dark and cold nights, far from you family." She truly sounds concerned, and I imagine her tending to her own child, curling protectively around her own baby, singing lullabies and smoothing back hair from a small forehead.

"Yes, Lady, I struggle," I whisper. "I am sorry, I beg your forgiveness. I struggle so much. I do not know how to serve you. I read my Bible every day, I think and think about Jesus's goodness, about Mary's holiness, and I pray, too. I pray so much. My knees hurt and my fingers are always so cold. I do not mean to complain, my lady, I know that my suffering is nothing compared to that of Christ on the Cross, or of Mary when she saw what they did to her son." I mean all of these words, but then I push past them into the harder words that I mean even more, the words that have clung to the back of my tongue with their sharp claws for so long. I don't know why these are the words that insist on being said now, but here they are. "I saw my own father before his son—my baby brother—died. I was in the corner of the room, I was afraid of all the blood. My brother never lived. But even so, my father was so sad, he had lost something, he knew it. But it was something he never had at all. Mary had her son for many years, so how much more terrible for her. But it was terrible for my father, too. Oh, I miss my family so much!" I clamp my lips shut so no more words will leak out. I already feel like all of my words are filling the cell, taking up all of this small space.

"Elinor, you do not need my forgiveness. I do not judge you—not for anything you do. I commend you for your strength—and your compassion. You have a generous and wise heart." I look up at her and smile, as she continues, "It is very cold tonight—would you like to join me on my pallet? Come, let's bundle up together to keep warm. Your midnight prayers are admirable, but you need your rest." I follow her over to her pallet, and she folds her small self around me, and pulls her blanket over both of us. I imagine we are baby birds in a nest, perched over the chasm of night.

Just before I drift into sleep, she whispers, "You are a good girl, Elinor, and—" she pauses, as if unsure that she should say more. But she swallows and continues, "you did that poor old woman a kindness. Sleep well."

And I do.

30

I WAS EXPECTING GRAND, arched ceilings, bookcase-covered walls, old wooden floors scuffed by centuries of feet—and I did get that, but only for a moment. The abbey library was open to visitors and retreat attendees, so it showcased the breadth and depth of Christian literature over the centuries, under just the kind of high, expansive ceiling I had envisioned, lined up neatly on solid shelves. The doorway on the far side of the room, across from the main entrance, was flanked on each side by a single bookcase: the one on the left held works of Jewish thought, the one on the right books on Hinduism and Buddhism. I noticed them because Brother Andrew, the archivist, led me through the long, gorgeous room of the library, across those worn floors, past the rows of books spanning the walls— *Regula Sancti Benedicti*; *The Seven Storey Mountain*; *The Practice of the Presence of God*— and to that second doorway, into a far less glorious place. "The archives are in here," Andrew explained as he unlocked the door to a separate, smaller room. "The library is open to visitors and residents, for contemplative reading and research, but the archives hold original manuscripts and more arcane material." Now we stood in a small room, not much bigger than the kind of walk-in closets featured in high-end American real estate. Metal shelving units along two walls, and dim overhead lightbulbs lit up the cool, windowless room, but only slightly.

Most of the shelves were stacked with file folders and boxes. Andrew's short beard was flecked with gray, and thick glasses perched on his nose. His fingers were quick and graceful as they pulled four boxes off shelf and put them on the single table in the middle of the room, and turned on a lamp on the table, which held a dim, incandescent bulb. He handled the materials with a practiced ease; careful, but not overly precious, like an experienced mother, well past the newborn stage.

I was a little disappointed to be working in such a sterile, modern setting, all metal and laminate, files and folders. I had imagined myself surrounded by leather-bound volumes and illuminated manuscripts splayed across massive ancient tables, in soaring rooms with ancient walls—something like Oxford's Bodleian Library. Or Hogwarts. Even as an academic—or maybe especially as an academic—I was susceptible to the American idea of Europe as somehow frozen in an earlier, more aesthetically pleasing, time. But now I stood in a chilly modern storage space, and watched Brother Andrew open the file boxes. I thought about the Instagram accounts I followed with names like @magicalmedievallibraries and @amazinglibrariesoftheworld and smiled, imagining this antiseptic room nestled among images of winding wrought-iron staircases and ornate gold-flecked ceilings.

"These files contain our oldest materials—the writings that we've managed to preserve from the fourteenth century. It isn't much—so much time has passed, of course, and a lot of material didn't make it through the church dissolutions under Henry VIII. And during the twentieth century, Wenfair donated most of its holdings to the British Library as well as some university libraries. But the abbots have managed to retain a few materials here. We aren't equipped for significant holdings, but the Lord watches over our modest treasures. I suppose having a trained archivist on site helps, too," he said with a smile.

When I looked confused, he explained, "in a previous life," he had earned an MA in Archives Management at the University of London. "I thought I'd live in a little flat near Russell Square, maybe work in the British Library. But another, more insistent voice brought me here." His smile softened as he continued, "I do miss London, though. A magnificent city! Still, I'm blessed and honored to be able to use my skills here at Wenfair. We are merely God's humble servants, but that doesn't mean our words aren't worth preserving."

Andrew unlatched a large file-folder box and pulled out a parchment sheet covered in dense writing and enclosed in a clear plastic folder. He also brought out a book, bound in faded leather, the edges of the pages yellowed. I leaned over the parchment sheet, and whispered the Latin to myself, peering at the dense lettering, caught the words *bovis*—or maybe just *ovis*—and *pullum*. Cow, or sheep, and chickens. A list of the abbey's livestock holdings, I supposed.

Andrew offered me a round magnifying glass with a sturdy wood handle, which I happily accepted. No gloves, though. "That's the accepted thinking, despite what you see in the movies," explained Andrew. "Gloves can actually do more harm than good. They might catch and tear, or transfer dirt, and can lead the wearer to be overly rough with the material, as it can be harder to get a proper grip on the page. I remember learning about the downsides of gloves during graduate school. I can still see the chalkboard listing the issues: '1. The Myth of Protection. 2. The Sanitary Illusion. 3. The Unfeeling Hand.'"

The parchment pages of the book were dry and a little rough beneath my careful fingers. An animal texture, not the smooth emptiness of modern paper. I thought about the long-ago creature who died so that its skin could be made into parchment; then the long-dead monks and scribes who wrote the words; and now me, under electric lighting, metal shelves at my back. For a moment I felt dizzy, unmoored by the sense of centuries stretching out behind me. The walls of the archive room seemed too close and small to be the repository for such vastness, for words that had been first put to the page hundreds of years ago.

"What is it, in particular, that you're looking for?" I nearly answered, "I'm not sure. I have no idea. A path? Guidance? Explanations? Meaning?"

In the face of my silence, Brother Andrew continued, "The abbot told me that you're a scholar of medieval Christianity. I'm happy to help you find whatever you need, as much as I can."

I replied, "Yes, my area of specialization is purgatory, but at the moment I'm interested in anything related to anchoresses, any of the women who were enclosed here at Wenfair. The abbot mentioned someone named Adela."

"Oh, yes—we think Wenfair housed a few anchoresses in the medieval era. We have very little original documentation from that time on hand here at the abbey. It's so delicate, of course, that we sent most of it on to other facilities for safekeeping. If you want to examine any of those materials at some point, we can reach out to the universities and museums. But for now this shelf, back here, holds our few onsite records from that era." He walked toward the back of the room, and stood before a shelving unit that

held two heavy-duty file folder boxes. He pulled one down off the shelf and opened it to reveal a bound leather volume. "Oh, this isn't what I was looking for, this is a hymnal. Gorgeous illumination throughout, and you can see how well the binding has held up. Would you like to take a look?"

I held my breath as I touched the leather and slowly opened it to the first page. "Several pages in the middle are rather loose, so best not to turn any further." I froze, terrified of damaging this centuries-old artifact with my clumsy American hands. The page of prayers opened with a large, lavishly illustrated letter "O" embellished with trailing vines and set into a gold background.

"I can't believe what great shape this is in—this gold still shines," I said. "And you just have this here in storage!"

"We do bring this out for display occasionally, when we have exhibits for the public. But we generally don't hold on to bound original volumes like this here. I wouldn't be surprised if, at some point, this heads to the British Library or another archive. We like to keep some of these original works here, at home, as we think of it. This is where this volume was born, after all."

"I understand wanting to keep some books, some things, for yourself." Yes, I could certainly sympathize with that.

"I've never closely examined these books and documents, so this is a treat and an absolute pleasure. I only glanced at these files when I arrived at the abbey, and a couple times since then. The archivist before me—Brother Duncan—who oversaw the transfer of many of Wenfair's materials to the British Library as well as the University of London."

I asked when that transfer had occurred, and Brother Andrew replied, "After World War Two. I believe there was a concern that the Abbey wasn't able to provide the sort of protection that a larger research institution could, going forward."

"So nobody has looked at these in over fifty years?"

"I suppose not," Andrew replied. "At least not in any great depth. I know it seems hard to believe, but since our archives are so small, we don't attract many researchers, and most of our visitors now are more interested in lectures, or simply breaks from their everyday lives." The monk had already lifted another box off the shelf. This one held another stack of parchment pages, each sheathed in a protective plastic layer as well, many with edges torn or sections ripped off.

"*This* is what I was looking for," he said. "These are old administrative records, and I think there is a listing of the names of the anchoresses in here." He gently lifted the encased pages one by one and set them before me. I examined faded Latin lists of land acquisitions, bequeathments of reliquaries, payments for and purchases of livestock of various kinds, death notices of various abbots, the naming of their replacements. The dry and daily doings of a living community, the hands that wrote these words long turned to dust.

Andrew scanned several of the documents himself; there were fourteen in all. We sat side by side in silence for several minutes, our eyes poring over the records, until he said, "Ah, here it is," as he set a plastic-encased sheet before me. "This relates to the anchoresses of Wenfair, I believe."

I read the lines at the top of the page. "*Terra suscipit terram*," I began, and then continued to translate. "Earth receives earth, and dust is converted to dust. All seeds are returned to their origins, and thus we ask you, most holy God, lead the soul of this your servant Alys from the filthy chasm of this world to her heavenly homeland, where she might bathe in the soft waters of rest." I looked up from the book. "Who was Alys?"

"The first anchoress we have any record of here at Wenfair. We think this must have started as a record of her care, but over the years the names of the following anchoresses were simply tacked on, as a running list."

I moved my eyes down the page, and onto the following one, as the anchoress records continued onto a new sheet of parchment. About halfway down the second page, I found her:

Lady Adela Webster of Kirkby. Her name was followed by the dates *1366–1371.* Five years of enclosure. It didn't seem like much compared to someone like Julian of Norwich, who lived in her cell for at least twenty years. But I thought back to my ten minutes in the darkness, and my stomach shuddered.

Beneath Adela's name and dates of enclosure, the writing was much less neat: it was cramped, and uneven. "Different scribes were probably adding to this record and updating it at irregular intervals," Andrew explained. "Just scribbling in notes and updates. Certainly doesn't make our job any easier!"

I peered at the dense, tiny text with the magnifying glass. "Is that a name? Mon . . . mouth?" I asked. Andrew looked to where I was pointing, took the offered tool, and as he examined the writing, said, "It looks like a financial record of some kind—someone named Monmouth made some kind of payment to the Abbey."

I touched the Latin words as I read: "*nam cur terrena* . . . for earthly care—yes, this must be a record of payments made by Adela's patron for her upkeep. But what does this say?"

Beneath her name was another line of text, but the writing was even harder to read. It looked as if it had been added hastily, with less care. The writing was messy, slanted, and faded. Andrew read aloud, "*Et eius servus et discipulus* . . . also her servant and student—I can't quite make out this next word."

I stared at it until I understood. "It's a name," I said. "*Elinor.*" A little ghost on my breath. The only lightness in the room. "It's her," I continued, "the girl who was enclosed with Adela. I think. Possibly. It must be."

"It makes sense," replied Andrew. "She is clearly meant to be linked to Adela—look you can see another name here, farther down the page—"

"It looks like 'Matilda,'" I said, squinting at where he was pointing.

"Yes, and look, there are dates after the name 'Matilda,' then the information about sums and payments. She must have been a subsequent anchoress. But see how 'Elinor' is written right under Adela's name, along with the records of payments."

"And no years, no place of birth, nothing, just—'Elinor.'" My heart thudded in my chest. I realized that my neck was stiff, and I could imagine how good it would feel to stretch and move, but I couldn't lift my eyes off that name. My back was hunched and rounded, my shoulders groaning and sore. But I couldn't move.

"I'm confused," I said to Andrew. "Father Michael told me that there was nothing known about the child who was enclosed with Adela, not even her name, but here it is. I think."

"We see what we're looking for," he replied. "I don't mean to sound dismissive, but I wonder how many people before you have been interested in learning more about that girl. Very few, I suspect. Perhaps her name is written nowhere else, and this single instance has been missed or overlooked for centuries."

Brother Andrew was probably right. For all I knew, someone at some point had, in fact, seen that name written there, but they may have thought it of no importance, not worth remembering or writing down. What was so special or memorable about the name of a long-dead, merely-holy-adjacent girl of no noble lineage?

"I'm glad that someone thought it was worthwhile to at least write her name here." I looked at it more closely, not the word as a whole, but rather at the singular shape and density of each letter itself. "It looks like it was added later, or quickly, as an afterthought."

Brother Andrew picked up the magnifying glass as he leaned over the page. "Yes, you're right—it is lighter than the text above, and the placement is a bit odd—the line is not quite straight, not quite aligned with the preceding lines. The poor quality of the writing here might also explain why the name was overlooked—I imagine my predecessors might have struggled to read this text, especially those who lived before the age of laser surgery, let alone reading glasses."

I wondered who would have bothered to write the girl's name here, in this document, where it wasn't required. I imagined a monk, tired at his desk in the scriptorium, his own back bent and aching as he kept his eyes on his work: a record of payments rendered for the care and upkeep, minimal as it was, for the monastery's holy anchoress. Say he finished his work late in the day, forced to cease by the setting sun, the candlelight insufficient for writing. But, before he gave thanks for the opportunity to work another day, before he headed to the evening meal, his modest portion of vegetables and bread, he felt compelled to name her, to include her, so that someone else, down the long years, would know Elinor was once here. Or, so that she was known, somehow, in her own time. He put her name to parchment and, in a small way, he made her live, if only in a single dry and dusty record, if only within the dark of many years.

Thank you, whoever you were, I thought to myself. *Thank you for thinking of her. Thank you for giving us her name.* The phrases Brother Andrew had mentioned earlier rose in my mind. *The Myth of Protection. The Unfeeling Hand.* I thanked this unknown monk-scribe for his small protection of Elinor, for holding her in his feeling hand. I wondered what his name had been.

The ligaments in my neck crackled when I finally lifted my head from the page and rolled it back and forth and around in circles. I stood and stretched my arms toward the ceiling. I wondered if Adela and Elinor ever sought respite for their curved spines, their prayer-crushed knees, their underused and weakened muscles, while my own back groaned and unwound itself. I looked to the closed door of the archives, ready to leave, to carry Elinor, or at least her name, back outside.

31

WENFAIR ABBEY, ENGLAND, 1371

I WAKE TO ANOTHER STONY MORNING, but I hear something I have not in many weeks: birds. These last several days, I have felt it, and now I can hear it, too: the world thaws again. I go to the window and peer out past the curtain, and wing-shadows flutter in the early light across the patches of grass poking out of the remaining snow. I look up but my eyes blink and water; they are not used to sun, not even this slanted half-light coming in the window. I close them and let the weak warmth rest on my cheek while I listen: the eager chatter and trill of a blackcap. The clear bell of a woodlark. Bright robin calls. And then, the happy clattering chirps of the wren. *I am here, it's me, Little Wren*, I long to call back to them.

—

Adela and I rise and kneel and sit, and rise and kneel again, through our morning of prayer and needlework. The curtain across the upper window is pushed aside, and there is Brother Joseph, sliding the midday meal on a tray toward us. Adela is still praying and makes no move toward him or the food, so I step over to the window and take it from him. As I do, my finger brushes one of his, and I flush warm in my belly, and lower.

"Good day, Miss. Are you well? Was your sleep peaceful?"

I remember curling up against Adela's frail body, her bony arms around me, and the heat in me cools, enough so that now I am able to answer calmly, "Yes, brother, thank you. I heard the birds this morning, I welcomed their wake-up call."

"Indeed, spring is truly upon us—the snow is melting and the roads are passable again. I've brought food for both of you. I know the Lady often refuses, but even so, the abbot thinks it best to offer it to her. But," he says with a smile, "if you were to eat it, I do not think that would be wrong."

I smile too, and then Brother Joseph and I pray together; we give thanks for the food, for this new day on earth, for a new season of birth and growth. Although my mouth faithfully forces the words, in my mind I imagine his hands clasping mine. I push that image away, focus more deeply on the words, on my mouth shaping and making them.

At the end of the prayer, to distract myself and cool my flushed cheeks, I ask him how goes his work in the scriptorium. His eyes shine bright as he says, "My letters flow more smooth with each passying day, says my teacher, Brother Richard. Even though my back aches, I am never eager to leave the scriptorium. It is so cold, but I do not mind. The way the letters form across the parchment, the good warm smell of the ink—I wish you could see it, Miss. Elinor." Now his cheeks redden as I reply, "I do, too."

"I know you are reading very well with Adela—I will write your name next time I can spare a bit of parchment, and I will bring it to you. Yes, I will do that for you, so you can see your written name."

This thrills me, and I grin wide. My name, inked in black on parchment? Something linked to me, out there, in the world, beyond me.

—

After Joseph leaves, I am somehow both relieved and desolate. I carry the tray over to Lady Adela. "Will you eat, my lady?" I ask.

Her lips are moving but there is no sound that I can hear. I ask again, but again hear no response. A surge of anger rises in me—she could at least respond! She is a mystery—all kindness and comfort last night, and now once again she is deep in herself, with no thought for the world around her. I grab the bread off the tray and carry it back to my pallet, where I sit and nibble like a squirrel.

Moments and moments. Still her lips move, her eyes stay shut. I walk back over and take some cheese as well.

There are footsteps at the window as someone approaches up the hillside path, so I walk back over to it and say, as I move the curtain aside, "Brother Joseph, the Lady has not yet eaten, please return later for the tray."

But it is not Brother Joseph at the window. It is the face of my father.

—

A breeze slips through the window past his face, and the heady, sour smells of home that he has carried with him rush at me: the damp scent of dirt, the sweat he wipes continuously from his brow. He is browned from the sun. There are lines beside his eyes, on either side of his mouth. Likely none of this is new, but I feel I have never truly seen my father before. He smells of earth, of home, and I want nothing more than to collapse in his arms, but there is, of course, a wall between us.

Tears rise up in my eyes. "Father, is it really you? I've missed you so much! Why haven't you come sooner? How is Anne? Why did you not tell me you were coming? Where is Margaret? Is she here? Is she well?" The questions pour from my mouth as if they are animals driven by their own instincts, utterly beyond my control, and the tears, too, pour down my cheeks.

"They are both healthy and well, they miss you. I did not know how to send word that I wished to see you. I told Father Everard once that I wanted to come here but he thought it best to let you alone, leave you to settle in here, rather than remind you too much of your past life. He told me that you were well, that the monks had told him so. But now that winter is past, I felt it was time for me to see you for myself, with my own eyes."

"Father, it is so dark, I am cold all the time—" I slide again into tears, into being a child, a little girl before my father. I look to the door lodged into the solid wall.

But then I look over to Adela. She sits on her pallet, head lowered, hands clasped in her lap. She has not budged at all during my talk with my father. I do not know if she is deep in prayer; perhaps she is asleep. More and more often, she drifts off and I do not even know she sleeps until I hear the rasping of her slowed breath. Her skin is yellowed, and her eyes bulge and yet seem, at the same time, sunk deep into her flesh, pressed against her skull. I force the air to slow in my throat. My heart, fluttering behind my flesh, calms along with my breathing. This breath helped me in that first dark night, and when I was distracted by Joseph's hand so near mine, and it helps clear my head now, too. I wipe away my tears and say, "Father, I'm so glad you are here. I worried you might have forgotten me."

"No, Elinor, I think of you every day, as do your sisters. Anne says Margaret cannot plait her hair as well as you." He attempts a smile but it barely shifts the edges of his lips. "City living is fine. It is louder, true, but Margaret has befriended a kindly woman who lives in the next house over, Mistress Barber, they often work at their spinning together. And there are many other children about, so Anne has plenty of playmates." I imagine Margaret sitting close by a kindly woman—not Mother—smiling and chatting, as they warm themselves by a shared fire. I see Anne running about town, dodging horses and carts, without a thought of me in her mind.

Father tilts his head to look past me, and his eyes widen when they land on Adela. He whispers, "That is her, then? The holy woman? I did not even notice her, it is so dim and she is so still. They say she'll be a saint. Is she all right?" He drops his voice even lower. "She doesn't look well." Adela remains unresponsive, deep in prayer, or sleep, or some other in-between state only she can reach.

I feel more tears pooling, ready to spill down my face, and a child's pleading begins to form in my throat: *I am cold, I am scared, I hate it here, I want to go home! Why does Margaret get to spin wool in a warm room with a sweet woman, why does Anne get to run where she wishes, under an open sky?*

But then I look again at Adela, so thin and sickly, and I think of all the other women, too: the supplicants on Mary's feast day, kneeling with us; the dim shapes of the night visitors; the old woman, whom I tried to comfort. Mother, on some long-ago night, tired down to her bones from another day's labor, yet holding herself back from sleep to tell Father that she wants more for me, some other kind of life.

I am no longer a child.

I reply, "Yes, that is the Lady Adela. She is not well. In her body, I mean. She suffers so much—she is the holiest person I have ever seen. And she is teaching me to read! When I am sad, she comforts me. I do not like to think of her being here all alone. I think I am of some service to her. And it is not so cold." I rub my hands together, which my father cannot see below the window ledge.

How are these words rising from my mouth? Part of me wants to stuff them right back down my throat. But part of me knows they are true and right. Father looks at me, and the lines and creases around his mouth and eyes seem to go soft. We say nothing: what can be said? I am in here and he is out there. There may as well be an ocean between us, not merely a wall. A shadow falls on him, and Brother Joseph's voice says, "Excuse me, sir, I have told Father Abbot of your visit, and he asks that you come see him in his study when you are ready to bid Elinor farewell."

I try to ask Father more questions about their new house, the other neighbors, how his work fares. He answers and makes his own attempts, asks me if I like reading, if we pray often, if the monks treat me well. But after several more minutes, our words slow to a mere trickle, then finally stop. There is so little to say. Have I ever simply sat with my father and talked to him? No clearing of dishes, no stirring of pots or ladling of soup. We are usually in motion, circling one another. Our words do not usually exist in such stillness.

Father reaches across the ledge and takes both of my hands in his, squeezes them. His rough hard hands are nothing like Adela's cold and thin ones, or Joseph's, which are smooth, save for the calluses along the sides of his middle fingers. But my father's hands are warm, and I cling to them as he says, "You are not forgotten. I will visit again. I am . . . proud of you. Your strength. Your godliness. Your mother would be so pleased to see you."

The warmth from his hands seems to spread, through my own hands, up my arms, across my face. But then he releases me, and I say, "Please tell Anne and Margaret how much I miss and love them. Make sure they include me in their prayers. And please— come back. When you can."

Before he leaves, Father looks past me toward Adela, frozen on her bench, and says uncertainly, with a nod, "My lady." He follows Brother Joseph away down the path, and I remain at the window, even when I can no longer see them.

There is a crack in the stone running across the ledge, and I drag my finger along it. I imagine the small crevice widening as I do—and then I do not feel that I am imagining anymore. I stare into the crack, I feel the rough rock beneath my hand, but then it seems the crack begins to widen and gape, until the entire window ledge falls into it, and there is only a dark expanse. I am staring into the darkness, which is everywhere and everything. No walls, no beginning, no end. I seem to have fallen into it. Except that there does not seem to be any "me" to speak of. I have become the emptiness. I am the dark, and I—or what remains of me—am at peace. I understand that I am nothing, yet also, I fill the nothing. I am the black and holding space.

A whistling call pierces what remains of me. And I

203

remember—it is a woodlark. It is spring, over there, in the living world. The blackness that is me arranges itself into shape, and I feel myself now to be a formed thing. I am the woodlark, I am all feather and breath, a sweet river of sound pours from my beak, announcing my being, the fact that I am alive and of this place. I am not a thing of darkness, no, I flap and rise, I call out my song, the sun on my wings—a shuffling sound comes closer, and then a hand on my girl-arm.

"Elinor, are you well? You have been standing at the window, still and staring, for some minutes now. I was resting but now I should pray. Join me, please." I blink back into my self, suck air deep into my throat with my beakless mouth. I look once more out the window before I turn my back on it and join Adela at her bench.

After we say our prayers, our devotions complete for now, I crouch down next to my pallet, pick up my distaff and, with the pointed end, scratch a line into the wall. I must mark the days. I should have been doing this the whole time I've been here. But it isn't too late to start keeping track of my own, small life. I scratch my presence into the stone. I am not nothing, and I am no wild and free creature. Or, maybe I am both of those things, and more. It may be that this one body holds my heart, and a wild song, and beneath it all, a calm embracing place. I suspect I am stepping close to the edge of blasphemy. I am a mere maiden in the dark as I focus on marking the stone with my sharp tool. I begin to acknowledge my time, my only mortal life, all of me here, now, in this moment.

I glance behind me, over my shoulder—I sense a gaze on my back. Adela watches me, but says nothing, only smiles, and returns to her book, her endless whispered devotions.

32

WENFAIR ABBEY, ENGLAND, 2018

"Aᴄᴄᴏʀᴅɪɴɢ ᴛᴏ Gᴏᴏɢʟᴇ, it means 'shining light.' Seems ironic for a child trapped in the dark of an enclosed cell," Father Michael said. We were in his office, and he had his laptop open. When I told him what Brother Andrew and I had discovered, he repeated the name "Elinor" aloud several times, as if savoring it. "Did you discover anything else about her, besides her name?"

I shook my head as I explained that Brother Andrew and I went back through the fourteen parchment sheets in that box several times. We spent the rest of the day in the archive, and by dinnertime my eyes were watery, my head aching, my neck stiff, my back moaning. "My goodness, I think I just heard every one of my bones pop," said Andrew as he stood and rolled his neck from side to side. But we found no other evidence of her. We explored the materials in half a dozen other files as well, although they led us far away from Elinor's time. Even so, I asked Brother Andrew if we might reconvene the following morning to go back through all of those materials, as well as perhaps a couple more boxes of documents.

But that second morning was fruitless. By noon I was re-checking records of sixteenth-century farmland expansion, even though there was no reason to assume there would be any further mentions of Elinor by that late stage in the archives. If she wasn't noted in her own time, why would a monk two hundred years later feel a need to mention her? Even the anchoresses themselves disappeared from the official records rather quickly. Other than her official record of upkeep, Adela's name only came up once more: upon her death, it was noted that she was buried at Wenfair Abbey.

"We didn't find any other references to Elinor," I told Father Michael that afternoon. "We have no idea what happened to her—was she released from the cell? Where did she go next? What was the rest of her life like? I know it's a long shot, but I was hoping we'd find something, maybe Adela's will, or a note about where Elinor ended up—something."

"Our records here are so sparse, and such a vast amount of time has passed, I'm not surprised we don't have anything," said Michael. "I wonder if it might be worth speaking with Agnes, the mother superior at Wilton, our sister convent. Wilton was founded around the same time as Wenfair, it's only about two kilometers away. Their archives aren't much bigger than ours, but our histories have aligned and overlapped through the centuries, and it's so close by, it seems it would be worth a look, if you're interested. They don't have a history of housing anchoresses, though, so I admit it's not likely to turn up much."

"Even so, I think it's worth a look. It's possible records got moved or shuffled around over the centuries, who knows?" I replied. Michael said he would call Wilton that afternoon, to see if they might receive me.

—

It was a pleasant walk to Wilton the next day, on a dirt path that ran alongside the two-lane road between the towns, a light trickle of cars accompanying me. I felt my leg muscles bending and stretching beneath the skin. A bird somewhere nearby sang a clear song. It sounded like a descending bell, the short bursting chirps sliding downward. I didn't know what kind of bird it was; I'm not sure I could name any bird other than a robin or a crow.

How easily my body was carried across an ocean, how easily my feet walked this new trail across the world. But all the birds were basically strangers to me.

I saw the cluster of stone buildings up ahead. I made sure my phone was silenced before I knocked on the convent door.

—

"Like Wenfair, we have a modest onsite archive," said the Mother Superior, Agnes, after she ushered me into the main convent building—massive gray stone, much like Wenfair Abbey, but fewer buildings, maybe three or four, as opposed to Wenfair's half a dozen —and as she settled me into a chair in her study with a cup of tea. I hadn't expected her to answer the door herself, but as she said, "We don't put too much stock in traditional hierarchies here." She also wasn't what I expected a head nun to look like: although she wore the traditional nun's habit, she also wore glasses with bright-red frames. I imagined her feet sliding gracefully along the floor beneath her robe. "And I'm afraid you may find the archives in a rather rough state, as we've been without a proper archivist for nearly ten years now. Sister Evangeline, God rest her soul, was our dedicated archivist for three decades, but we haven't found a proper replacement for her since her death. And, in all honesty, Evangeline found the standard upkeep of the archive . . . overwhelming, I think, in her final years."

"You don't need to apologize to me, Reverend Mother. I'm just happy to have the opportunity to look at these primary materials—that's not something I have much access to as an American. I'm just an adjunct professor back home, in a small department; you welcoming me here to your convent, and your archives, is more than I could ever hope for."

She tilted her head and smiled at me. "As I understand it, your research is quite intriguing—Michael mentioned your interest in the anchoresses. As far as I know, Wilton didn't house any anchoresses, but there certainly was cooperation and communication between us and the abbey. We haven't had an academic researcher express interest in our archives for several years."

"Really? I was impressed with the holdings at Wenfair—it's incredible to me, to have materials hundreds of years old just sitting right there, at your fingertips. I imagine you archives are similar."

"I think perhaps we don't quite appreciate it enough ourselves," the mother superior replied. "It's so easy to fall into a focus on the quotidian—the leaks in the ceiling, sorting out reservations for upcoming retreats and tour groups—we are less cut off from the concerns of the world than you might think! The archives are overlooked perhaps, but in many ways they are the heart of the convent; they are our history, our story over time. I'm glad you're here to explore them."

As she led me through the great central hallway, we passed two nuns, each carrying an unwieldy cardboard box full of canned food. "Good morning, Reverend Mother," they said in unison, briefly bowing their heads. One continued, "We'll be leaving soon for the shelter, we're just packing up the last of the donations for the food pantry."

As we continued on, we turned a corner and I heard women's voices from behind a thick wooden door. "Choir practice," said Agnes. *Why wouldn't this be enough for Adela, or Julian, or any of those enclosed women?* I thought. But then I answered my own question, thinking back to what Agnes had said before: *we are less cut off from the concerns of the world than you might think.* Even this was too much community, too much of the world. Did Adela and the other anchoresses find the solitude they needed in the cell? I thought about that small window in the cell at Wenfair that looked out onto the world, the hilly path leading down to the village below.

At the end of the hallway, the abbess opened a door and beckoned for me to enter before her. The library was large enough to hold half a dozen rectangular tables, each of which had four chairs. Two of the walls featured floor-to-ceiling bookshelves crammed with books, some of which looked impossibly old, with their faded, dusty covers. The other two walls held shorter shelves, presumably because of a couple of small windows high up on those walls. It was a musty, woody room, and as I inhaled, I felt peaceful, at home.

A nun in her forties, seated at one of the tables, rose as we entered. "Sister Sophie, this is the professor I told you about, Elizabeth Pace." As we shook hands, Agnes continued, "Professor Pace, Sister Sophie is one of our newest arrivals to the convent. She came to us as a novice three years ago, and has taken her temporary vows. We hope and pray that she will be guided to take her perpetual vows at the end of the year." Sister Sophie smiled as Agnes continued, "and speaking of that service—Sophie has a degree in library and information studies, and has undertaken to review and organize our holdings. Perhaps she might even find herself called to step into the role of Wilton's next archivist."

"I would be honored to answer such a call, Reverend Mother," replied Sophie. "But for now, I'm very happy to assist Professor Pace with her work."

"I'll leave you to it for now, then—I'm due to greet a tour group shortly."

After Sister Agnes left, I waited for Sophie to usher me to the archive. But she simply stood smiling at me, and it dawned on me: *this* is the archive. That is, there was no separate, modern room. This room of stone and wood held all of the convent's history that remained in print and parchment.

"Is there something in particular you're looking for? How might I assist you?" asked Sophie. I explained my interest in anchoresses, especially Lady Adela and her child assistant, Elinor. Like everyone else I'd spoken with so far, Sophie was shocked to learn of the young girl.

"It's incredibly difficult to wrap one's head around, isn't it? It seems like such a cruel fate. . . then again, some people would say the same thing about a nun's life these days—it seems so anachronistic, so limiting to most people."

"Do you find it limiting?" I asked before I could stop myself.

I felt my cheeks flush as I hurried to add, "I'm sorry, that was so rude—"

But Sister Sophie merely smiled as she said, "No need to apologize, I understand. Believe me, my own family had all sorts of questions—and much ruder ones! 'Why do you want to go lock yourself up with all those old white ladies?' It's hard to explain, but here at Wilton, because so much external noise—expectations, pressures, temptations, distractions, not to mention social media—has been erased, I find myself able to expand so fully and completely into myself, and into God's love. At any rate," she continued, gesturing to the walls around us, "this library offers enough noise and distraction for me! All of these books, all of these authors and voices—it's become so cluttered in here, I imagine them all shouting, calling out to me. No disrespect to Sister Evangeline, of course, God rest her soul—but given the age and state of some of this stuff, Wilton is way overdue for a thorough reorganization and cataloging of the library. And your visit has, I think, made this clear to the Reverend Mother. As you work, I'll do all I can to assist you, and to catalog the materials appropriately."

I still couldn't quite grasp the reality of it: all these invaluable books, some hundreds of years old, stacked on top of one another, squeezed into every crevice of available shelving. But then I thought of the nuns in the choir, singing their devotions. The others making deliveries to a food pantry. And Agnes's mention of a visiting tour group. This isn't a museum, this isn't a relic frozen in time. This is a living place. A community. A home. I walked over to the nearest shelf and picked up a heavy, leather-bound volume. "I guess the best way to begin is to simply dive in," I said to Sophie, as I opened the book.

33

WENFAIR ABBEY, ENGLAND, 1371

*W*ITH SPRING HERE, so close yet beyond my grasp, I feel a yearn-ing for a new beginning. A longing to shed, to become clean. It's nothing holy: I want a bath. Where I might have hesitated months earlier, now I boldly ask Adela if I might make soap so that we can wash ourselves properly, beyond the splashes of water that have been the extent of our rare winter baths.

"Yes, that sounds quite nice—although I do not see how we can fit a large tub or basin through the squint or window."

"I will find a way, my lady." When Joseph next comes, I ask that he bring us tallow, and several bowls, as many as can be spared. I put aside a portion of ash from the fire in one bowl, and mix it with water. Adela watches me from across the cell, but then comes closer, asking, "how does this ash turn to soap?"

"I mix the ash and water to make lye, and then combine that with the tallow—the fat." I think of the sheep I hear and sometimes glimpse down the hill, and know that one of them was slaugh-tered to give us this tallow. *Thank you*, I whisper inside. I don't let the words out—Adela would surely consider it a pagan act, or blasphemous, this offering of gratitude to an animal in death, but Mother often did something similar, saying, "This creature gave its life so that we might be nourished, we should at least acknowl-edge its sacrifice."

A day later, and we undoubtedly make a strange scene: we stand in the middle of the cell, facing a row of six deep bowls filled with hot water, as well as one that holds the soft soap, and a small pile of our rags. "We can dip a cloth into the water, then into the soap, wash ourselves, then dip another cloth into a bowl of clean water to rinse away the soap and dirt," I explain. I begin to remove my stockings, as well as my cloak and outer tunic. It is too cold to strip fully naked, but I wash my feet and legs and reach up under my skirt to clean the part between my legs, too. I rub the soaped cloth against my skin and it comes away brown, leaving my skin freshly pink.

Adela watches me and copies my movements. She dips a corner of a cloth in water, then soap, and touches it to her leg.

"You must scrub harder, my lady." *Does she not even know how to wash herself?* "Would you—may I assist you, Lady Adela?" I ask. She probably had maidservants to help her wash in her old life. And I do not know how much, or how little, she washed herself in the days and years before I joined her here. If she bathed at all. Perhaps she considered bathing a luxury, or an indulgence of the sinful flesh.

Adela holds her bare leg out before me. A bone enclosed in a thin coat of skin. I kneel before her and prop her ankle on my knee. "Perhaps sit on your pallet, lady, so you do not lose your balance and fall," I say, and as she sinks down, I feel the muscle beneath the skin ease and soften. I move the cloth back and forth, up and down her leg, front and back. Her heel is cracked, and dirt has settled into the split skin. Her toenails are flecked with brown spots. I slide the cloth between her toes, around her ankle, and she sighs.

"That feels wonderful, Elinor, thank you." She removes her tunic and unbuttons her chemise, slides out an arm for me to wash as well. I wash her piece by piece, limb by limb. The cloth turns black. Her cleansed skin, I notice, is not pink like mine, but rather yellow. It is slow work, washing one body part, drying it, redressing it, then moving on to another part. But of course we have time enough for twenty such baths if we wish. All we have is time, and these dirty bodies, trapped in stone.

After I wash her feet and legs, her arms and hands, she dips a new clean cloth into the soapy water and brings it to her face. "Might heaven feel like this? Warm, and clean, and soft?" she asks as she wipes it across her brows and along her neck.

In my old life, I bathed in the brook in the woods behind our house. My sisters and I would carry a small tub of soap with us, and let the running water wash over our bodies, carrying away the soap and the grime. The cool water felt wonderful in summer, but the first bath in the spring was always a cold shock.

I finish with a warm cloth to my face. I move over to the window and tilt my head so that the spring sun lands on my closed eyes, my smiling mouth, my clean body.

But I am startled by an awful barking sound—Adela is bent over, coughing so hard her whole body shakes. She stumbles, knocks over one of the bowls of water. She brings her washcloth to her mouth, and when her hacking finally stops, she takes the cloth away from her lips, and we both see it is spattered with blood.

34

—

WILTON CONVENT, ENGLAND, 2018

"*I*F YOU FIND YOU DON'T NEED A BOOK, just leave it on that table," said Sophie, motioning to the one next to me. "I'll focus on orga-nizing them roughly by date. I'll start my hopefully-not-futile attempts at cataloging over here." She motioned to the wall of shelves behind her as she continued, "and if I find anything from the era you're interested in, I'll bring it to you." We turned away from each other, and began to lift and open books, back to back, the only sound the rustling of timeworn pages in slow, careful hands.

After half an hour, I paused to stretch, listening to my muscles creak and ripple as I swayed my neck from side to side. Another half hour or so after that, I blushed when my stomach growled— it sounded incredibly loud to me in that quiet place, but Sophie either didn't hear it, or politely ignored it. I continued to lift books from the shelves one by one, carefully opening them only to find a nineteenth-century study of the Holy Trinity, or an eigh-teenth-century missal (a notable find that excited Sister Sophie). Important and interesting books of considerable age, but nothing close to what I was looking for. And what, exactly, was I looking for? A pristine fourteenth-century codex with the clearly writ-ten title, *All About the Wenfair Anchoress*? Or maybe *This is Elinor's Diary from her Time in the Cell with Many Many Details that Explain Everything About Her*? If Wilton had any six-hundred-year-old manuscripts, would they be lying around in a messy library, in pristine, readable shape?

Unlikely. But still, I kept looking, just in case.

—

At some point, I noticed that the light of the sun had settled on the back of my neck, where it hadn't been before. It was shifting across the day while I remained before these shelves, centuries of dust settling on my hands, my back groaning from the repetitive reaching and lifting and setting aside. My stomach was grumbling so loudly now that I was sure Sophie must hear it. How much time had passed? Just a couple of hours, I thought, although I wasn't sure—my body wasn't attuned to the movement of the sun in any meaningful way, and my iPhone was in my bag, on the floor next to my chair. I wondered if Sophie needed to pray the liturgical hours, but she seemed intent on her cataloging. Perhaps the nuns at Wilton didn't follow the canonical hours? What time was it, anyway? I bent and turned to reach for my tote bag, to fish out my cell phone, and as I did, my elbow knocked hard against a thick book with a green cover that promptly fell off the table and onto the floor with a thud.

"Oh, god, I'm so sorry," I said, wincing at both the pain in my elbow and the fact that I had said "god" in front of a nun. I knelt down to pick up the book and saw that, thankfully, it wasn't a very old volume—an annotated New Testament from the 1920s. I was at eye level with the second-to-lowest shelf, and figured I might as well take a look at what it held. As I skimmed the titles, I noticed that there were actually several books stuffed behind the first row of books, pushed back against the wall. I leaned over the top of the first row of books to peer at the second row, and saw that a small red volume seemed to be caught, held upright, in a small gap between the shelf and the wall, above that second row of books. As I strained to grab it, I only managed to loosen it enough for it to drop to the floor behind the shelf.

Mortified at my clumsiness, I turned on my phone flashlight and looked more closely at the back of the overstuffed shelf. I could see now that there was more space back there, between the shelf and the wall, than I had realized—the shelf wasn't flush against the wall. I knelt in front of the lowest shelf, and began to pull the books off of it gently, in order to reach the small book behind them that I had managed to cause to fall with my graceless movement a moment before.

Sophie came over and bent down next to me, and I showed her the gap between the shelf and the wall.

Sophie pointed out that, just one case over, there was no space at all between the wall and the bookcase, and said, "my guess is that, with time, things have shifted. Or maybe these shelves weren't all built at once, as a single unit. If they were added on by different people at different times, perhaps not everyone was careful—or skilled enough—to line the shelving up properly."

I slowly moved several books off the bottom shelf and reached back, my shoulder pushed against the shelf, my head turned to the side, straining, and pulled the fallen book out from the gap between the wall and the bookcase.

Except that what I had managed to grab wasn't the little red book I had knocked down behind the shelf. Instead, I held a much smaller volume, which fit comfortably into the palm of my hand. Maybe six inches long, it was enclosed in a leather cover, or case, faded brown. I undid the button on the case and saw another cover, a wooden board. There was a dark stain of some kind, prob-ably water, across the bottom half of the book. The stitching was loose, so loose that the wooden cover was only half-attached to the parchment pages inside, the bottom corners of which mostly looked to be ripped or stained, or both. The pages looked ready to crumble to dust at the slightest touch.

"What is it?" Sophie asked, her voice barely above a whisper. It looked old. Very old.

"I don't know, but I think we better get the mother superior,"

I said. I could barely hear myself over my thudding and bouncing heart.

———

Several minutes later, the three of us were gathered around the little book, which was now perched on one of the library tables. I had walked slowly over to the table with the book balanced on my hands, practically holding my breath as I did so. I felt like I was taking part in some of Catholic processional, something ancient and holy, what with my open-palms, supplicant position, and the presence of the two nuns beside me.

"Would you like to try and open it, Dr. Pace? Do you think we should?" asked Agnes.

"I—well, yes, I would, but I'm afraid I'll damage it even more."

"Try," said Sophie, her eyes wide and shining. "This is so exciting, who knows what it could be?"

I thought back to what Brother Andrew had said, about how gloves were discouraged, that they offered a false sense of protection. As long as I was extremely careful, I could at least try. With the leather casing unbuttoned and opened, I slid my pinkie slowly beneath the wood cover and began to lift it away from the pages beneath it. The first few stuck to the cover, and I didn't dare try to separate them. The first page that wasn't stuck to others was badly water damaged, but the illustration it displayed was still rather clear—although there were some stains and fading across the illustration, it was clearly a kneeling woman, praying. She was bent in the stiff way that people so often were in medieval illustrations, her lower half not quite in proportion to, or correctly aligned with, her upper half. She was beneath a window, and another figure was above her and the window. "It's an angel," said Sister Sophie. "See the wings, and it's holding a horn or bugle of some kind."

Now that I could see the style of the illustration more clearly,

I ventured a guess. "I think this could be a book of hours. A personal book of prayer. Generally, only upper-class women, nobles, would have something like this. See, this illustration, this woman—it's probably supposed to be the owner of the book, whoever she was."

"The style, the illustration—it looks ancient," asked Sophie.

"Yes, I think this could be really, really old. Thirteenth- or fourteenth-century, even."

"Glory be to God," whispered Mother Superior Agnes. "Could it really?"

"Yes, I think so," I said, growing more confident. I turned to another page. "See how the first letter here is so large, and decorated? Medieval scribes were known for this kind of decoration." I pointed to the faded vines enwrapping the large "D" at the beginning of the first line. "I can't read this, it's too small and faded, but it's definitely Latin, I can make out enough letters to know that much at least."

"Is that a snake?" asked the mother superior, pointing to a tiny creature in the margin. "Perhaps a dragon? I think those are wings," replied Sophie.

I went to turn another page, but the next few were stuck together. This possibly hundreds-of-years-old artifact could easily disintegrate beneath my hands, no matter how careful I was. So I said, "We need to stop, before this whole thing falls apart. I think this might be a medieval book of hours, a personal prayer book. We need to get this to a safer location for proper study. Is there a cool, dim room? Someplace with low humidity? A lamp and a magnifying glass would be great, too."

"Let's switch off the overhead lights, and I'll get you a magnifying glass and a lamp, Dr. Pace. I'm not sure where to move it," said Agnes.

"Does the convent keep records of its holdings? It would probably be good to check those, just to see if there's any record of anything like this," I said.

Sophie agreed to start checking the convent records, as I

said to the mother superior, "Also, we should reach out to someone with the appropriate tools and training. The University of Reading is the closest university, right? It would be a good idea to call them. They might be able to send someone to take a look at this. But while you call, and check the holdings, I'd love to look at it more myself in the meantime." The directions rolled clear and smooth off my tongue.

They both left, and for a few minutes, I was alone with the book. *Who did you belong to?* No ordinary nun would own a book like this, not at a time when books were so rare. Only a devout noblewoman would own something like this. Someone like Adela. But Adela was at Wenfair, not Wilton. What noble lady visited Wilton and left her prayer book behind? I turned back to the frontispiece. I stared at the woman drawn there. I waited. I looked.

Who are you?

35

WENFAIR ABBEY, ENGLAND, 1371

THE DAYS BURST WITH BIRDSONG FROM FIRST LIGHT UNTIL DUSK. The songs of robins and blackbirds and wrens weave together into a blanketing music. The village below us has stirred back to life too: a cart clatters by on the village path, children shout as they run along the roads. I imagine sun on crabapple trees, light trickling through leaves. I hear a hum outside the window, and peek out to see a fat bee flying by. In the clearing outside the window, violets poke out of the ground.

I envy all growing things, and thus I am sinful. I must fill my heart and mind with prayer. And yet, somewhere I cannot see, a sheep calls to its lamb, and I ache for wool, and clover, and Mother.

—

"How long has it been, Elinor, since you came here?" Her cracked voice little more than a whisper behind me. I turn away from the window and see her seated on her pallet.

"It was the beginning of the summer when I arrived, Lady. We've passed through autumn and winter together, and now here is spring—nearly summer again, I think." Or, I should say, *there* is spring. Out there, beyond these walls, spring blossoms into summer. I drag my foot across the hard-packed dirt floor, where nothing roots or grows. I have spent close to a year in this small, tight darkness. Something black inside me shudders at the thought.

"Another year passed of the new leaves turning red, then brown, then the bright white cold, and now here we are in the budding of the world again. So it always goes. Around and around, down here on the ground, never ascending any closer to the heavenly kingdom until we are finally freed of these seasonal bodies we inhabit." She is seized by a coughing fit, and when it ends, she says in the same flat tone, "I wonder, Elinor, if I should not have brought you here."

Something in my chest drops. It is like there are two Elinors under one skin: one of us wants to say, "I accept this path that God has set me on," while the other one longs to shout, "No, you should not have, I am young, I should be in the world, I should be with my family!" There is a place of splitting under my skin, or so it feels, a tightening and a pulling, and I imagine the two Elinors, arguing. I cannot open my mouth; I do not know which of us will speak if I do.

Adela begins to pray. "Lord Jesus Christ, only begotten Son of the Father, bless us sinners in the darkness. We seek the light of your forgiveness, the compassion of your understanding." She pauses, and the next words are less sure, less rote. It is like they stumble on their way out of her mouth. "Jesus, show me how to lead this child. I thought this was what you wanted: a young disciple, a simple girl to set on the path. But did I misunderstand you? I thought you had spoken to me, but was that foolish human pride? I thought you said, bring her here, save her . . . and I felt so alone—" Adela is whispering now, her words buried. With us.

I do not know what to do, so I kneel at the bench and try to pray for acceptance of my station, my fate. No, my *gift*—that is what Father Everard would call it. The honor and gift of serving one so holy as the Lady Adela. The words she has given me, the letters I can now read on the page. The prayers that I say along with the monks now, as my body settles into the given hours:

Prime, Terce, Sext, None, Vespers, Compline. When I first came here, I did not know the meaning of the word "Vespers." Now I mark the devotional hours as they pass with ease, sure of each one's place in the daily procession, until we begin again, at the first hour. The seasons mean little to me in here; we do not have green grass growing in the melting snow in here, but we begin again every morning, and with each sunset we grow closer to—what? Am I one day closer to walking out that door? I glance at Adela, eyes closed, still murmuring, one day closer to what she wants: a heavenly union with the Lord. I cannot bring myself to be happy on her behalf. But if she dies, I am released. I may walk out of this cell, into the world, and never return. I want to leave, and I do not. I want Adela to live, and I want to go home. I want, I think, too much.

—

New calves calling to their mothers in the fields below, and daisies sprouting along the path beyond the window. As life thrives again in the outside world, Adela seems to collapse in on herself. She turns away from this existence, and from the nourishment it offers: she barely pecks at her single meal of the day. She more frequently prays while laying on her pallet; I am not sure that she can easily walk the few steps to the prayer bench any longer. Indeed, she increasingly spends entire days resting on her pallet, her eyes closed or staring up at the ceiling, seeing nothing, I think, or seeing something I cannot. Her lips move, and I hear the scratch of her whispers, but I can't understand the words, which is just as well, as it seems to be a private conversation.

I sit on my own pallet with her book of hours on my lap. Adela doesn't seem to have any need of it; the words and prayers are stored somewhere deep in her, and she mutters them into our little room. I have made a small routine for myself: after I read five psalms, I stand and stretch, then I take ten steps in a circle, and then I go to the window and let myself look for several breaths.

I am able to complete my routine many times each day. When Brother Joseph delivers supper in the evening, I tell him about my pattern, and I see concern flicker in his eyes.

"Elinor, I will come to you more often—I will start visiting you after Compline, before retiring to bed for the night. Not for confession, but merely to talk. You can tell me about what you have read that day, or learned. And I will tell you more about my work in the scriptorium. And I have not forgotten my promise to write your name, I have not been able to spare the parchment just yet, but I'm sure I will soon." As I reach to take the platter from him, he lets go of it, and stretches his arm forward, rests his hand over mine. Heat roars over my flesh, races up and through every part of me. I cannot move. I look up at him and when our eyes meet, he pulls his hand away. "I . . . I beg your pardon, Miss. I will return soon."

After he leaves, I feel unable to move. My hand seems to sizzle where he touched it. But then Adela begins to cough, and I turn to carry Adela's portion to her bedside. She gasps and shudders; I stroke her arm until she calms. She does not even acknowledge her meal, nor me, as she continues to lie there on her pallet. So many nights her supper has sat cold and wasted on the tray. So tonight I kneel at her side, hold a spoonful of broth to her lips.

"Please, my Lady, won't you sip some broth, at least? It will help you keep up your strength."

Adela continues moving her lips as she tilts her head toward me. I catch a dull stench, something like iron, like death on her tongue. As she keeps mouthing her unheard words, I slip the spoon between her lips. Most of the broth dribbles down her chin. I wipe it away with the hem of my dress.

I lean in closer to her, and the thick, rust smell is stronger. Is this the stench of decay, or the scent of devotion? "My lady, what are you saying? I cannot hear you."

My face nearly touching hers, I can finally hear it: "We fly to Thy protection, O Holy Mother of God. Do not despise our petitions, but deliver us from all dangers, O Glorious and Blessed

Virgin. Amen. We fly to Thy protection, O Holy Mother of God. Do not despise our petitions, but deliver us from all dangers, O Glorious and Blessed Virgin. Amen. We fly to Thy protection, O Holy Mother of God. Do not despise our petitions, but deliver us from all dangers, O Glorious and Blessed Virgin. Amen."

And then, new words, unfamiliar. "What, my lady? What did you say?"

"Wilton Convent." Her eyes roll toward mine. "Wilton. The sisters there. It sits in a valley. It is green with God's bounty. There you will learn and pray. And you will write. There is nothing to keep a woman from being a scribe. I know you can put God's Word into ink. In the sun. In the light. Go there. Elinor. Go."

"Yes, my lady," I said, although I don't know what I am agreeing to. Is she telling me to go to a convent? As if I could simply get up and walk out the door! I think she does not know what she is saying.

"And—for you. A gift. Please take it. Keep it." She lifts her hand and points at her prayer book, still lying on my pallet, where I left it when our meal arrived. Her finger wobbles, her whole hand quivers.

"My lady, that is very generous. But I can simply share it with you, it is still yours." I am secretly greedy for the little prayer book— my hands long to grab it, hold it close to my chest, never let it go. But I feel I should protest, hide how much I want it, how much I want something that is only mine, that I can hold in my hands.

Her eyes move back toward the ceiling—or, toward something beyond or behind it which I can't see—and she begins again: "We fly to Thy protection, O Holy Mother of God. Do not despise our petitions, but deliver us from all dangers, O Glorious and Blessed Virgin. Amen. . . . The book is yours, Elinor. Please, take it. You will use it well. You will honor the Lord all of your days, I am sure of it."

"I will cherish it. But I feel I do not deserve such a lovely thing."

Adela's eyes lose their cloudy look as she looks at me and says, "Elinor, you are special. You are strong. If I have caused you pain, please, forgive me."

"My lady, you do not owe me any apology. You are the special one, not me. And we should not be speaking in this way. You are strong, too. You will be fine." But her eyes have rolled away again, back toward the ceiling, toward something I cannot see, as she begins to whisper the prayer again.

When Mother died, it was a rush of blood and terror—the midwife calling for more cloths and towels, Margaret rushing back and forth with her arms full of whatever the midwife demanded, my mother pale and still, my father frozen in the doorway, Anne in my arms, her face pressed against my chest, me trying to soothe her while also straining to see what was happening. But here, with Adela, it is quiet and dark. I do not know this kind of death, if that is what this is. It is slow and bloodless. Is God calling his beloved home? Or will he make her healthy and well again, and keep her here with me?

If she dies, I am free. Forgive me, Lord. My heart cannot help but quicken at this thought.

I kneel next to Adela's pallet and begin to pray with her. After several moments she starts to cough, forcing an end to the prayer, and when the hacking finally stops, she closes her eyes and whispers, "I wish my mother was here."

I place a hand on her forehead and make soothing noises like my own mother used to make when I was flush with fever. She grabs my other hand. It is hot and damp but I hold it tight. "I am not afraid," Adela says, looking at me. "I am ready to walk through that door, to go from this world, to the next and better one." She closes her eyes and begins to pray again. I whisper the words with her. My eyelids start to fall, heavy. The last thing I remember is her mouth still moving.

—

The weak half-light of earliest dawn, and I am stiff and sore, having fallen asleep half on and half off Adela's pallet, my head slumped against her chest.

She is very still. She has escaped.

*

I should call for help, but I crawl over to my own pallet where I sit very still, mere steps from Adela's body. Her cheeks have caved into even deeper hollows; I can see the shape of her bones. I know I should pray. But I simply keep looking at her body. The fingers curled, the eyes unseeing. They should be closed, coins placed on them. But I have no coins, and a man should do these things. So I merely sit with the body. I watch over it. Someone, I think, should recognize it. This body that Adela loathed, it held her here in this dark stone place, it breathed so she might speak and pray.

I clasp my hands together, feel my own warm skin. But then I notice the prayer book next to me on my pallet, and I pick it up, and hug it to my chest.

The larks and finches begin to stir, to call and cry. I look to the window and see sunlight seeping around the corners of the curtain. I hear the yell of a shepherd, maybe one of the monks, calling to his flock, urging the sheep toward another pasture. I have never seen the fields where the abbey sheep spend their days. I don't even know which one of the monks is the shepherd, or if a local boy or farmer tends them.

The whole great world. All those lives, those living beings, unburdened by stone, by the weight of the devotion that drove Adela here.

—

There is movement at the window. A shadow approaches. Footsteps.

I rise to tell Joseph that she is gone.

36
—

WILTON CONVENT, ENGLAND, 2018

*W*HILE PHONE CALLS WERE MADE, and Sophie went to find the tools I needed for further study, I sat, alone, with the little book of hours. I compared the convent library with the college library back home. This time here in this library felt sacred, too, but in a different way: not in the regular, rhythmic way that my research visits to the college library did, but in a more singular—transcendent?—way. At the UNNY library, I was hidden away, deep in the stacks, surrounded by crisp volumes neatly arranged on metal shelves. Here, I felt not so much hidden as cloistered, held; huddled between old stone walls, surrounded by lopsided piles of books in various states of repair and decay. I inhaled the rare moment. Right now, nobody else besides Agnes, Sophie, and I knew of the existence of the book of hours. It seemed likely that nobody had been aware of this book for a long time. Who was the last person to murmur these prayers? What hands last touched these pages? Bones, ash, dust.

My thoughts scattered, unmoored. I couldn't make sense of this. I forced myself to focus, to follow the available path of partial information, half-clues, and educated guesses. This was what I was trained to do. I needed to figure out, first, who this book belonged to. It seemed likely it dated to the thirteenth or fourteenth century. It would have to have been a noblewoman's book;

at that time, only the upper classes could both read and afford to have a manuscript written, illustrated, and bound.

The only scrap I could cling to was the record of Adela's residence at Wenfair. Not Wilton. This little book could have been moved from Wenfair to Wilton. So many years and generations, the shuffling of books and papers across institutions, not to mention the shared history of the monastery and the convent. There was surely movement of people and materials between them. There were surely women from wealthy families who attended church services at Wenfair or Wilton or both. Perhaps a devout and wealthy lady bequeathed her book of hours to her favorite church, a much-admired monk, or a favorite nun?

What did I have, besides this floundering in the darkness of the past? This book, right here, the object laid before me. Parchment, leather, wood, thread. Stitched and bound, illustrated and inked. I turned the book over so that the back cover was visible. It, too, was water stained. I opened it so that I was looking at the final page of the book—I was afraid to open any of the central pages, worried they would stick and rip, but the last page inside the back cover laid flat, facing the leather casing. I stared at this final, lefthand page. As well as the yellowed marks and patches from water damage, there were gray smudges along much of the bottom. But nothing legible: no clear words, no drawn or penciled images.

I kept looking. I picked up the magnifying glass, squinted, and leaned in close to the ancient page. Faint lines scratched into vellum. One word in the bottom right corner still visible, still readable, just barely, just possibly: *Elinor*.

Was I just seeing what I wanted to see? A servant child would not own a book in the fourteenth century. There was simply no way this could have any connection to that girl in the cell with Adela at Wenfair.

But then again, this name wasn't inked into the frontispiece. The first page featured an illustration of a lady, presumably the owner of the book, as custom would have dictated. This scrawled handwriting in the back of the book was possibly, probably, not that of the original owner.

I made myself think through all of the contingencies and counterarguments and what-ifs. "Elinor" was a fairly common name in the medieval era. Was that really an "E"? A university would have to perform an extensive examination process to determine when the book was written and made. Other highly trained sets of eyes would review the name inked onto the bottom of the final page, to confirm or reject my analysis. I would need to then compare the possible and likely dates of the book of hours against Adela's time at Wenfair Abbey, and try to untangle a clear chronological thread between Wenfair and Wilton, Adela and Elinor, this book and its multiple owners.

But first, before all that, I was alone with this small and aged book, an ancient half-ruined thing that was once the daily companion of an unknown woman—or multiple women. Before the tests, the dating, the scrutiny, all those weeks of analysis, there was this moment: me, across an ocean, far from home, surrounded by stone and the words of the dead. So many possible directions in which to go, each leading to a different answer, but I was certain that this book had belonged to the anchoress Adela, and had then, somehow, been passed on to her young companion Elinor.

I thought about leaving Wilton, running out the door, the book clutched to my chest. I didn't want to let anyone else in. I wanted to lock everyone out and discover what I could from this book by myself. Just me and this book. I could protect it. I could keep it safe, couldn't I?

Julian. Jutta. Hildegard. Adela. Elinor. And so many more, so many women who yearned for more, who died, their names disappeared.

I told myself, *it doesn't belong to you. Your job is to bring it into the world, not hide it away. You are one moment in the cycle, one minute in unfolding time. And then you let go. None of this belongs to you.*

Sophie returned with a flashlight and another magnifying glass, and I showed her the faded name on the last page. She held her breath as I carefully said each letter: "E—L—I—N—O—R."

"Do you think it's her? The girl in the cell?" asked Sophie.

I knew I should maintain rigorous academic doubt, say that it was impossible to know without further study, examination, comparison. More eyes, more opinions, further investigation.

But I simply said, "Yes, I really do."

I see you, Elinor. I know that you lived. This might be both the beginning of my knowledge of you, and the end. This might be all of it. All of you. But even if I never figure out how your name came to be in this book, or where you ended up, where you lived, when you died, even so, I see you.

We catch hold of what light we can. We carry holy names in our mouths.

37

WENFAIR ABBEY, ENGLAND, 1371

*S*HE IS NOTHING LIKE MY MOTHER. Even in death my mother looked alive. Her belly still swollen, even with the baby removed. Her skin pale like Adela's, but her cheeks full and round. She looked tired, but not entirely done with this world, and I confess I let myself think that she was merely sleeping, and would wake soon and call for me.

Adela, however, is gone. Her body, her unloved prison, has released her yearning soul. She is not here. I am alone. I told Brother Joseph this morning when he brought my meal, which he set down hastily on the ledge so that he might cross himself and whisper, "Grant her rest." I wanted to cry out, *What about me?* They will release me. I am not an anchoress. I am not holy, I am not special, no matter what my mother or Adela said. A twelve-year-old girl locked in a cell brings no glory to an abbey. And who would pay for my upkeep, my soup and bread?

Brother Joseph rushed off to tell Father Hugh. A few moments later, the abbot peers through the squint at Adela on her pallet. He speaks the prayers for the dead over the body—no, call her Adela, she is no mere body. Although Adela herself would agree that this shell she has left behind is a mere burdensome thing, mere flesh.

But it is all I have left of her. No—there is also the book. It slipped to the floor when I stood to tell Joseph. I step over toward Adela's pallet, pick it up from the ground, and return to my own pallet, clutching it to my chest. My movement seems to remind the abbot that I am still there. "Elinor, are you well? What happened?"

"I do not know, Father. She was praying, we were praying together, and I fell asleep, and then I woke and she had . . . gone." A new thought seizes me. "Father Abbot, what about last rites? There was nobody here to pray for her at—the end!"

"She received last rites when she entered the cell. Her enclosure was, essentially, a living death. Still, we will pray and bury her with full rites. She deserves that," replies the abbot. He continues, "But, are you well, Elinor?"

I have no way of answering this question. Am I well? I am locked in a cell with a dead body of a woman I . . . admired? Loved? I cannot find the right word. It has slipped beyond my reach, into the dark.

"Yes, Father, you do not need to worry about me." I sound so brave, much braver than I feel. It is like when I spoke with my own father when he came to see me: I am more and more able to say the words that are best for others to hear. This, I think, is what adults do.

"I will instruct the monks to begin unblocking the door so that we may release you, after they have completed the prayers at Terce. Joseph, please bring her something more to eat. Elinor, after Terce, we will work as quickly as we can."

The monks leave, and I sit with what is left of Adela, and all I hear is my own breathing.

Then, footsteps return: Joseph, sliding a tray of bread and cheese through the window for me. I take the bread and nibble it, but I taste nothing. Joseph does not stay. He smiles at me, but keeps his lips shut. What can he say to me, chewing on bread in the morning next to a dead body?

Now I hear, again, the psalm recited at Terce. I remember when I first arrived, those many months ago, and the Latin rolled past me, beyond my grasp. I grabbed for and held what I could. *Tree. Chaff.* Today I pray along with the unseen monks, the Latin confident and clear on my tongue: *That person is like a tree planted by streams of water, which yields its fruit in season and whose leaf does not wither—whatever they do prospers.* I see the brook in the woods where I bathed and waded with my sisters. I see trees thick with apples and pears. I hear the drowsy buzz of bees among the sweet fruit dropped to the ground. I make myself turn the words into these pictures, I make my eyes see the water, the trees, the apples, the bees, so that I do not see the wracked body on the other pallet, the yellowed flesh. I want to cover her with a blanket. But I cannot bring myself to close the small distance between us.

After Terce ends, I hear the brothers gathering, the shuffle of feet coming close. Brother Joseph peers through the squint. "We are beginning to unblock the door, Miss," he says. "We are loosening the bricks from the mortar on our side." I hear a scratching behind the blocked door. The monks will say the full Office for the Dead over Adela's body, starting tonight at Vespers, but first, they need a body over which to pray. And so unseen men on the other side of the wall begin the work of unburying and unlocking what remains of Adela—and me. It's a weird resurrection: her living body, when enclosed, received last rites, and was considered dead to the world. Now she is being brought back into the world, only to be prayed over and buried, again.

Adela's flesh is tight across her bones. Her thin fingers curled to claws. It seems strange to offer prayers over such an empty husk. But it also feels disrespectful not to pray at the passing of such a holy woman. I open the book of hours, and my eyes fall on this prayer, which I whisper: *O Thou who art the Sun of Righteousness and the Light Eternal, giving gladness unto all things; shine upon us both now and forever, that we may walk always in the light of Thy countenance; through Jesus Christ our Lord. Amen.*

I repeat it many times as I hear the continued scraping of mortar and brick. The wall must be torn away from the other side of the door before it can be opened. I stop speaking, and sit on my pallet clutching the book to my chest.

I look at the ceiling, and then at the bench beneath the squint. The hard, pressed floor under my feet. A whole dark little world.

The sound beyond the door shifts: now it is not so much a scraping, but rather a cutting, slicing sound. The bricks have loosened, and now they are being removed. There is a sliver of light, now, at the base of the door. It begins so small, no bigger than a worm. It lengthens, but so slowly. There are at least two hours until the monks are due to pray at Sext. Will the door be opened before then?

The hours, it seems, have wrapped me in their embrace. Will their hold endure outside in the world, or will I leave the little hours behind? Out there, will I pause at Vespers, or know when Matins comes? Or do I leave this pattern of prayer behind, return to days of work and rest?

As I hear the brick being cut away, a wild flush of terror rushes up from my stomach, rages into my throat. I know I have been here for a long time. Although each day passes in a predictable way, I have not been able to track the weeks and months. Yes, I started scratching in the stone when my father visited, but I had already failed to mark so many days by then. Too much blend and blur. All I have is the rough mark of seasons: spring has passed into summer proper. I've heard the new calves in the village calling for their mothers, caught the sugar scent of honeysuckle on the breeze.

I think about the women who have come here. The old woman I sat with and listened to. In this small cell I have learned about a whole other world out there, in the dark, where I never looked before. I hold all their prayers and lamentations and confessions now that Adela is gone. I think of them and I feel less lonely.

I exhale and watch the specks of dust tremble in the air. I can see them because now the whole of the door is outlined in light— the little worm has grown and now it snakes its way around the wood and into the cell. The cell is not bright, but it is less dark than before.

I realize my hands are clasped very tightly around what is now my book. I loosen my hands, let the book slide into my lap. I bring my hands to my face. I feel my own bones under the skin—skin still warm and living. I whisper the words of the psalm again: *That person is like a tree planted by streams of water, which yields its fruit in season and whose leaf does not wither—whatever they do prospers.*

Could I be such a person in the world? I imagine a stream, flowing fast with snowmelt, and I want so suddenly, more than I have ever wanted anything, to lower my hands into that rush and flow, to drink the freezing water, to feel the cold burn, then numb, my tongue.

I am still here. But I have not withered. Might I yet prosper?

There is a knock at the door, a foolish politeness. "Miss?" calls a voice. Brother Joseph again. "Miss, we have unblocked the door, we are working to open it. It is very stiff, but we are beginning to loosen it on its hinges." I look at Adela's body, I hear the door groan and scrape the floor as it slowly opens.

I do not turn away from her. I pick up my book. I let the light from the opening door land on the side of my face—no mere streak now, it widens, it pools. I do not turn toward it, I do not scramble for the door. I am strong. Like a tree planted by streams of water. I keep my eyes on her.

The light gathers as the door opens, my eyes twitch and water at the new brightness, and something in my chest breaks open. I cry and cry, I cannot turn my face the outside world. It is too bright. My eyes reject the light. How can something I have wanted so badly also hurt? I rush over to her body and kneel at her side, on the ground next to her pallet. I want more than anything to leave this cell, but I am also afraid. Can I live in the light? Can I live in the city with Father and my sisters, all the noise and people? Will they point at me and say, *there she is, the one who was locked up with the holy woman, but she's nothing special herself so they let her out*? I lay my head on Adela's chest and repeat, over and over, *shine upon us both now and forever, that we may walk always in the light of*

235

thy countenance; shine upon us both now and forever, that we may walk always in the light of thy countenance and then there is a hand on my shoulder and it is nothing like Adela's, it is firm and warm with the blood that flows within it, and the abbot says, "Elinor? Please rise, your time here is finished."

I turn away from the body, I take one-two-three-four steps across the cell, but I keep going, because the door is open, I stumble across the threshold, still holding my book, and I do not stop, I walk up the nave of the church, out the door, up another hallway, I am still walking, so many steps, I cannot stop until my feet encounter dirt, or grass, I cannot abide a built stone floor. Here is an open place, it is so green, it is summer, the birds toss insistent song at my ears, the sounds everywhere and overwhelming, my eyes blink and cry in the sun-bright air, the honeysuckle scent floats over the village stench of manure, this is the day the Lord has made, every breath I suck into my body is a clean and holy gift, I am crying, I am glad, I am blessed and I stand in the shine and ripeness of the world, I fall onto my knees, onto the green, green grass, the land meets me, holds me, spreads beneath my open palm as I keep hold of my book with just one hand, reach for the ground with the other. My ears are full of hum and buzz, and down here on the good land I see the bees dipping into and out of the clover. I inhale the sweet fresh air, and that welcome stench of distant shit—and of a male body coming near. A smooth palm extends toward me and with my tear-blurred eyes I see a young monk. "Miss, are you well?" His childish voice squeaks on "you" before dipping back down on the next word. "You are Mouse!" I say. "It is you!" And I laugh and laugh as I lay my whole self flat against the ground, my back against the solid earth, and through the tears rolling down my face I see Brother Joseph smiling at me, I see the young monk who reached for me, a confused look on his face as he stands above me. I clasp my book to my chest while I lie on the green green grass, while the bees dance their devotions all around me, while they do the good and godly work they are meant to do.

38

—

STILLBURNE, NEW YORK, 2018

I COULDN'T STAY IN ENGLAND, at the convent, with the book, as much as I would have liked to; my airline ticket was nonrefundable. The University of Reading had sent over an archivist and a medieval studies scholar, who both agreed that my initial guess about the book's status and origins were probably correct. They would take it back to the university for further examination. Before I left, I carefully moved the little book to an archival storage box, and then handed it to the archivist, Charlie, who said, "We'll take good care of it, and you will come back for further study, won't you? As soon as we authenticate the dates and provenance, I'll email you." I smiled back and thanked him, emptiness heavy in my hands.

A couple days later, I was home. It was late afternoon, and I was standing in my own room, removing clothes from my suitcase and hanging them up in the bedroom closet, the air conditioner in the bedroom window humming. Nick watched from the doorway, then leaned against the frame as he said, "What did Helen say?" He knew I had called her from England, and she had said she would email me as soon as she had a chance to speak with the administration and the head of the School of Humanities. I had just gotten a response from her. I read from my phone, a plastic hanger still in my other hand. "She agrees that I should submit a book proposal to the editor who approached me at Kingmore, and she'll let Reading know that UNNY will support me as ongoing lead researcher."

"Meaning . . . ?"

"Meaning that UNNY will pay to fly me over to be part of the examination and analysis of the book."

"OK, they're willing to buy some plane tickets so they can say their faculty member made this big discovery—but what about making you a permanent member of that faculty?"

"She wants me to come in for a meeting next week 'to discuss your future with the University.'"

Nick crossed the room and put his arms around me. "Babe, I'm proud of you. They're going to offer you a tenure-track position, how can they not? I know there will be the usual procedures: an open call, you'll need to apply—but they won't let you go now, they know they need to offer you something to keep you."

I turned my head to rest my cheek on Nick's chest, and as I did so I saw *Purgatorio* still on my nightstand. I thought back to being in this bed, after the miscarriage and the blacking out, staring at those pages, watching the sun leak weakly into the bedroom. Getting out of bed, putting one foot in front of the other. I blinked as I felt something hot and thick settle in my chest.

"Are you crying?" asked Nick, pulling away so he could look at my face. "What's wrong?"

"Nothing. Everything. I don't know. Does that cover it?" I forced a frail smile and put down the hanger so I could wipe my eyes. "I'm excited, of course. 'Excited' barely begins to cover it. It's just a lot, lately." I placed my forehead against his chest, looked down at our feet, our toes just touching. "I have a confession to make. I stole a book from the college bookstore. Months ago. I went back and bought two more to make up for it. I don't know why I did it. I just wanted something, I wanted everything in that book—it was Sloane's book, and I wanted to be her, I wanted her work, I wanted the anchoresses, I wanted our baby"—I started to cry harder, and Nick's arms tightened around me—"I wanted to have something good, and special. Something mine."

Nick, still holding me tight, said, "I get it. We're always digging around, looking for a new angle, trying to carve out a new little space for ourselves, for our work. It's hard to hold onto anything that feels real, that doesn't feel dusty and ancient and already pawed over. It's ok."

I wiped my eyes with my sleeve as I said, "Thanks babe. Anyway, what if it really is her? Elinor, I mean? Did she end up at Wilton? Is that what she wanted? I hope she was happy, eventually, whenever she left that cell. If she did leave it."

I let go of Nick and reached over to pick up *Purgatorio*. I opened it to the extensive endnotes section in the back, and the first words I saw were "the debt we owe." The endnote went on to clarify, "i.e., the debt of purgation that we, as sinners, owe to God." Well, yes, to a fourteenth-century mind that would be the foremost debt, the one overriding all others. But what do we owe to a stranger, to the long dead, to the never born?

A name in the mind, in the mouth, on the page. Something held, something seen.

"Let's celebrate. I'll let you buy me a drink," I said.

"Sounds great, should we drive, or would you rather walk?" Nick asked.

"Let's walk," I said, "I just have to send a couple emails first."

—

Dear Emma,

I hope you're having a great summer! You probably aren't checking your school email much, but I just wanted to give you a heads-up that, this fall, I'm going to be working on a big research project and I think it could be a great opportunity for you to assist on it. I'd love to tell you more about it if you're interested, so reach out whenever you get this.

Thanks!
Professor Pace

Hi Sloane,
How are you? How's your summer? I kept meaning to check in with you after the conference, but the second half of the semester got so busy—same for you, I'm sure!
You really inspired me to think more about direct research, and the importance of it. I just got back from a research trip to the UK, and I think I may have found something huge: a book of hours, an actual 13th- or 14th-century bound manuscript, that very likely belonged to an anchoress! And it might include evidence of a young woman, a child assistant, who was enclosed along with the anchoress—like Hildegard and Jutta. I'm going to be working with some people at the University of Reading on the analysis, but I'd love to keep you in the loop as the research progresses, and get your opinion, at the very least, on whatever turns up.
Look forward to hearing from you!
Liz

I didn't know if or when I would get a tenured position at the university. I didn't know if or when I'd get pregnant again. But I knew I was part of something bigger than this mere body of mine, in this small moment in time.

"I'm ready," I said to Nick. With one hand I opened the door, and with the other I took hold of his, and together we stepped into the lateness of the day. We began to walk the familiar path, the everyday sidewalk, the first stars just barely visible in the sky.

39

WENFAIR ABBEY, ENGLAND, 1371

THE NEXT DAY, Adela is buried in the monastery graveyard. Her diminished bones deep down in the earth, but her soul far away from here, with God. I stand before her grave and think of my mother, because of course she has no marked grave, being a common person, being only my mother.

I feel the slight wind across my shoulders, I see the shifting light as a cloud moves before the sun, the green moss that clings to the headstones.

After the funeral, after dinner, I am standing at the window in the room where I spent my first night at Wenfair before my enclosure, leaning out over the ledge, my face turned up toward the stars. Adela's prayer book—my prayer book— is on the pallet, where I can see it. I don't like to have it out of my sight. There is a knock at the door. Joseph. "Father Hugh wishes to speak with you, Miss." I follow him down the long hallway, past the herb garden. I smell sage, mint, chamomile—somehow, each is distinct in my nose, and yet they also overlap and blend in the dusky air. I used to heat and blush at Joseph's approach, but now that I see him whole, I warm to him differently. Only as I would to a brother, I think. He has been all kindness to me, and I feel such gratitude, and only that. I do not know how or why this feeling has changed, but so it is. Perhaps my body is so full and flush with all I see and hear and touch—birdsong, sunlight, moss—that there is no room left for those old feelings any longer. Perhaps I left that heat in the cell, a small warmth for the stone to absorb into itself.

"Joseph," I say, "thank you for all your kindness toward me. It has been a help to have a friendly face. To have a friend."

He turns toward me, slows and stops. "It has been an honor and a pleasure, Miss. You have conducted yourself with honor and grace. We are told that women are the weaker sex, but I do not think I have your strength. I am sorry, however, that I have not yet written your name for you. I will amend that." He walks on, opens the door to the abbot's chamber, and I look at him as I step through. "God bless you, sister," he says with a smile.

The abbot motions for me to take a seat across from him, near the flickering fire. I gaze into the hearty flames, see orange lap at red. I blink and water rises in my tender eyes. I wipe it away as Father Hugh says, "Elinor, I hope you are comfortable and managing well enough. I imagine this all feels familiar, and yet also quite strange." I want to say, *I have missed one of every season. I am dizzied by the scent of chamomile. The birds offer an unceasing shriek, yet I welcome their sounds. This fire is a gift from God.* But I say nothing, and glance down at my intertwined hands, the dirt-edged fingernails. I scrubbed them so hard with the dampened edge of my skirt before I left the cell, but it was little use.

Abbot Hugh continues, "I wish to know what you will do next, and if we might be of any assistance to you. You served the lady very patiently and well. We have dispatched a messenger to your father, so this time before his arrival is an opportunity for you to prepare for the next stage in your life."

I think about an unfamiliar new house in London, shoulder to shoulder with many others, the voices calling, the animals scurrying in the streets. I imagine a town square full to bursting with women and men offering to sell me eggs, good cloth, cheese. All of it presented to me, simple in the sun. It sounds exciting, but it also sounds like too much. And then will come the marrying, and the childbearing, probably sooner than not.

I gather my breath and my strength, I lift my eyes, and I say, "Father, I wish to go to Wilton."

"You wish to join the convent, take the veil?"

"Yes, Father. I wish to pray, and learn. And read. Are there many more books I might read?"

"Yes, Elinor," the abbot says, smiling, "there are many, many more books for you to read."

Do I sound greedy? "I wish to be of service, too, Father Abbot. I can write. I can become a scribe." His mouth opens so I speak more quickly, to get all my words out before he can release his. "Adela is teaching me— taught me—to read. And she told me I could become a scribe. I can learn to write, Father, I'm sure of it, if I can practice."

Abbot Hugh sits back, brings his hand to his chin, and begins to nod slowly. "Yes, the sisters at Wilton would be fine teachers for you. And they do have a small scriptorium."

"I want to be able to see my family. But I also want to study and learn." Part of me cannot believe I am stating, what I want, so clearly and simply, to this powerful and holy man. But I also feel Adela and my mother, ghostly at my side, encouraging me as I sit between their guiding spirits.

He asks, "What, precisely, do you wish to write, child?"

"I want to write—all of it, Father. The trees, the birds, the mice in their burrows, the goats in their barn. This is the world the Lord has made. I want to praise it—" he raises his eyebrows and I hastily add, "I want to praise Him. I will honor the Lord and all He has created."

The abbot smiles again and says, "Then so it shall be. I will speak to the abbess at Wilton and arrange for you to travel as soon as they are ready to receive you."

"If I may request it, Father Abbot, might I stay here until I go to Wilton? I want to see my father and my sisters, but where they live is not my home. I have never been there. It might be difficult for them if I were to be home with them for some time, only to

243

leave again. Especially for my smallest sister." I will miss my sisters and father, and part of me cannot fathom these words I am saying. *You could be going home! Home! What are you saying, foolish girl?* But I am warmed by the fire, and by the thought of a world of women, where I might walk freely, where I will read in the sun, not stone. My mother, Adela, the heat of these flames, this great and holy world: all support me, and the clean clear words coming out of my mouth.

"Elinor, I believe you have some of Adela's generosity of spirit. You think of the needs of others so naturally. So be it. You are free to walk the grounds and visit the gardens. You will be a fine addition to Wilton, praise be to God."

I thank him as he dismisses me. Outside the door to the chamber I pause, unsure of my next step. The hallway stretches dark before me. I breathe in deeply, filling my body with evening air. The smell of mint wafts over from the herb garden in the center courtyard and catches in my nose. I follow as my feet lead me out from under the roof and into the garden. I make my way to the center, where a statue of Mary, holding the infant Jesus, stands. She gazes down at him in her arms, while he reaches a fat little hand toward her cheek. In the middle of the garden, several paths meet. It is like I am at the center of a great wheel, with each spoke spinning out from me. I extend my arm and bend to brush my fingers across chamomile. I turn toward another path, and grasp feathery fennel. Over here, the delicate, yellow flowers of rue. And there, and the soft leaves of sage.

I spin and bend and turn, I mark a slow circle, the many paths into the darkness, all these unseeable futures before me.

40

To: chen.l@neup.edu
cc: lanham.s@wolverton.edu, Emma.williams@unny.edu
From: elizabeth.pace@unny.edu
December 5, 2018, 4:02 pm

Dear Ms. Chen,

As you may recall, we met briefly at the Kingmore Conference on Medieval Studies. At that time, you invited me to send you a book proposal centered on my work on the medieval development of purgatory. However, my research has taken what I think is an exciting new turn. I thank you in advance for bearing with me as I briefly present an entirely new area of study, and an astonishing development, to you.

This past summer, I made a very notable discovery during a research trip to Wenfair Abbey and Wilton Convent in the United Kingdom. I have recently returned from another trip to the UK to follow up on this discovery, along with fellow medieval scholar Sloane Lanham, and we feel that our work merits development into a full manuscript. I've taken the liberty of attaching here a brief abstract of the book we're proposing. If you are interested, we would be happy to provide you with a full, standard book proposal.

We hope very much that you might be interested, and look forward to speaking with you further at your convenience.

With best regards,

Elizabeth Pace, PhD
Assistant Professor
Medieval and Early Modern Studies Program, Department of Religious Studies
University of Northern New York

Sloane Lanham, PhD
Associate Professor
Department of Religious Studies
Wolverton College
Author, Holy Enclosed in the Dark: Anchoresses in France and Italy, 1100–1400 *(Princeton University Press, 2015)*

My Steadfast and Devoted Child: Medieval Anchoresses and their Child Helpmeets

BOOK ABSTRACT

The anchoress is a subject of renewed and intensive research interest, given her rich and layered location at the intersection of gender, Christianity, and medieval devotional practices. This is evidenced particularly by the positive responses to *Holy Enclosed in the Dark: Anchoresses in France and Italy, 1100–1400*, by Dr. Sloane Lanham. A far less studied figure, yet equally compelling, is that of the child servant of the anchoress.

Occasionally, when women chose to be locked in a cell adjacent to, or built into the side of, a church, a young girl was also sent into the cell along with her, or brought into the cell at a later date. It is not entirely clear what the extent of the relationship between holy woman and child companion was; while the anchoress was expected to oversee the spiritual development of the girl—and, often, to teach the girl basic literacy skills, centered on reading the Bible—it remains something of a mystery as to what was expected of the child in turn. The anchoress had few traditional domestic duties or expectations; chores would have been minimal in a ten-by-twelve-foot cell.

Our interest in the figure of the anchoritic child helpmeet has been spurred on by a recent, and very exciting, discovery: during a research trip last summer to Wilton Convent in England, Dr. Elizabeth Pace discovered a fourteenth-century prayer book. Ongoing study and analysis of this rare artifact (at the nearby University of Reading, where we have been working with their excellent archivists and medieval historians) leads us to believe that the book originally belonged to an anchoress, Lady Adela Webster, a noblewoman who enclosed herself at Wilton from 1366 until her death in 1371. What makes this discovery even more exciting is that we strongly suspect, as we will argue in our book, that Adela was accompanied by a child in the cell, and she gifted this prayer book to that child. Although it is not entirely clear precisely when the child joined Adela in the cell, our analysis of the book has led us to conclude that this devotional object was given to a girl named Elinor who, after Adela's death, entered nearby Wilton Convent, where she took vows and assumed the name Sister Francis. If we are correct, then we have, for the first time, conclusively determined the name of one of these enclosed child servants, and an item that belonged to her throughout much of her life.

Dr. Pace's recent article, "Purgatory is a Cell of Stone: The Liminal Place of the Anchoress in the Twelfth through Fourteenth Centuries," proposed that the anchoress, in her performance of extreme devotion, embodies the state of purgatory; her physical self inhabits a space that is neither the heavenly realm nor, for practical purposes, the earthly one. Rather, she inhabits a "third place"—as Martin Luther dubbed purgatory—and in situating herself, bodily and spiritually, into a separate, third category, she undermines the dichotomies underpinning so much of medieval society: not only does she reject the heaven–hell binary, but she also exists outside the Madonna-whore, virgin-mother dichotomies narrowly available as life categories for medieval women.

And yet, as we now hope to posit in *My Steadfast Devoted Child*, the presence of a young female handmaiden seriously destabilizes the "third way" of the anchoress. Does the presence of a youth inherently reposition the anchoress into the role of mother, teacher, and/or spiritual advisor, to some degree?

The specific example of Elinor/Francis illuminates and deepens the study of the anchoress and the child(ren) who served and assisted such holy women. In their destabilization of accepted categories of sex and gender, and their movement into and through unsettled and liminal spaces, Adela and Elinor offer a specific, personal, yet potentially widely applicable and far-reaching opportunity to (re)consider the pathways open to women (or not) in the medieval era.

In undertaking this project, we also hope to shed light on this forgotten young woman, who moved from the darkness of the anchorhold at Wenfair, to a position of some prestige at Wilton Convent, but who has, until now, been lost to obscurity. We hope that our continued study will further illuminate the life of Elinor/Francis, and encourage others to join us in this exciting new area of research.

41

—

WILTON CONVENT, ENGLAND, 1430

*M*Y FAVORITE PRAYER IS THE ONE FOR MORNING, with which I greet every day: *O God, who has folded back the mantle of the night to clothe us in the golden glory of the day, chase from our hearts all gloomy thoughts, and make us glad with the brightness of hope.*

I offer prayers throughout the day; like monks, nuns follow the canonical hours. I join my voice with those of my sisters at the established times each day. Oftentimes, when I turn to my prayer book—the one Adela gifted me all those years ago—I think of her, and I pray for the peace of her soul, although she hardly needs my intercession. Sometimes I pray for the women who visited the cell at Wenfair at night, who choked out their despair, their sins and griefs, their fear in the face of their growing bellies. And the farmers' and merchants' wives who came to the abbey church on feast days, longing for rounded bellies of their own, who beseeched us for prayers to bring them babies. The same source of despair and love, of ruin and joy.

At Wilton, I do more than pray, as necessary as that practice is. I read to the sisters who lie ill with infirmity or age. I sweep floors and pick herbs from the garden. Indeed, I am in the gardens as much as is possible. I am always praying, with both body and breath. A hand held, a turnip pulled from the summer dirt—these are also acts of devotion. I know some of the other sisters find it odd that, despite my age and seniority, I am eager to tend the sick, and work in the garden, with the young nuns and novitiates. My ears catch all such whispers, they remain fine and glorious instruments, sharpened in that long-ago cell and never dulled since, even in my old age.

I put aside a portion of my daily bread, and offer it to the wrens and other birds. I chose Francis as my religious name because, like that great saint, I exalt all living things, and I too am especially fond of birds. I know this edges close to blasphemy for some, this devotion to the low creatures of this fallen world, but did not the beloved saint from Assisi himself say, "Be praised, my Lord, through all your creatures"? I am glad for the rumbles of my belly if it means that the birds might thrive.

When I am kneeling in the dirt, or lugging a wagon uphill, I pray, again, these words of the good saint Francis: *Be praised, my Lord, through our brother sun, who brings the day; and you give light through him. And he is beautiful and radiant in all his splendor! Of you, Most High, he bears the likeness.*

This how my year in the cell marked me: I loathe too much stillness, and I long to be outside in the sun and the breeze as much as possible. And, as I remind the younger sisters, there is no shame or drudgery in hard, bodily work that is done well in the support of this community. It is all a form a prayer, a form of service, a form of communion.

But my first and holiest duty is writing. I spend as much of my time as I can in the scriptorium, and when I write the words of the saints, the words straight from Heaven, when I sit at my bench and raised table, and ink the truth of the lord onto parchment, that too is prayer. The quill between my wrinkled and bent fingers still feels like home. I remember Adela telling me, "Focus on the words, and the fear will fall away." If I am scared, aware my time here cannot be much longer, I write, and my heart calms.

Rarely, there is word of an anchoress arriving at another convent or church or abbey—the mother superiors of the orders correspond with one another, across kingdoms, even, for what are the borders and boundaries of man to God and his most devoted servants? Our Mother Superior will add the name of the anchoress to the list of those to whom we offer our prayers. I speak the holy woman's name, and as I do, I see Adela's face.

Few people alive know of my time in the cell with Adela. Mother Superior knows, and one or two of the older nuns. My sisters, of course, but Margaret has been gone for many years, dead in childbirth, may the Lord protect and keep her. Anne lives in Fossbury still, near her grown sons and daughter. When they were children, Anne would bring them to visit me every summer, when the trip takes only half a day. When the youngest, Maud, reached twelve years, I had such terrible dreams—I saw the girl standing immobile while a tower grew up around her, until I could not see her, could only hear the sound of a woman crying, calling my name.

But of course Maud is grown to full womanhood and herself a mother now. And to most people I am simply Sister Francis, the nun who is always found either in the scriptorium, or walking the gardens. The nun who finds it hard to sit still, who even at her advanced age squirms on the prayer bench, her eyes drifting from the icon of Mary, to Christ on the Cross, to the window, to the sky beyond the colored glass.

Mother Superior has encouraged me to write down my story, and Adela's, as much as I can. She says there is value to be gained from reflecting on this unique gift I was granted in my youth. There is edification here for future readers, but also the task focuses me, and offers me opportunities to thank God for the many good paths he has set me on. When I copy the psalms, or the gospels, scratching the ink into the vellum letter by letter, I believe I am offering something, if not holy, at least devout and true. But this manuscript, my own words, is nothing sacred. It is merely the faded memories of an old nun, who struggled in the dark with a holy and tortured young woman—Adela now seems so very young to me, steadfast and unchanging as she is in death. I have aged far beyond her. I am the one left here, likely for not much longer, to hold her name aloft. My father is dead, Monmouth is dead, as is the priest, Everard. I write Adela's name and pray that her soul is rested, that it enjoys the peace her poor bones could not. I have here while I write, as I always do, her book of hours, which I often read from when I wish to offer what prayer and comfort I can to her glorious soul.

I have a confession. I offer it here. After Adela passed on to the heavenly realm and gifted me with the little book of prayer, I scrawled my own Christian name on the last page when I got to Wilton, and had learned to do so. I wanted to see my name, my self, attached to something solid. When I scratched those letters into the vellum, I felt as if I were seeing myself for the first time. After those months in the darkness, I saw my own name, stark and true on the page. I know this was a vanity on my part. It was a foolish and impulsive act. Still, I hold some compassion for that girl, who wanted only to feel herself a living thing, someone who mattered, who lived.

I am no longer that girl, of course. So many years have passed. And yet it is not so hard to put myself back in that dark place. Indeed, I see that when I write of my time in the cell, I write as if it is happening right now, in this very moment. Mother Superior set me this task not in order to exalt myself, of course, but merely to recognize Adela's great devoutness, and to offer a path, a guide, to future anchoresses or nuns who might wish to read of my experience. I do see that in my writing, I have tended to wander into the dark thickets of my own mind, into the confused and struggling thoughts of that girl who, I can hardly believe, was me. May God forgive the foolish ramblings of an old woman.

I suspect that time overlaps and retraces its own steps. Or curls in on itself, protecting both what has happened and what is yet to come. Last year, a merchant knocked on the convent door during a storm, seeking a night's shelter and rest. In thanks he gifted us a small portion of black pepper, as well as a shell, from the sea coast, which curves into itself, a spiral traced along the hard, yet delicate, surface.

I do not understand time. I see that the hand holding this

quill is wrinkled and worn, but cannot see how this has come to pass. I mean no sacrilege with my womanly musings, I am merely too feebleminded to understand God's great plan.

Brother Joseph would say, "Sister Francis, it is not your place to understand. You have been given the gift of language, an ease with words that seem to flow directly from your heart to the parchment. Simply write, and worry not what will happen after we have all turned to ashes and dirt." He was so wise, my friend Joseph. We exchanged letters and occasional visits after I left Wenfair, up until his death some years ago. Those hot, girlish feelings I once felt for him settled and cooled into something warm and nourishing. We saw each other, and that was enough. May the good Lord grant him eternal rest, and let perpetual light shine upon him.

These words, this parchment, may very well die along with me. It may all fade and wither with time, blown to dust. That is most likely. Or, even more likely, these words will be erased and written over by some man with something more important to record. Parchment is precious; women's words are not.

Or it may very well be that, someday, someone across the years will find this, and will see me. Not that I deserve such recognition. It is merely my foolish womanly heart, yearning for a moment in the everlasting sun.

Adela's prayer book. This parchment, inked with my memories. Will any of this last?

I see time like never-ending water, stretching across the world, holding us aloft, waves carrying us toward unseen coasts. I feel myself a sailor, although I have never left England and never will. But in my mind, I have traveled from one small stone place to this greater one, I have walked through darkness, and now I keep my eyes on the light ahead. I hold oceans in my mind and in my heart, I hold the stone and chilly places, I hold the women, I hold the birds that sing, and all of this I offer to God, the most holy on high, and also, I offer it to you, whoever you are, if you find and read my words, whenever and wherever you may be, whatever far shore you might stand on.

Acknowledgments

Endless gratitude to Anne McGrath for her insightful editing, which vastly improved this book, and her unwavering support for me and this story. She understood Elinor and Liz, immediately and deeply.

Many, many thanks to Colin Rolfe for the gorgeous and perfect cover design.

This novel began as a seed of a short story in Julie Chibbaro's writing workshop way back in 2015. She was, and is, an astute and thoughtful guide. I'm also eternally grateful to Robert Eversz, whose finely tuned editorial eye helped me see where this story needed to go; Nerissa Nields, whose writing retreats are the warmest, most nourishing experiences; and Elizabeth Cunningham, for wise support and excellent conversation.

Shoutout to the Friday afternoon Weeding and Pruning writing group—Elaine, Tom, Linda, Mimi, and Cheryl—for invaluable advice, critique, and insights.

Special thanks to Dr. Amy Damon (Macalester College) and Dr. Maggie Dickinson (Queens College, CUNY) for clarifying and explaining various aspects of academic administration and faculty life; and to Professor Eddie Jones (University of Exeter) for his helpful answers to my questions about medieval anchorite cell layout. His translated and annotated volume, *Hermits and*

Anchorites in England, 1200–1550, was an invaluable resource—but of course, any errors in this book are entirely my own.

Thank you, Mom, for listening to me and loving me unconditionally. Also, thanks for babysitting.

And finally, all my love to Sam, Alex, and Elliot. I wouldn't want to be walking this path with anyone else.

Kristen Holt-Browning is a novelist, poet, and freelance copy editor and proofreader. Her poetry chapbook, *The Only Animal Awake in the House,* was published by Moonstone Press in 2021. Her poetry and fiction have appeared in several literary journals, including *Hayden's Ferry Review, Hunger Mountain,* and *Necessary Fiction.* She holds a BA from Connecticut College and an MA from University College London. *Ordinary Devotion* is her first novel.

www.ingramcontent.com/pod-product-compliance
Lightning Source LLC
Jackson TN
JSHW020017141224
75386JS00025B/564